Love Means No Regrets

by

Toni V. Sweeney

The McCoys, Book 1

Cover Art by *Lisa Dawn MacDonald*

The Wild Rose Press, Inc.
PO Box 708
Adams Basin, NY 14410-0708
Visit us at www.thewildrosepress.com

Publishing History
First Edition, 2024
Trade Paperback ISBN 978-1-5092-5555-9
Digital ISBN 978-1-5092-5556-6

The McCoys, Book 1
Published in the United States of America

Author's Notes

Information on Regency gentlemen's behavior, fashion, and manners may be found in *The Beaux of the Regency, Vol 1*, by Lewis Saul Benjamin.

~*~

Trademarks Acknowledgement

The author acknowledges the celebrity names, trademarked status and trademark owners of the wordmarks mentioned in this work of fiction.

Chapter 1

London, Summer, 1850

"Good morning, sir."

That was too cheerful and bright for a head having indulged in too much wine the night before.

Donal McCoy forced his eyes open, found the source of the greeting, and glared at the blurred figure silhouetted in the bedchamber's single window, his valet now flinging the external shutters outward.

Bright sunlight flooded in, making him wince. It was too much for his pounding head. With a groan, he closed his eyes and rolled over, rooting into the mattress and burying his head beneath a pillow.

"It's a beautiful day, it appears," Rollo continued.

Donal moved again, this time lurching onto his back. Tossing the pillow aside, he sat up, hand shielding his eyes.

"Not for my headache it isn't." He squinted at his valet. "Dash it all, man, close the bloody shutters and put a stop to that blasted sunlight."

He didn't attempt civility. He was in pain, the sunshine was blinding, and as usual when Donal was discomforted, he became more British in his curses than his peers.

Rollo hastened to obey. With a resounding slam, he pulled the shutters closed.

Not appearing the least insulted by his master's curt command, he hurried over to seize the flung-away pillow, plumped and returned it to the bed, saying as Donal leaned against it, "Came in foxed last night, did we, sir? Perhaps had a little too much of the heavy wet?"

"Bite your tongue," Donal groaned. "A gentleman never drinks malt barley. Besides, you'd know the answer to that if you had waited up for me as a good valet should."

"I *did* wait up, sir," Rollo replied, a note of reproof in his tone. "Until near three. After that I'm afraid I fell asleep. When next I awoke, you were already here…face down upon the bed."

"Whereby you, being so considerate, didn't awaken me and help me under the covers." Donal pulled up comforter and sheets, tucking them around his bare waist. "Who undressed me, then?" He gave the valet a stare with one brow raised suspiciously. "I didn't bring home a…guest…did I?"

"If you did, she managed to escape before I got here, sir."

"Then it appears I was more sober than I thought, if I did it on my own." Donal leaned back, thankful once again he'd had the good foresight, even while sailing three sheets to the wind, not to be indiscreet and bring one of his doxies to his home.

"Will you have breakfast now, sir?" Rollo turned to the little table where he'd placed the tray after entering the room and before seeing to opening the window.

"Such as it is, I suppose."

Taking a deep breath, Donal affected disinterest not wholly feigned. The twinge in his temples was immediately echoed in his vitals, his appetite vying with his headache for attention, to see which would lose.

"It's as you like, sir." Rollo swept the cover off the silver cloche dome and laid it upside-down on the tray. Tiny beads of moisture trickled down the interior of the little lid. "Two slices of well-buttered toast and a cup of chocolate."

Donal didn't speak, waiting for the outcome of his inner turmoil.

Appetite won out.

He seized a slice of toast and bit into it, speaking through the mouthful of bread and melting butter. "Good, as always. Rollo, you do have a way with toast."

"Thank you, sir." Rollo bowed in gratitude, one hand to his heart.

"Makes me glad I requested in my advertisement for a gentleman's gentleman one who could also cook." Donal gave the valet a sideways glance as if he suspected that bow was a bit sarcastic.

Sometimes he thought he allowed Rollo a bit too much familiarity. Other times, he was certain of it. Then again, exactly how much was too much when the man was privy to all his secrets and had seen him staggering drunk, stark naked, and flat on his back snoring like a pig in the mud?

"Just as I'm grateful you take most of your meals out, sir." That was Rollo's subtle way of saying he didn't really like to cook, even toast.

"Hm, quite so," Donal agreed, absently. "I can't envision you wearing an apron and wielding a ladle all day. Too many other tasks to tend to, and that reminds me, I've been meaning to ask…" He waved the toast as if in emphasis. "Do I have a dining room?"

"Most assuredly, sir." Remarkably, Rollo didn't

appear surprised by this question.

After leaving university and establishing residence in London courtesy of the allowance supplied by his father, Donal, wishing to escape the smallish confinements of college rooms and the usual bachelor digs, had let a townhouse, in Chesterfield, Mayfair. It held the usual *accoutrements* of downstairs rooms plus two bedchambers on the upper floor, a completely unnecessary arrangement for someone never having guests.

Since Donal rarely spent any time at all in the lower part of the house, he couldn't be expected to be familiar with what that level held.

"How big is it?" Donal munched, finished the toast, and picked up the second slice as he spoke.

"Quite small, sir," Rollo replied. "Only large enough for perhaps an intimate dinner with fifteen to twenty of your very closest friends."

"I see." Donal finished his toast and gestured at the chocolate pot. "As if I'd dare have that many here unless I planned on demolishing the place preparatory to its renovation. Pour me some chocolate."

There had been a bit of a to-do when Donal first requested chocolate as his morning beverage.

Rollo had argued it was a lady's drink. Donal replied he liked the taste and why should he be deprived of it simply because of his gender? If Rollo truly feared a smirch on his master's reputation, he should simply button his lip and never speak of his employer's breakfast habits outside the home.

Rollo gave his attention to the chocolate pot. It was a beautiful example of Sèvres porcelain, and silver-lidded. The valet had been in charge of ordering the dining and kitchenware for his master and, knowing Donal's penchant for the latest, elected to follow the trend of Neo-Classical styling instead of the usual chocolate container with its pear-shaped bulbous bottom and three legs. He'd seen to the preparation of the liquid that morning…grating the tablets, crushing them in a mortar and pestle, then heating the resulting powder with cream in an open pot and blending it with a *molinet* or chocolate mill.

Now he made the final touch as he unscrewed the finial plugging the hole in the lid. Letting it fall free on its small chain, he raised the lid, inserted the handle of the *molinet* through it, then reclosed the top. A few brisk rolls between the palms of the hands raised a heavy froth.

Rollo removed the *molinet* and set it aside, reinserted the plug, and completed the ritual by pouring the chocolate with its head of froth into a high, narrow china cup.

"Where is it, exactly?" Donal returned to the subject of the misplaced dining room.

"It's that closed door down the hall and just off the parlor, sir."

Rollo set down the pot, placing the cup into a chocolate stand whose small center was a cup holder preventing the chocolate from spilling. He presented the cup to Donal, who accepted it with a nod.

"Hm…" Donal sipped chocolate, set down the cup, and decided, "I suppose I should come down some day and eat there, so I'll know where it is."

"Give me one day's warning, if you will," Rollo requested. "I'll open it and have it dusted and prepared." He picked up a newspaper lying beside the chocolate pot. It looked as if it had been opened, then refolded. "Here's the morning paper, sir."

He presented it with a bow. Donal reached for it, then jerked back his hand.

"Did you iron it?"

"To take out the creases, yes, sir."

Thus assured, Donal took the paper, peered at the headline, then checked for crumples. When he'd first learned of the newspaper-ironing practice, he'd thought it the most harebrained thing he'd recently heard of, but if the British did it, he, in his attempts to become one of them, would request it also.

"What day is it, anyway?"

"Wednesday, sir."

"Wednesday? Oh damn…that means tonight's Almack's." Donal swallowed the last of the toast and washed it down with a gulp of chocolate.

"You don't wish to go?" The way Rollo said it meant he already knew the answer.

"I'm afraid I have to, as you very well know," Donal retorted. "You're aware I received a letter earlier this week from my father."

It was the latest of many letters written by the elder McCoy. In each, he'd reminded his son he hadn't paid all those years' tuition for Donal to venture forth from the halls of academe and settle himself in London as a man about town without something productive to show for it, that something being finding a wife and supplying a grandchild.

According to Quinton McCoy, that was the entire reason for Donal to be living in London. He noted his son's bachelorhood as a state to be lamented, while at the same time mentioning second son Padraig's rapid tumble into becoming a near tearaway, and commending his brother for his own abstinence from excess.

Donal's silent reply to that had been to wonder how one could be a man about town and not yield to excess at some time or another. He supposed the way was not to get caught at it…and as yet, he hadn't.

"However, before then," he continued, "there's some shopping to do. I've a new evening suit ready at the tailor's. Didn't you say he sent word round yesterday?"

"Yes, sir, but I'd planned to fetch it," Rollo answered. "You don't wish me to?"

"I think this time I'll go myself. I want to be certain he doesn't make some mistake in the suit's design. Even if stovepipe trousers are now acceptable and the incident happened some time ago, when I get to Almack's I don't want to be barred entrance because of a fashion mistake such as the Duke of Wellington made. I have no wish to be considered a dandy or a fashion-setter, but I don't want there to be anything wrong with my clothing that might get me kept out. I can't afford that, especially now. You may come along, if you wish. I'll need someone to carry my packages."

"Yes, sir." Rollo managed to keep the expectation of boredom out of his voice. "And afterward, sir?"

"I think I'll be coming back here." Donal made it a decision of the utmost import. "I believe I'm going to rest a bit. I shall probably need all my strength for this coming evening."

****

Donal Callum Seamus McCoy was the eldest son of a landed Irish family.

The McCoys weren't nobility, not this branch, anyway. They didn't spring from the Scottish Clan

Mackay, who were descended from the royal House of Moray, but had been galloglasses, coming across the sea to Ireland in the mid-thirteenth century. Descendants of Vikings who intermarried with Celts, they were called *Gall Gaeil,* or foreign Gaels, by the Irish. In those times, the McCoys were a feisty lot, always spoiling for a fight, and with the added penchant for choosing the wrong side.

During the first war of Scottish independence, the branch of the family that would later produce Quinton McCoy and then his son Donal, lost their lands. It was joked that the use of martlets on their family crest, signifying someone who'd lost his estate, had no doubt been bestowed by one with the Sight, foreseeing their future loss. Nevertheless, the crest for their part of the clan retained the argent and sable coloring of the original as well as the martlets, with a variation in arrangement. Being warriors, they didn't sit around and bewail their deprivation, however. Instead, they hired out to fight for the O'Neills at the battle of Calmeirge, when that clan wiped out the McLoughlins and went on to rule most of the western half of Ulster.

Liking what they found in their new country, a good many decided to stay after the fighting was over. They left Ulster, travelling south, and eventually were granted land in County Tipperary, where, though no longer titled, they led the lives of near-nobility. The clan McCoy was well-liked, and as landed gentry, well-received and looked up to in that part of the country.

Soon, most of their land had been lost through various ancestors' wastrel gambling habits, and quite a few had gotten themselves killed for proving to be better lovers than fighters. By the time Quinton's father was born, the McCoys had gone from wielding their claymores past pushing plows to doing nothing more strenuous than riding a horse round the estates. A nobleman favored by the English became the landholder of most of what had been McCoy land, but the family was so established in the country they were still looked to in settling disputes and caring for the tenant farmers.

That was how Callum McCoy became the steward for the then landlord, and after him, his son, Aloysius, and now his grandson Quinton was estate agent for the current lord. It was also why Quinton sent his sons to England to be educated. Though it galled his proud Irish soul, he saw the advantage in kowtowing to one he felt was a usurper of his own lands as well as a toady to the English. Quinton quickly realized getting a British education for his children was the best way to keep the family successful.

Unfortunately, Donal got more education than that.

In his studies, he was a model student, earning grades with which no father could find fault. He was praised by his teachers and lauded by the faculty in general. From observing his school chums, however, he learned a good many other things that would hold him in good stead later in life. Among them was the ability to hide his true feelings as well as his real nature. One trait would enable him to tolerate those in Society he needed but abhorred, while the other would keep him from being ostracized by that same Society. Though it took a while, young Donal was eager to succumb to the entertainments a young man might seek once shed of his parent's domination.

When he arrived at Eton, Donal soon found himself the object of ridicule and mockery. The other lads laughed at his accent, tempered now from an Ulster-tinged one into a Munster tone, as well as his way of expressing himself. They made jokes at his expense. One proctor even tied a tally-stick around the boy's neck, and with permission and the agreement of his instructors, made notches on it every time Donal pronounced something the way he always had and not as his schoolmates did. At the end of the week, the notches were added up and the total determined whether or not he would be allowed privileges with the others or would stay in his room with extra studies.

That lasted through one month. Being a smart lad, Donal observed and copied. Within another thirty days, he'd modified his lilting Irish brogue into a refined British drawl, such a good copy of his schoolmates' accents he was mistaken for one of them until his name was learned. Even then, someone would wonder aloud why a youngster with an Irish name sounded so much like an Englishman.

When Donal returned home for his first holiday from school, Quinton swore he couldn't understand a word the boy said, whereupon Donal replied he had best get an interpreter, for his new manner of speaking was here to stay.

"Let's face it, Father." He ignored Quinton's slight wince as he replaced his usual familiar epithet of *Da* with that more formal title. "You want me to succeed, and I can't do it if I sound as if I'm still pushing a plow through the sod."

Quinton could only agree as he saw his plan for his eldest had succeeded too well.

Even that early, Donal had resolved to stay in England and not return to Tipperary except for holidays.

He'd seen quickly enough where the opportunities lay, in social advancement as well as the pleasures he'd discovered.

Now, however, his father's letter insisting he begin thinking of marriage might put a halt to that more enjoyable part of his life.

Chapter 2

"Beg pardon, sir." Rollo appeared in the doorway. "Mr. Josslyn is here and wondering if you can receive him? I explained you were at your *toilette*."

Donal paused, razor in hand. "Tell him to come on up. I believe he knows the way."

With a bow, Rollo disappeared again. There was the sound of voices below and someone tromped up the stairs. In a moment, Ashley Josslyn, tall, blond, and dressed to dandified perfection, stood framed in the doorway.

Removing his low-crowned hat, he looked in, then flinched dramatically. "I say, Don. Didn't expect to find you shucked. Thought you'd at least be wearing your trousers and braces."

"Am I offending your sensibilities by appearing only minimally dressed?" Donal kept his attention on his task, leaning forward to peer into the looking-glass. He touched his chin, studying the coppery bristles adorning it.

"Minimally?" Joss laughed. "You're starkers, man."

"Nonsense," Donal denied. "I've a towel around my neck."

"True." Joss allowed that was so. "Well, it doesn't bother me a bit, as long as no one sees and mistakes us for a couple of mandrakes."

He didn't move from the doorway, however.

12

"I assure you, Joss, you're not my type, besides being the wrong gender."

"Thank God for that, is all I have to say." Joss quirked a blond brow. "By the bye, what *is* your type exactly…in a woman, I mean?"

"What else would you mean?" Donal tilted his head, gently skimming the razor up his throat. He flicked suds and a swathe of whiskers into the basin and touched the blade to the underside of his jaw and the curve of his chin. "I'm afraid my taste in women is fairly simple. She must be alive and have a willing cunny."

"Couldn't have said it better, myself." Joss continued wavering as if uncertain whether to enter or go back downstairs to the parlor. He twirled his hat in his hands.

"Quit dithering and come in." Donal glanced his way, then turned back to the mirror over the wash stand. "Rollo, I know you're out there," he called. "Come chaperone us and put Master Joss' conscience at ease."

The manservant appeared behind Joss, looking over his shoulder. "I can do that if you'd like, sir, but I hardly think either your virtue or Master Joss's is in danger. One can't guard what's nonexistent."

"Rollo, I believe I'm insulted," Joss exclaimed.

"That's your privilege, sir." The valet smirked. In Joss's presence, the master-manservant demeanor was also briefly laid aside. He looked to Donal. "Would you like me to help you finish your shave, sir?"

"No, thanks." Donal glanced at him and back to his reflection.

Shaving was one thing he'd always done himself. Though he wouldn't admit it, he had a fear of being seized with a sneezing fit at the moment the blade

13

touched his throat and suffering accidental exsanguination. At least if he were the one holding the razor, he'd have enough time to deflect it before the sneeze occurred.

"I believe there are enough tasks here for you to attend without that." He waved a hand to the clothing on the chair.

Without another word, Rollo picked up the shirt and neckpiece, inspecting them for food or wine stains needing laundering.

Joss still hovered.

"Oh, come in, Joss, and stop being such a prude." Donal slung suds off the blade, swished it into the basin, then applied it to his left cheek.

****

Ashley Charles Albert Josslyn was Donal's best friend. They were the same age and, though one was English and the other Irish, both had similar backgrounds. They were each from the gentry, eldest sons sent by their fathers to make a small entry into the Society to which their male parents were eager to gain access, as well as paving the way for their younger brothers.

They'd met while at university. The college had a surfeit of students that year and the dormitories were full. Donal's rooms contained two bedchambers and it was the practice for seniors to let extra space to freshmen in such an event.

One day, he was startled to hear a knock at his door and discover a young man his own age, asking, "I hear you have an extra bedroom. Would you consider keeping a pig?"

Donal did consider. If Joss didn't take umbrage at

being termed *a pig*, then he would agree to sharing his digs.

The two found they had similar interests, and stayed friends through graduation and beyond.

Though fairly subdued at Eton, once at Cambridge, Donal, along with Joss, fell in with a crowd champing under the rules and regulations placed upon them by their parents. In the absence of their curbing presences, they sought to break free from those bonds.

There had been a rumor his father had been a wild youth, quickly married off by grandfather Aloysius to nip the would-be libertine in the bud. Quinton never spoke of that, but Donal had heard the servants whispering belowstairs. When given an opportunity to enjoy his own freedom, he told himself he was simply following his father's unspoken example.

Drinking, gambling, and whoring, merely dabbled in while at school, followed in wholehearted and swift succession. Soon the young Irishman discovered within himself a desire to experience even more delicious and carnal satisfaction. He was smart enough to realize word of his attempts to satisfy what he considered the depth of his passion mustn't get back to his father, however.

While many of his fellows threw caution to the winds, becoming admitted rakehells openly chastised by their families and Society in general, Donal kept his own propensities well hidden. He wasn't about to let his leanings interfere with his studies, no matter how much he enjoyed gratifying them. It was only during his leisure time, after studies or anything academic had been completed and set aside, that he allowed his carnal yearnings free rein.

Generally with Joss in tow, he did so only in specific

places where his identity wouldn't be questioned. Even after he left the university and took up residence in London, he kept up this masquerade.

To that end, when the urge for physical satisfaction became overpowering, each was careful to keep himself hidden by wearing a black colombina completely covering the features. Thus assured of anonymity, they reveled wholeheartedly, tipping ladybirds, and occasionally daring the indulgence of *ménage a quatre* while swapping their women back and forth as the mood dictated, or joyously joining in the occasional minor orgy with six or eight of their *camarades des plaisirs charnels*.

Donal and Joss might be rogues, though secret ones, but they never became true libertines. Indeed, they would've been shocked had anyone suggested they were. Neither had an inclination to taste the forbidden as did those *débauchés*. While others loudly and blatantly proclaimed their disdain for Society's mores as they dabbled in the unsanctioned, Donal and Joss made the decision to clandestinely revel in the lesser excesses available to them.

Both sought only the satisfyingly carnal, a deep abiding craving for the physically sensual act of sex as it involved females. Neither visited the third story of the brothel where mandrakes, followers of de Sade, and others of the more extreme leanings satisfied their desires, nor did they imbibe in the tears of the poppy or other decadent and habit-forming gifts from the Far East.

Though their vices weren't as condemnable as others, each felt it his duty to keep them hidden because of his father's wishes for him to be accepted into the English world. For Joss, this meant only Donal, Rollo, and his own valet were aware.

In Donal's case, the same held true. Only those three knew the well-mannered young gentleman appearing at Almack's and other clubs, one any mother would've allowed alone in her daughter's company, was the rake celebrating nightly in the most notorious districts of the city.

****

"To what do I owe this early-morning call?" Donal asked.

"Just wanting to make certain you arrived home in one piece."

Joss tossed his hat into the chair Donal's clothing had recently vacated. It was the latest fashion, low-crowned and wide-brimmed, a style affected by artists and other bohemian types, as well as the very young. Dropping into another chair, he leaned back and stretched out his legs, clad in dove-gray trousers, before him. His black low Wellingtons peeked from under the hems.

"You were so foxed when you left the Church, I wasn't certain you'd make it into your curricle, much less arrive home. Why do you insist on driving that thing yourself when you know you're going to drain every bottle in the cellar?"

"I'm touched." Donal paused long enough to give his friend a sarcastic little bow, then concentrated on his image, flicking more suds into the basin.

"Not to keep harping on the subject, old chap, but would you mind covering a bit of your anatomy?" Joss put a hand to his eyes, then spread his fingers, peeping through them. "Seeing all that glaring-red man-fuzz is a bit off-putting."

"My apologies for being so hirsute." Donal reached for a towel from those on the dresser top, flipped one open, and wound it around his hips. "There. Does that soothe your sensibilities?" As Joss nodded, he continued, "You've no room to talk, you know. I swear I've never seen so much yellow hair in my life, other than on a herd dog."

"Perhaps that's why we're such good friends." Joss sighed in mock resignation. "Because we're so overburdened with hair."

"As for my handling the curricle," Donal returned to the subject. "I think you were more than worried. Don't I have a vague memory of you personally helping me into it and placing the reins in my hands?

"Yes, well…can't have my best friend driving off and perhaps overturning and killing himself, can I? After all, neither of us can afford a scandal, and you doing something like that would definitely call in the Peelers. If you're dead, I'll be the one bearing the brunt of the whole thing. So far, we've managed to keep our adventures away from the gossips' knowledge as well as out of the newspapers. I'd like to keep it that way."

"Once more, your concern, especially for my part in *our adventures*, as you term them, is touching."

This time it was Joss who gave Donal an ironic dip of his head.

"Pardon, Mr. Donal," Rollo interrupted. "Do you wish me to lay out your usual evening clothes or will you be wearing that new set tonight?"

"New dunnage?" Joss looked interested. "Going all-out, are we?"

"The new ones." Donal dropped the razor onto the dresser top and reached for a third towel, wiping his face.

"Otherwise, I wouldn't have bothered fetching them today."

He laid the towel next to the basin as the valet approached with his shirt, dropping it over his head.

"Got to look my best as I make my first assault," he said, as he pulled down the shirt, thrusting his arms into the sleeves.

"So you *are* going to Almack's tonight?" Joss questioned.

"You know I am." Donal's answer held the inflection that it should be obvious.

He stood still while Rollo closed the neck of the shirt, maneuvering tiny mother-of-pearl ovals through the upper placket's buttonholes.

"No time like the present to start my campaign."

"You're actually beginning the hunt?" Joss looked disbelieving.

"Have to. You were here when I got that letter from home." Donal accepted drawers from Rollo, pulled them on and tied them, then took trousers and stepped into them and buttoned the front panel. "My father's making matrimonial noises. If I don't find myself a wife soon, *he* will."

"Damn, Donal, I'll say it again...you're only twenty-four," Joss protested. "Is he trying to tie you down before you've even gotten out of the stable?"

"My dear Joss..." Donal raised his head as Rollo wound the length of linen around his neck and proceeded to fold and tie it. "Careful, Rollo, not too tight. I want to be able to breathe."

The manservant loosened the knot a bit.

"If we're going to use equine metaphors...getting into harness doesn't mean there won't be any midnight gallops with willing fillies other than the old mare in the round pen."

Rollo seized a comb and applied himself to Donal's mad thatch of curls.

"I suppose." Joss' answer was slightly uncertain. "I'm thankful my father isn't putting on the screws."

"Yet," Donal added, ominously.

"So…" Joss ignored that, immediately speaking with near-false brightness, as someone wishing to cover a friend's *faux pas*. "Got any plans after your initial entry into the fray? I hear there's a card game going on at Remy's."

"Not tonight." Donal surveyed himself in the standing glass near the wardrobe, inspecting the magnificent folds of his cravat, then touching a finger to the forward-swept coppery curls at his temples. "After associating with so many nubile but untouchable virgins of the *ton*, I'll be desperate for some time at the Church."

"Going to dab it up with a few of the followers of Venus, eh? I can't help but agree." Joss looked eager. "Why don't we meet and go there together?"

"Splendid idea."

"In that case, I'll bid you farewell and leave you to your morning tasks." Joss took his hat from Rollo, who had retrieved it from the chair.

He perched it on his head, giving it a smart pat to settle it.

"You'd best hurry, for the morning's nearly gone. No, don't bother seeing me out," he continued as the valet went to the door, stepping back so he could walk through. "I know the way well enough."

He tapped the manservant on the chest.

"Keep him out of trouble, Rollo."

"I believe it's a little late for that, Master Joss," Rollo replied.

Joss' laughter trailed back up the stairs.

Chapter 3

Standing before the triptych cheval glass in the shop of *Wellsby, Tailors*, Donal frowned as he studied his reflection. He was certain both the tailor and his valet saw a well-appointed young gentleman of the *ton*. What he saw was a fox-haired Irish upstart about to muscle his way into their Society.

Which image is the correct one?

He'd accepted the shirt Wellsby brought out, questioning, "Silk? Not linen?"

"It's the latest thing," he was assured.

Donal slid it on with misgivings. He'd heard of no one wearing a silk shirt before. That was for smallclothes or ladies' garments. Still, if Wellsby said so…

Next came the vest, and again Donal had arguments aplenty. Not only was it of white satin with a notched collar, but the embroidery…it wasn't gold thread as he'd requested but *white* also?

"I say, Wellsby, didn't someone or other write up a set of rules saying a gentleman could wear a white waistcoat only under the most desperate of circumstances?" He gave the tailor an askance look.

"That may be true, sir, but this is more understated. Simplicity but refined without drawing attention to itself." Wellsby tugged the vest points over Donal's waistline, smoothing the front. "They look. They aren't certain they see embellishments. They look again. At *you*, sir."

"I see." Donal watched his image intently.

Yes, he understood what Wellsby meant. When he moved, the design became visible. When he stilled, it took a keen eye to observe it. That should make him the center of attention, but in a good way.

He had no argument with the trousers, but when he slid his arms into the evening jacket and settled it across his shoulders…

"Satin lapels? They're the correct width, and they curve around my shirtfront properly, but…I want to look elegant, not like a dandified toff."

Again, he was assured satin lapels were the latest thing. From Paris *couturiers*. That seemed to be Wellsby's best argument. As usual, it always swayed Donal into accepting, which he did with a nod.

"This, however…" He fiddled with the neckpiece, if he dared call it that. "I'm afraid it won't do, Wellsby. It's too small."

He wondered why Rollo hadn't made any comments or protest. The valet was always up on the latest styles. Could it be he approved?

"I assure you, Master Donal." At last Rollo spoke. "A cravat wrapped around the neck and knotted into a bow is the current ultimate in evening wear."

"Oh? Quite so, then." Donal released the cravat, patting the breast of the jacket. "Those inner pockets? You made them deep?"

Wellsby nodded. The tailor had questioned that at the time, fearing it would ruin the smooth line of the jacket's chest, but, as usual, he had done as Donal asked.

"Good." Donal thrust fingers inside each pocket as he spoke. That was where he planned to put his colombina and his *préventif*, the mask in the right pocket, the condom in the left. "Wouldn't want anything falling out when I bow. Now…the hat?"

He touched a hand to an errant curl aiming a spike of hair at his cheek. Better ask Rollo to do a bit of a trim…not too much, of course, didn't want to look as if he'd just been to a sheep shearing, but perhaps an eighth of an inch off the temples. Briefly he wished his hair wasn't such a bright shade of red. Ginger, perhaps, or deep auburn…why did it have to be flaming copper, as blatant as a rising sun? Everyone would be looking at him, all right, at the man whose head looked like a Guy Fawkes bonfire.

Wellsby distracted him from that thought by presenting the top hat as if it were a jewel on a silver salver, its brim resting in his palms. Donal considered it.

"Bit tall— Don't tell me," he went on before the tailor could speak. "The latest style? From Paris?"

"Exactly." Wellsby bowed, looking relieved he didn't have to point this out.

"Silk?" Donal brushed fingers over the brim, adding, "Also."

"Silk is coming into use for a good many things nowadays, sir."

With a sigh, Donal placed the hat on his head, settled it, and turned to Rollo, arms widespread. "Will I do?"

"If not, there should be a complete reconstruction of the rules," Rollo told him.

"You'll have every man there envious and every woman…" Wellsby left the rest unsaid, as it might be too indiscreet.

"Well, then…" Donal turned toward the disrobing rooms. "I'll just slip back into my own duds, you can box these, and Rollo, you may have the pleasure of carrying them for me." He called over his shoulder. "I'll expect a billing at the end of the month, of course."

A gentleman never paid for anything then and there. Wellsby's bow acknowledged this.

In the carriage, with the various boxes on the seat beside Rollo as he sat across from him, Donal said, "Once we're home, I'm for that nap. Going to need all my energy tonight. Don't bother me until it's time to start readying myself."

Chapter 4

Almack's was ablaze with lights. Thousands of candles would be sacrificed in a brilliant immolation that night to keep the various rooms bright as day. Donal strolled through the crowds with ease, nodding to this group, bowing to that one. Joss had met him outside and they walked together. There had been no problem gaining admittance.

He was again thankful he'd attracted the favor of one of the Lady Patronesses of the establishment. Though they no longer had the power they'd carried earlier in the century, the seven women making up the committee still decided who among the men of their acquaintance would or would not make the grade and become members. Good breeding and deportment were generally the rule of thumb because the club had been organized to keep out the *nouveau riche* abruptly inundating Society at the beginning of the century. Now, however, a good many of that class found themselves admitted because their behavior eclipsed that of more noble members.

The lady in question, with whom Donal had the most innocent of passing acquaintances, had a soft spot in her heart for red-haired men. From the moment she was introduced to the copper-haired young Irishman, he became a favorite, though at that point they'd only spoken once or twice. She'd even provided him with a voucher for gaining admittance, paying the fee of ten guineas herself.

Donal showed his gratitude by arranging a moment alone with his benefactress where he offered her his gratitude for the gift, then waited for the suggestion that she wished to be repaid in a more personal way for this favor. It wouldn't have been much of a chore, since the lady was still relatively attractive though over a score older than he. He was more than surprised as well as grateful when she waved away his thankfulness, stating she was only too happy to help someone she thought worthy of gaining access to Society.

He later learned from Joss, a great supplier of gossipy titbits gleaned here and there, that the lady's first sweetheart had been red-haired and also from the middle class, thereby assuring the romance would go no further. After that, Donal always made a point to speak to his patroness whenever he saw her, and if they were both at Almack's on a Wednesday night, asked to be graced with a dance.

He and Joss sailed past the supper rooms with their day-old bread and dry cake. Before leaving home, Donal had asked Rollo to whip him up something filling but quick to eat. He didn't want a growling belly providing embarrassment or diverting him from his mission by demanding a detour to the dining rooms to quiet it.

Not that the bread and cake weren't good. The thinly-sliced bread served with butter was tasty, and though he'd never liked frosted pastries, dry cake, minus all that slapped-on sugary sweetness, was pleasing enough to his palate, especially the lemon-flavored kind.

The fact that only lemonade or tea were served as beverages, with occasionally ratafia and orgeat, was also a strong deterrent. Donal wasn't too fond of almonds, and both drinks contained the nut. Ratafia was an almond-flavored cordial and orgeat sirup was an almond emulsion simply too sweet to take more than a sip.

He definitely needed something stronger and more alcoholic tonight.

Joss made a few comments about his attire, and Donal reciprocated. He'd always thought his friend's garments the epitome of current fashion. Seeing the way his companion's own neckpiece was wound, knotted, and fluffed to hide both his collar and shirt-front in a pouter pigeon effect, made him wonder again if he shouldn't have argued with Wellsby a little more about his choices. After Joss declared his remarks mere politeness because his own tailor hadn't such good taste or more insight into Parisian fashions, he felt more assured.

The dances were already starting in the ballroom. He could hear music, a lilting melody of some kind, perhaps a waltz. Donal was too young to remember when only *contredanses* were allowed. By the time he arrived on the scene, the dance program had been enlarged to include the quadrille and then the waltz, which by that time had lost its scandalous reputation of being known as "the hold-close dance."

Nowadays, a young man could dance a waltz with a young woman without asking both parents' permission beforehand and being watched closely by them for any impropriety as it was performed. Of course, one still asked parental permission as well as the young lady's, but that was more or less a mere formality, especially where other dances were concerned.

Not many couples were on the dance floor yet. Most

of the young women sat on the sidelines, on settees and small sofas arranged around the edges.

Donal stopped, looking around, scanning the crowd. He saw groupings here and there, the men mostly standing, fathers, uncles, and sometimes brothers hovering slightly. The girls themselves glanced around surveying the crowd, most eagerly, a few shyly. Usually they were seated with their mothers or sometimes a married older sister, or barring that, an aunt or some other duenna type.

One had to brave those guards to get to the prize.

His gaze settled on one group consisting of two gentlemen standing behind a crimson velvet settee, while on it sat a woman and a girl who was a beauty by any standards. The woman surely was her mother because there were still remnants of faded splendor and a strong resemblance to the girl, giving Donal a good idea how the young lady would look in twenty years.

Not bad, he told himself. He decided he could accept living with someone ageing that gracefully. When he himself was in his forties, he expected to look much as his father did now…still well-appointed, fiery hair mellowed by streaks of silver. They'd make a handsome couple, he thought.

The girl was looking around impatiently, with occasional irritated glances at her mother. Abruptly, she glanced in Donal's direction, looked away, then back, and smiled.

Rescue me, that smile seemed to say. *Come over here, introduce yourself, and whisk me away.*

He drew in a deep breath, and stopped so quickly Joss nearly barreled into him.

"Have you sighted your first quarry?" Joss

recovered. He'd been looking in the opposite direction and hadn't seen the girl.

"That one." Donal nodded, averting his gaze quickly so it wouldn't be obvious.

Joss turned. The girl was now looking away, pretending she was unaware of their scrutiny.

She's a quick one, Donal thought.

"Ah…"

"*Ah?* What does that mean? Exactly?" Donal searched for a nuance. "What do you know?"

"It means nothing, except the young lady is guarded like the Crown Jewels."

"Interesting." *No matter. I like a challenge.* "Why? Tell me more."

"Her father's some minor baronet or other. No one, really, as far as importance is concerned, but she does have a fairly good dowry plus a fortune which he's publicly announced he intends to divide between her and her brother. She's a good catch." Joss leaned closer. "If you can get past the watchdog." He nodded at the older woman. "Her aunt, her mother's sister. The mother's deceased, some ten years ago."

"You've quite a bit of knowledge about them," Donal remarked.

"Family of a friend. The brother, actually."

"Do I know him?"

"You've never met him." Joss gestured. "Shall I make an introduction?"

"If you'd be so kind."

Together, they made their way through the crowd to the red velvet settee.

****

Several hours later, Donal decided to call it a night.

He felt he'd acquitted himself well as a sporting but relatively mild-mannered man-about-town. He'd been introduced to several young women, danced with them all, ingratiated himself with mothers and fathers alike, then proceeded to make his initial choices, and received permission to call on each.

Now he'd had enough. Holding all that desirable young femininity in his arms, feeling the movement of supple nubile forms under his hands and occasionally brushing against his own body was engendering a need demanding to be fulfilled.

A glance across the floor to where Joss was whirling a lady about made him think his friend felt the same way. Joss glanced over her head, caught his eye and jerked his gaze toward the exit while raising his brows. Donal nodded and turned his attention back to his partner as the music ended. Bowing, he escorted her to her seat, made some innocuous murmur, and hurried away to join his friend.

As they left, Donal felt satisfied with the way the night had played itself out.

He'd started the hunt, found his prey, three of them, and now would proceed with stalking and perhaps trapping one of the lovely creatures. Then, hopefully, his father would be satisfied and he could get on with his life.

If not, if any of the three managed to elude and escape him…then there would be more of this pleasant agony. He felt certain he wouldn't fail, however.

****

They decided to take Joss' curricle and leave Donal's, coming back for it later.

"Is this to make certain I get partway home safely?"

Donal asked.

"You see through me, don't you?" Joss didn't attempt to deny it.

Donal decided he must've been pretty high into the wind the night before, even more than usual, if Joss was being that cautious.

"That reminds me." He spoke again after a few moments of riding in silence, watching Joss' hands, the left loosely clasping the reins, the right holding the whip. "Soon I need to make a trip to our friendly neighborhood chemist, and visit his supply room."

Joss turned toward him with a raised brow.

"My *préventif* is getting a bit thin," he explained. "I need to purchase another. Pity I didn't think of it earlier. I might've stopped by while I was out shopping."

"You're still using that thing?"

He couldn't tell if Joss' answer was surprise or disappointment. At the suggestion of Donal's father…and for that, read *order*, since Quinton McCoy had written his son and told him if he decided to have any *untoward alliances*, he'd best make certain they were *safe* ones…he'd talked Joss into accompanying him. The chemist had also been recommended by Quinton, though Donal still had no idea how his father knew of such an establishment in London, since as far as he was aware his parent had never been across the sea to England and definitely hadn't gone to school there. He wondered if his father had dared inquire of such a place of Lord Alisdaire, the noble for whom Quinton was steward. "I thought you might've done away with it now that you've a mistress."

"My dear Joss…" Donal's manner was patronizing to cover his astonishment at this rather naïve statement.

"I especially need it now."

"Why, don't you trust Nellie?"

"Not particularly. After all, she's a beautiful woman and has had plenty of admirers. Never know when one might come sniffing around and tempt her to betray me. Anyway, simply because she knows ways to keep herself from getting planted doesn't mean she will. To tell the truth, I don't particularly trust anyone."

"I hope you don't include me in that mix." Joss looked worried. He glanced at Donal and back at the horses.

"Of course not." Donal smiled. "After all, we're partners in crime, aren't we? Isn't there something called 'honor among thieves'?"

"Don't know that I like being called a criminal or a thief…" Joss muttered. He studied the reins, rubbing the handle of the whip against the leather lines in his left hand. "…since perhaps the only law we've broken is when we bought those *préventifs.*"

"You haven't stopped being careful, have you?" Donal's expression held concern.

"Of course not." Joss voiced his usual complaint. "It's just that the things are damned awkward…having to interrupt a vigorous dabbing to put it on, and…"

"I admit the ol' nebuchadnezzar doesn't dance as well when it's in costume, but better to make it work a bit more energetically than to sire a bastard…or get the glim, the French pox, or something worse. Any of which would definitely get us booted out of Almack's, I might add, as well as probably causing disinheritance, and other unpleasantness."

"Please." Joss shivered and looked around as if fearing someone might've heard.

They'd passed a couple of hansoms and one or two late-night coaches. On the streets, a few tavern celebrants were wending their drunken way homeward. A couple of midinettes huddled together on a street corner. Ordered by a patrolling Peeler to "Hurry on there," the two women scurried across the street, directly in front of the curricle.

Joss pulled the horses up short to avoid running them down.

"'ey…watch it there!"

One raised her head, shaking a fist. The other caught her arm and dragged her to the opposite curb.

"Damned dollymops. I could've killed both of them." He flicked the whip and the horses started up again.

"Lucky there was a patrolman on the scene, wasn't it?"

"Was it?" Joss didn't look as if he thought so. "I can hear him now: '…and where were you headed, sir?' 'Well, Constable, my friend and I were on our way to a brothel to have a little sport…' '…and you were in such a hurry you trampled two women?' Oh yes, that would go over well."

"You, my friend, worry too much." Donal patted Joss's shoulder. "It would've been his fault. He sent them running in front of us."

Joss thought about that a moment. "Somehow I doubt he would've seen it that way."

He shook his head and resumed their previous conversation. "Anyway…it was a fortunate day when your father suggested that little device. I'm still surprised *my* father didn't mention it. He's so damned concerned with my reputation…*his* reputation." He looked thoughtful. "Don't you think it odd? One is called the *Préventif Française,* and the other is called the French pox?"

"That's only appropriate." Donal's shrug said he hadn't given it much thought. "The French gave us one, they should also give us the way to prevent it."

They both laughed at that.

"Donal, why are you going to the Church with me, when you've a mistress who's the most toothsome bit this side of a pastry shop?"

"Variety, my friend."

"Ah yes, the spice of life…good ol' Cowper. Glad he wrote that."

"Where women are concerned, it's definitely necessary. Can you imagine anything drearier than being with the same woman day in and day out…oh damn, I've just described marriage, haven't I?" Donal pulled a rueful face.

Each laughed uproariously at that, seeming to find it exceedingly funny, and neither was drunk yet, having had only lemonade at Almack's.

"Guess you'll really need Nellie and the ladies of the Church after that fateful event, won't you?" Joss asked, in sympathy.

"More like *fatal* event. Damn it, Joss, I don't want to get married." For a moment, Donal sank into moroseness.

"Why is your father pushing marriage on you, anyway?" Joss slowed the horses to a walk. There were no other vehicles in this section, and if they were going to talk overlong, he didn't want to arrive at their destination too soon. "He hasn't gotten wind of your extracurricular activities, has he?"

"Nothing like that," Donal denied. "He was married young…twenty, I think…and I think he truly believes I should be, also. I heard some backstairs babble that he was a bit of a rip while a youngster, but I seriously doubt he got a chance to experience much before being caged, so he doesn't realize how I want to spread my wings a bit before taking that plunge." He paused. "Either that or he thinks I'm a chip off the old block and is trying to prevent it. Anyway, according to his timetable, I'm long overdue for a walk down the aisle."

"He also doesn't know how much of a wide wingspan you've already attained, my avian friend." Joss looked up, pulling slightly on the reins. "We're here."

Before them stood a large four-story mansion, its many windows gleaming with light.

"No more of this dreary talk." Joss slid out of the curricle, tossing the reins to a waiting groom. "Let's plunge with abandon into the joyous worship of the goddess of earthly love."

Donal followed, digging into his right breast pocket. He brought out his mask and proceeded to tie it around his head. It was of black silk, covering his face from his hairline to just above his upper lip. There was no way by looking at him anyone could guess his identity, though he had a vague discomfort that any acquaintance seeing that red hair would know exactly who was behind the mask. After all, how many fox-haired young gentlemen could there be in London?

Nevertheless, it gave him some peace of mind and a sense of anonymity, no matter how false, so he continued wearing it when he visited his favored dens of iniquity.

Joss put on his mask also. Once it was secured, they made their way up the stairs to the front stoop.

Chapter 5

With a groan, Donal settled himself at his desk in the study.

Lord, what a head I have this morning!

Considering the things he'd done the previous night, he was surprised he wasn't near-comatose. Two bottles of wine and two willing ladies of the evening…and how stimulating all four had been. He decided his current discomfort was worth it.

Upon awakening, he'd refused his usual breakfast fare. The thought of toast and chocolate made his stomach rival his head in rebelliousness even worse than the day before. He ordered Rollo to take away the tray and brew a large pot of coffee. Managing to crawl from bed, he forewent his usual morning ablutions for the moment. Just then he didn't trust his own hand with a razor, he was so coopered. It was a struggle simply to pull on clothing.

At last, dressed in trousers and shirt and wrapped in his dressing gown, he slumped at the desk, staring at the sheet of foolscap before him as if he had no idea what it was.

Looking almost as ill, though natty as ever, Joss arrived a few minutes later, along with the morning post. Donal wondered why he was there and not snoozing off his own wine-head.

Did I ask him to be here? Why would I do that?

Joss himself gave no explanation. As if he were expected, he simply strolled in, nodded a greeting to the valet, and sprawled in a chair, waving a hand at the coffee.

"Pour me some of that elixir, Rollo."

When he received it, he accepted it with a slightly shaking hand and, after balancing the cup and making certain the liquid didn't splash, went on, "Don't mind me, I'll simply huddle here and suffer in silence."

Stay silent he didn't, however.

Gesturing to the letters lying by Donal's left hand, he asked, "Aren't you going to read those? Don't let me stop you from your morning routine."

"They can wait." Donal spoke quietly when he really wished to snap, *Not so loud,* though in reality Joss was nearly whispering.

He ignored the two folded sheets. He knew what they were. He recognized the handwritings on the outside.

"One's from Colin, probably wanting to come for a visit before going from Eton to university, and the other… It's from Father, no doubt bewailing more of Padraig's escapades."

Donal's youngest brother was eighteen, just graduating from Eton and preparing to go to Cambridge. Donal had left school as Colin was arriving, so they'd had very little association. Nevertheless, during Colin's first year and Donal's last, he pulled a few strings and managed to make his younger brother his fag, preventing Colin's mistreatment by some other senior.

Though he made the youngster work as industriously as any freshman in running errands and performing other chores, he took the boy aside and gave him a few pointers, attempting to assist him in settling in and avoiding trouble, especially in the matter of his accent.

Colin, being the good lad he was, did his best to follow Big Brother's advice, though he, like his father, very frankly told Donal he didn't like the way he'd "gone over to the British side."

As a result, Colin practiced an odd dichotomy of dialect. While at school, he spoke as his brother did, and when at home, he sounded as he always had.

As for his other sibling…

Padraig was a troublemaker and always had been. He'd been sent to Eton, also. Though Donal hadn't been master to Padraig, he attempted to guide his younger brother.

All efforts had been vehemently rejected.

Not liking how he was treated because of his Irish accent but disdaining to change as Donal had, upon completing his three years, Padraig chose to go to Oxford instead of Cambridge. There, he became part of the "South Nation," that section of the student body including the Irish, the Welsh, and English people living south of the River Trent.

A bit defiantly, to Donal's way of thinking, he offered as his excuse that he didn't want to turn out as his elder brother had.

Padraig was a good student, but he was also one for pranks and misbehavior. News of his practical jokes, tricks, and other adventures, most unfortunately concentrating either on the female sex or cony-catching in some form or other, spread to Cambridge where Donal was enrolled. Padraig had the dubious honor of being one of the few students called before the university proctors and sent directly to the vice-chancellor for verbal chastisement. No amount of threats were successful, however, nor did letters to his father work any wonders.

Only Quinton McCoy's position as Lord Alisdaire's steward and a letter from His Lordship himself saved Padraig from expulsion.

Even with that specific brother so far away, Donal spent a good part of his terms apologizing for him as his reputation was bunted far and wide. At the same time, he was grateful he himself was by then well-established enough for neither his teachers nor his friends to believe he would act the same way.

Relieved he had everyone so gulled but fearing Padraig's acts might somehow bring his own behavior to light, though his brother was at another college, Donal had even taken upon himself the task of writing and cautioning Padraig in what he was doing. The warnings were brushed aside, and Donal was nothing short of relieved when he received word from his father that Padraig had finally committed the ultimate in embarrassment and disobedience—though he never outright mentioned the specific crime—and had been requested to leave the university before graduation.

Though he felt he should've been apologetic, Donal loudly rejoiced he was no longer even vaguely in his brother's vicinity. Except for a couple of visits after Donal moved to London, which were mercifully short, and during which Padraig never spoke of the reason for his abrupt dismissal, they hadn't seen each other since.

"The letter can wait," he decided. "Just now..." He stopped, wincing as another pulsation, no doubt triggered by the sound of his own voice, speared through his temple.

"I say, sorry I had to pull you away from your fun last night." Joss' voice seemed to come from very far away. It sounded hollow.

Glancing at him, Donal saw he had his coffee cup raised and appeared to be drinking and talking at the same time.

"It was getting more than late and those two girls you were drubbing looked to be exhausted."

"Only two?" Donal shook his head, then stopped as that made his brain joggle painfully. "I could've sworn there were four."

"You *were* seeing double then," Joss exclaimed as if vindicated. "I knew it." He considered. "Sometimes I worry about you, Don. Can flushing the old system that many times be healthy?"

He set down the cup. Rollo poured more, for which he was given a grateful glance. When Donal didn't answer his last remark, Joss peered at the paper lying on the desk.

"What are you doing anyway, and why can't it wait until later? You don't appear in any condition to do anything of import just now. Hadn't you better delay until a clearer mind prevails?"

"Possibly so, but I need to get this done immediately. Doing it should get myself into a better frame of mind and body. Stage Two of the hunting expedition goes into effect today."

"Oh Lord…so I didn't imagine that." Joss groaned and drank more coffee. He watched Donal scribble something, slinging ink as the quill traveled from inkpot to paper. "That's your battle plan?"

"More my list of prey."

"May I?" Joss held out a hand which by now was

remarkably steady.

With a nod, Donal handed it over.

He studied it. "I say, isn't this a bit cold-blooded? Writing everything out as if it were a laundry list or something?"

"Is it? I'd think it would be the best way, all things considered."

Donal had divided the sheet of paper into three sections, separated from each other by long vertical lines. In each division, there was a heading.

The first read: *1) Araminta Bradley*. Under it were the listings: *Pro—beautiful, can make fairly intelligently-spoken small-talk, baronet's only daughter. Con—accustomed to the best, conversation subjects mostly fashion and clothing during limited exchanges with her, baronet's only daughter.*

"Yes," Joss agreed. "I can see how being a baronet's daughter would be both an asset and a disadvantage for you. She'll expect only the best."

"Luckily, Lord Benton's a very *minor* baronet, so perhaps there wouldn't be much protest against the son of Irish gentry asking for his daughter's hand, especially since Father's associated with Lord Alisdaire."

"Quite so," Joss agreed. He looked at the next entry in Donal's script, quite legible in spite of his hangover. "Amelia Smythe-Bolton? Really, Don?"

He read what was written by that young lady's name: *2) Amelia Smythe-Bolton. Pro—pretty, halfway decent conservation, graceful in deportment, substantial dowry. Con—giggles more than I like, indulges in pastries, opinionated, buck-teeth?*

"I agree with your assessment here. She giggles at everything. While you were dancing with her, I kept checking to see if you were being bold enough to tickle her publicly."

"I think it's mostly nervous habit." Donal dismissed Joss' observation. "It remains to be seen how long I can bear that. The pastry habit worries me. I wouldn't want to be bound to a woman who's attempting to transform herself into a jelly dumpling. At the moment, I'm leaning very strongly toward Miss Bradley."

"Don't lean too far just yet," Joss cautioned. "After all, you only danced with her once."

"That might be enough." Donal held out his arms as if placing them around someone's waist.

One barely missed striking his coffee cup. Rollo hurried to move it out of harm's way.

"Thank you, Rollo."

The servant nodded.

Donal fell silent, thinking again how it had felt to hold Miss Bradley as they moved about the dance floor. He'd managed to ask both her and Miss Smythe-Bolton for waltzes, the most acceptable way to have each nestled in his arms with no outcry from anyone. Miss Bradley settled into his embrace quite comfortably and easily. In fact, she'd snuggled closer than was expected, looking up at him with a smile that missed being a suggestive smirk by little more than a control of her lips.

An instant before he whirled her into the first set, she actually leaned against him so their bodies pressed together most improperly, making him visibly flinch as the flounces of her gown and the stiffened crinoline underneath brushed against his nether anatomy. Thank God he had absolute control of it in public. He was also grateful they were moving in the steps of the waltz so she had no occasion to do more.

He couldn't help but wonder what else she might've attempted had the music not started then. What if he'd been able to maneuver her into a quiet corner or a secluded spot? He decided he had to be guarded around Miss Araminta Bradley, who just might be the type to lead him into some act he'd enjoy but would have consequences heading to the altar more hastily than he wished.

As for Miss Smythe-Bolton…

He'd studied her mother while he made the customary small talk with her father. The lady was gaunt and thin, with an overbite that might once have been charming but now increased because of her thinness into what appeared to be a gigantic set of central incisors. Miss Amelia had the same dental problem, which currently was fairly attractive, but if she aged as her mother had…

Would I be able to tolerate looking at those overgrown front teeth forever? As it was now, whenever he glanced at Lady Smythe-Bolton that was all he saw…those large rabbit-like tushes. As for the giggles…

"This last one, however…" Joss paused, shaking his head.

"You have some argument with that one?"

"*Felicity Melton*…" Joss didn't answer, instead reading his notations. "*Pro—pretty.* That's all? Nothing else to commend her?"

"Her uncle's in manufacturing," Donal replied. "*Nouveau riche* to be sure, but a likeable enough fellow, or the Lady Patronesses seem to think so."

Ignoring that, Joss read on, "And the Cons aren't much better…*timid, clumsy, deferred to both uncle and mother for every decision, greatly to be pitied.*" He looked up, tossing the paper onto the desk. "Scratch that one off the list right now. Why did you put her on there in the first place?"

"I'm not so sure." Donal was thoughtful. "About removing her name, I mean."

"I was with you, remember? Introduced you to her uncle? She barely spoke a word the entire time, and when you asked her to dance, they both had to give permission. Then she tripped over her feet as she stood. On the dance floor, she stepped on your toes at least thrice. I saw you wince, and also witnessed the condition of your evening slippers afterward."

Joss glanced around as if expecting to see the damaged slippers sitting in the study, begging for medical treatment.

"The girl's a social disaster. Trust me. You'd be beating your head against the wall within a week of living with her."

"I wonder…"

Felicity Melton was small, delicate, and fair, with ash-brown hair having a glint of gilt, and the most guileless blue gaze, almost colorless in fact, with nothing remarkable about her to attract the eye, and yet…

There had been something about the girl, some aura sending an unfamiliar stab of protectiveness through Donal. It unsettled him because he hadn't felt such a sensation since the time he was a child and viewed the coach dog's puppies or watched his sister's cat play with its kittens.

Felicity had stumbled, yes…but he'd caught her by the elbow, steadying her. She'd smiled at him and that smile did things to his long-hidden sensitivities.

During the waltz, she unbent, daring to speak to him,

telling him how she loved to dance but rarely did because her mother felt they should both continue being in mourning for her father who was dead five years now. If this hadn't been her first season and her uncle hadn't insisted, she was certain her mother wouldn't have allowed her to attend at all.

Before she could say more, the dance ended and Donal escorted her back to the divan where he settled her beside her morose and unsmiling maternal parent. He saw how the light glowing briefly in her cheeks, giving her a high color, was immediately snuffed, and all he could wonder was what else she might've said to him had the waltz lasted longer. He also had a vague wish to make that glow return.

Thinking of that, he shrugged and merely said, "I suppose we shall see. Right now, I'm favoring Miss Bradley, however, so there will probably be no problem."

"More than *favoring*, judging by your expression." Joss made lasciviously hungry sounds, with appropriate leers.

That startled Donal, since he was still thinking of Felicity Melton.

"In the meantime…" He stood, unbuttoning his dressing gown. "I must get ready to begin the hunt. I've permission to call on Miss Bradley this morning and am expected there before eleven. So…" He turned toward the study door. "Unless you plan to come upstairs and watch me dress?"

"I'll forego that pleasure, thank you." Joss was on his feet so quickly it appeared he'd been goosed. "I had enough trouble getting you into your clothes last night." He sniggered. "Took the two girls and myself to do it.

You kept pulling things off as fast as we got them on."

Donal didn't answer, thinking he didn't remember a bit of that and wondering if Joss was merely fabricating at his expense. If not…

Maybe I'd best temper the drinking a bit if I'm beginning not to remember things. He didn't want to commit some act that might get back to people who mattered.

"Perhaps we'd better take Rollo with us next time," he suggested mildly. "I daresay he never has trouble getting me dressed."

He glanced at the valet.

"Only if I'm allowed a chance at a dolly beforehand, sir." Rollo bowed.

"I'll think on it," Donal promised. "See yourself out, Joss."

He went up the stairs.

"Will I see you later tonight?" Joss called from the front door as Rollo opened it for him.

"I doubt it. I've a feeling I'm going to need Nellie's company tonight," Donal replied. "As solace for my suffering."

After all, this might be called a *social engagement*, but to him, it was going to be a minor ordeal. Sitting in a stuffy parlor, having tea with a young woman guarded by a watchdog of an aunt while making the most innocuous conversation was never a pleasant task on the easiest of occasions, especially when he preferred a good glass of wine and a vigorous bed-romp.

Briefly, he cursed his grandfather for not allowing Quinton a bit more free rein before his own marriage and felt anger at his father for wishing the same early shackling of his eldest.

Chapter 6

"Lemon or cream, Mr. McCoy?" Lady Alistair inquired, hand poised between the little bowl holding lemon slices and the silver cream pitcher.

"Neither, thank you, Your Ladyship." Donal accepted the cup and saucer and held it close a moment, making it appear he was savoring the aroma.

In truth, he rested his thumb against the delicate shell of the cup, testing the temperature to determine if the tea was so hot it might burn his mouth. If the heat emanating through the delicate china was any indication, it was scalding.

"A man who enjoys his tea unadulterated. You have the same opinion as my husband, as well as my brother."

"Quite so." He lowered the saucer and gave Her Ladyship his attention.

"I prefer sugar *and* lemon in mine," Araminta spoke up as she received her cup from her aunt, who'd prepared it without asking her preferences.

"That makes it more lemonade than tea," Lady Alistair commented.

Araminta didn't answer. Instead, she sipped daintily, appearing not to be affected by tea hot enough to boil taste buds. Lowering the cup and peering into the liquid, she exclaimed, "Oh!"

Instantly, Donal was on the alert, asking hurriedly, "Too hot? Did you burn your to-…"

He managed to avoid the word *tongue* just in time. That was too personal a word to use on such short acquaintance.

"…your lips?"

"Oh no, nothing of the sort." She laughed away his concern. "I simply noticed the tea is the same color as the fabric I ordered for my new ball gown. What kind of tea is this, Aunt Elspeth?"

"Lapsang Souchong," Her Ladyship answered promptly. "It's a black tea," she added helpfully.

"How odd." Araminta studied the contents of her cup. "It looks rather a dark crimson, I'd say."

She held the cup up to the light and nodded.

"Yes, it's the exact color of that bolt of watered silk Madame Toulouse showed me at her shop last week. I suppose that's why it reminds me of this tea, because it's watered, just as the tea is. Don't you think so, Mr. McCoy?"

She directed this last question at Donal, who was beginning to wonder if he'd wandered into a dress shop by mistake.

"Oh…uh…yes, surely," he stuttered, not certain what answer to give and opting for a vaguely agreeable one.

"She told me the color would contrast beautifully with my hair." Araminta brushed fingers over the bouquet of corkscrew curls at her shoulder. She gave Donal an expectant look.

"I'm certain it shall." He drank tea to forestall further statement. He decided he liked its smoky flavor, with definite hints of peat, paprika, and whiskey, though he was thinking he might soon prefer a cup of the latter.

Since her hair was dark, he would've thought any

color except black, or dark brown, would go well with it but wasn't about to say so. This was a time to be agreeable, not contradictory. Besides, what he knew about women's fashions and *accoutrements* could be put into a thimble. He much preferred women out of their clothing rather than wearing any.

****

Upon arriving at Lord Benton's townhouse, Donal had been received easily enough. He'd supplied his calling card, which the butler accepted, placing it on a small serving tray and leaving him waiting in the foyer while he inquired if Miss Bradley or her aunt would receive him.

Lady Alistair remembered her brother giving his permission to call and welcomed Donal graciously, one might even say *eagerly*, while Araminta acknowledged his presence with a demure smile fading to a slight pout as he sank into a chair opposite her aunt instead of sitting on the divan beside her after she moved over invitingly. She was radiant and more than beautiful in a topaz-yellow morning gown, her hair simply coiffed in a chignon with a bouquet of corkscrew curls gathered over her right shoulder.

Tea was served and the ordeal began.

****

A platter of cake was offered.

Donal tried not to grimace as he accepted a small plate on which rested a thick slice of sponge cake with a drizzle of lemon icing. Setting down his cup and saucer, he took the small fork and cut off a corner, tasting it with the same hesitation he had the tea.

It was surprisingly good, but would've been better without the icing, which was extremely tart, perhaps because of the addition of lemon zest and juice. Donal swallowed the bit and without setting down the plate, reached again for his tea to wash it down.

The lemon flavor remaining on his tongue made the tea extremely flat and tasteless. He decided he preferred tea over cake and began to cut the latter into small sections which he scattered about the plate so it appeared to have been eaten. The desire for that whiskey became stronger.

"Do you like the cake, Mr. McCoy?" Lady Alistair asked, having noted how he was busily cutting it apart with his fork. "It's an Alistair family recipe."

"Oh yes, it's very tasty," he lied. "Reminds me a bit of the cake they served at Almack's the other night…minus the icing, of course."

Almack's was much better. He didn't add that.

"I daresay," she rejoined, placing an overly-large portion into her own mouth and chewing. "I believe the addition of lemon peel perks it up a bit. Almack's is always a bit bland."

"Indeed." Donal was frantically searching for something to say instead of mere monosyllables. He'd never thought himself at a loss for words, but this innocuous conversation was becoming more of a test of his patience than he'd expected. He told himself to remember his father's admonition.

There was another silence.

"I'd like to express my gratitude to His Lordship for allowing me to call on Miss Araminta today," Donal told Lady Alistair. "Is he not joining us?"

"I'm afraid my brother is away on business at the moment, but my dear Mr. McCoy, you were so polite and acted so reserved at Almack's, how could he not give his permission?"

"You're as gracious as he, my lady." Donal was startled to feel his cheeks heat in a bit of a flush at this flattering but completely erroneous description.

"Nonsense. The moment I saw you…and I daresay you weren't very difficult to notice, with that red hair and all." Lady Alistair smiled. "You were like a handsome beacon lighting up the ballroom."

"You flatter me…" Donal began.

"I agree," Araminta interrupted. "Your hair's the most wonderful color. Do you have much trouble finding clothing to compliment it?"

"Clothing? Well, I…uh…"

"I imagine you've a great deal of greens and rusts in your wardrobe," she continued. "Brown frock coats with fern-green vests…tan trousers and mahogany-colored Hessians…evening suits with emerald green embroidery to match your eyes…"

"Actually, I'd never thought about that," he admitted. "I usually leave that sort of thing to my valet. The man has a talent for making the proper selections."

"He certainly does," Araminta agreed. "You are most beautifully attired, Mr. McCoy." She paused, then added, "You must suggest to him adding moss green to your clothes chest."

"I…I certainly shall." Donal wondered what Rollo would say if he dared do such a thing. Probably nothing to be uttered in polite company.

He applied himself to drinking his tea, which was now cooled to a non-lethal temperature. Lady Alistair and Araminta sipped their own.

Silence reigned again.

"Oh!"

Once again, the exclamation by Araminta made him jump. This time, however, he didn't inquire about the heat of the tea, mainly because she was currently concentrating on the cake. Instead, he simply looked at her.

"Is there a problem?" he dared ask.

"Oh, goodness, no." She trilled a delicate little laugh as if to say, *Silly man*, and explained, "The icing. I just realized how well this color would complement the new morning gown I'm having made." She held up her plate, gesturing with her fork at the remnants of cake and the strip of frosting adorning its surface. "See?"

Having never seen the mentioned gown and therefore no idea of its color, Donal merely nodded.

Encouraged, Araminta explained, "It's the most lovely shade of dark green…silk with sateen insets, of course…"

"Of course," Donal murmured. That seemed safe enough.

"The hem will be bordered with appliqués in pale yellow and lime green, as will the sleeves and neckline. They'll also be decorated with ribbon and bowknots, and I think this is the exact color I wish for the ribbon." She glanced at her aunt. "Don't you agree, Aunt Elspeth?"

There was a murmured assent.

Using her fork, Araminta cut the strip of icing from the cake, then speared the cake and thrust it into her mouth. Swallowing, she returned the fork to the plate and set it on the tray.

"I'm going to save that bit of icing and take it with me when I go to Madame Toulouse's for my fitting on Monday. That way she can see the color I want and order the proper shade." She sighed heavily. "It's so dreary when one asks for a color, waits for it eagerly, and then when it arrives, it's either too dark or too pale."

Ordering a batch of ribbon by showing the dressmaker a bit of cake icing?

Donal had never heard such idiocy. If he wanted something a specific color, which was rarely, he simply gave Rollo some vague instruction, such as "Order me a blue cravat," and let it go at that.

Aloud, he said, "Oh, definitely," and added, "There's nothing so disappointing as waiting for something and then finding it lacking when it's gotten."

"Exactly," Araminta agreed. "Like that time I wanted a new gown the same shade as the apple blossoms in the orchard at Winterside…that's our country estate. I gathered a bouquet of branches and took them to Madame Toulouse, but she was never able to match that pale pink precisely."

There was another sigh and a sad shake of her pretty head.

"I was so disappointed. I mean…really. A dressmaker should be able to match something as simple as apple blossom pink, don't you think?

"I should hope so," Donal replied, and mentally shook his head.

Lord deliver me from this inane conversation.

He'd hoped to be able to speak to Miss Bradley a bit more privately, expecting her aunt to absent herself, if not from their presence, at least moving away so their conversation couldn't be overheard. The parlor was large enough. She could've sat at the other end of the room where they would be in plain sight but their words inaudible.

That was not the way it would go, apparently.

"Excuse me, ma'am?" A maidservant, in black broadcloth and starched white apron and cap, stood in the doorway. She held a large bouquet of pink roses.

"What is it, Judith?" Lady Alistair looked her way.

"There's a delivery of flowers, ma'am." She gestured with the bouquet. "It was brought to the tradesman's entrance."

"Flowers? From whom?" Her Ladyship was up and out of her chair with remarkable alacrity, hurrying to the door. "I wasn't expecting any delivery."

"There's a card." Judith plucked a small envelope from among the blossoms.

Her Ladyship took it from her, opened and read, then sighed. A smile lit her face, making Donal see what a beauty she'd once been. She pressed card and envelope against her ample bosom.

"That dear, dear man..." She glanced at Donal in explanation. "Tomorrow is our wedding anniversary, and Lord Alistair has sent me this lovely bouquet. One rose for each year."

"Twenty-four roses," Judith supplied, helpfully. "My uncle's so thoughtful. He buys Aunt Elspeth the most beautiful gowns."

"Come, we'll get a vase and put them in the parlor." Returning the card to the envelope, Lady Alistair turned Judith and guided her back into the hall. She paused, looking back. "Please excuse me, Mr. McCoy. I trust you'll be the gentleman while I'm gone."

"You needn't worry, Your Ladyship." Donal didn't dare bridle or look insulted. He definitely wasn't going to do anything that might reflect badly. Not at this stage of the game. "Miss Bradley and I will have a pleasant chat while we await your return."

With a nod, she was gone, Judith trailing behind.

As her footsteps died away, Donal looked back at Araminta. She had picked up her cake again and was toying with that final bit of icing, working it back and forth with her fork. Her head was down, but she was looking up at him through dark lashes with what he could only describe as a *calculating* expression.

"I suppose…"

That was all he managed to say.

She dropped the cake plate onto the table so quickly it bounced. The fork was slung off the plate and flew through the air, striking the teapot and rebounding to land among the lemon quarters. Stabbed by the tines, juice squirted and Donal dodged…as Miss Araminta Bradley flung herself at him.

He was startled into immobility by her slight weight across his knees as, billowing skirts hiked up high enough that he could've seen the ruffles of her petticoats had he not been so stunned, Donal found himself immersed in voile and organza flounces. The skirts floated around him like a dense cloud. Miss Bradley settled onto his lap. Her hands went to his shoulders, mouth coming down on his in a kiss, a very determined, if inexpert, kiss, seeming to beg for better instruction.

She released him, leaning back. Automatically, his hands caught at her waist to prevent her from falling to the floor.

"Miss Bradley…" Donal took a deep breath.

She dove in for another kiss, this time leaning against him, the tops of her breasts, modestly displayed in the neckline of the morning gown, brushing against his chest.

That made his body react. *Give me more*, it

56

demanded. *I like where this is heading. The girl wants it, lad. Let's have a go.*

The nebuchadnezzar wanted to get into the act, too, rising against the weight resting...no, *writhing*, against it. If Donal parted his thighs the least bit...

The girl would definitely get a surprise.

Those looks of the other night at Almack's came back to him. Miss Bradley did indeed possess passion as their brief dance had hinted. She was practically begging him to assist her in unleashing it. They were alone, her aunt was out of the way for a bit, he could...

No, I can't. I have to keep playing the gentle suitor. I can't do what I want to do, what she'd obviously like me to do...or what she thinks *she'd like me to do...*

He had a feeling Miss Bradley would be in for a rude awakening and a bit of a shock if he followed through. He wondered if, in between ordering apple blossom-colored fabric and trying on dresses, she read romance novels. Feeling he was letting a golden opportunity pass by, he pushed her away.

"Miss Bradley, please." He was appalled by the prudish lilt to his voice.

She was disappointed, if the way her lower lip protruded in an immediate pout was any indication. Bosom heaving, she was breathing heavily. Donal was gasping also but more from being unable to breathe because her kisses had shut off his air supply than with any extreme arousal. He wasn't about to let old Neb take over and ruin his chances.

"Whatever are you about?" Oh, God, he sounded like the oldest male virgin on the planet.

Clasping her about the waist, he scrambled upright, gained his balance, and set her on her feet. Her skirts fell in graceful folds as they slid away from his body. She looked disappointed, startled, then a bit angry.

Donal released her and took a step backward, not a minute too soon.

"Araminta, dear, look how lovely they are."

Lady Alistair was back, holding the vase of roses. She looked from her niece to Donal.

"Were you leaving, Mr. McCoy?" She noted the rapid rise and fall of his chest and the slight color in his cheeks. "Araminta? Is something wrong?"

By now, her niece was very composed. She turned an inquisitive countenance to Donal.

Are you leaving? it questioned. *If so, please don't tell.*

"Oh, no, Lady Alistair," he assured her. "I was merely…" He glanced around hurriedly for some excuse for being on his feet, saw the fork skewering the lemon wedge and reached for it. "…going to try a bit of lemon in my tea."

He seized the fork, plucked the lemon from it, and picked up his cup, squeezing the wedge. Juice trickled into the liquid with gentle drops.

"I thought you liked your tea unadulterated," Araminta pointed out, relaxing.

"Variety," he answered quickly. "I'm always ready to try new things."

"Oh?" The look she gave him was *come-hither* to say the least, very interested at most.

Donal was thankful she was turned away from her aunt so Lady Alistair didn't see that expression. He felt an internal shiver as he realized what it suggested. Clutching the tea saucer, he sat down quickly.

Araminta, you are a lass after my own lascivious

heart.

"Your tea must be cold by now." Lady Alistair set the vase in the center of the table and reached for the teapot.

Donal held out his cup and she refilled it. He drank gratefully, only wishing it held something stronger. He certainly needed it now. He turned his attention to the roses.

"How very thoughtful of Lord Alistair to send you flowers."

"Isn't it?" she agreed. "Such a surprise. He's always done things like that."

"They're a lovely color," Araminta put in. "I'd like to have an afternoon gown that color." She had recovered now, stroking a blossom. "Perhaps we can save a few petals for me to take to Madame Toulouse to match…"

She was off on another diatribe about roses and the fact that she had two other afternoon gowns which were exact equivalents of roses in the Bradley garden.

Donal sipped his tea and remained silent. He endured the tale of three more pieces of apparel which he wasn't certain were tea dresses or morning gowns or something else altogether, before deciding it was time to make his escape.

"Lady Alistair, Miss Bradley…" Setting down his cup, he rose, pulling his watch from his vest pocket and consulting it. "It's fast approaching afternoon, and I fear I've a few errands that must be seen to."

A nice way of saying *I've got to get out of here.*

"So soon? Oh dear, where did the time go?" Araminta commented.

"Yes, it does fly when one's having such a pleasant time, doesn't it?" Donal thought that the epitome of understatement as well as a bold-faced lie.

We could've had a much more pleasant time if you weren't such a foolish virgin, my dear. In that moment, he felt such a yearning for Nellie, he almost cried out.

Missing his sarcasm, Araminta took his statement for more than it meant and smiled broadly and rather indiscreetly.

Lady Alistair tugged the bellpull near the hearth and the butler immediately appeared. "Mr. McCoy is leaving now. Please escort him to the door."

She turned to Donal, holding out her hand. "You must come again, Mr. McCoy. You're a wonderful conversationalist."

Donal took her hand and bowed over it.

Don't you mean I'm a wonderful listener? He really hadn't a chance to say much and doubted if anything he could've said would've been listened to by Araminta unless it involved clothing or the colors of fabrics and such. He released Lady Alistair's hand and turned to accept her niece's.

"Yes, Mr. McCoy," Araminta echoed. "Do come again." She fluttered her lashes and whispered, "Please."

Donal bowed but didn't answer. He hurried away.

At the door, he accepted his hat and gloves from the butler and was shown out. His curricle was still tied to the iron-ringed post—but had he expected it wouldn't be?

Donal untied the reins and climbed into the curricle. Automatically, he snapped the whip and sent the team trotting smartly away. He didn't return home but simply drove around for a while with no definite destination in mind.

He had planned to go directly to Nellie's afterward

but decided he needed to think a bit before proceeding with his evening.

Yes, he definitely had to think about what had happened and make a decision about Miss Araminta Bradley and whether to continue pursuing her or not. The girl was a real beauty, putting the other two on his list to shame. They would never be able to best her in the looks department.

However…

That intelligence he'd thought he saw, as well as her conversational skills… She might be beautiful and probably would stay that way even as she aged, but that incessant obsession with wearing apparel…

Lord God, I'd never get a word in edgewise unless I prefaced it with some comment about clothing. Donal envisioned himself beginning every sentence with a reference to a style or fashion and wondered how long it would take for him to run out of topics. Since he left his sartorial needs in the hands of Rollo and Wellsby, it wouldn't be long.

He thought about that little episode while Lady Alistair was off finding a vase for her roses. If that was a hint of what was hidden in her niece's well-rounded bosom, Donal would be in for some high old times in the bedchamber. She was a smoldering coal, waiting to be fanned into flame. He had an idea Araminta would be willing to learn quite a few things her husband would be more than eager to teach her.

Mentally, he amended his list.

Pro—beautiful beyond a doubt, dowry, baronet's daughter, as fiery a piece as Sophie at the Church, could probably singe my eyebrows if I stoked the fire…

It would be nice to be a baronet's son-in-law, but he

doubted he'd last a week under that constant barrage of fashion statements. After that, he'd either shoot himself or her to shut off that incessant chatter, and if that didn't happen…if Araminta's desire for clothing matched her conversational bent, he'd also be bankrupt in a short time from buying the many garments she talked about…and no amount of passion and lack of inhibition in the bedroom could make up for his loss of money, or his sanity.

With a great sadness, Donal envisioned his list and Miss Bradley's name on it with a thick black line drawn through it.

So sorry, my dear. I do hope you find someone who shares your interest in clothing and giving his hair a good scorching between dress fittings. I'm afraid I won't be the unlucky gent, however.

With that thought, he sighed heavily, considered himself fortunate to have discovered what he needed to know so quickly, and turned the team's head toward home. Once there, he did a quick in-and-out, dashing to his study to pen a note to Miss Smythe-Bolton asking to come to morning tea the coming Saturday.

Giving it to Rollo with orders to deliver it that night, he dashed back to the waiting curricle and aimed himself for the little mews house he'd leased for Eleanor Nordin.

Chapter 7

Riverview Mews was nowhere near a river. In fact, it wasn't in sight of water of any kind except that which fell from the sky and turned the cobbled streets into unspeakable, smelly slush as it mixed with the general dirt and debris, and the dung deposits left by horses pulling the cabs, lorries, and other vehicles.

When it rained, pedestrians crossed the streets as infrequently as possible. Sidewalk cleaners generally made a frugal living running ahead of walkers and sweeping their paths clear of unpleasantness, thus saving their footwear, but those workers prospered in more ways than one after a thundershower.

The house itself was small and modest. Nothing of its aspect hinted that a kept woman, once an inhabitant of the infamous Church, lived there. Donal wanted it that way, so Nellie didn't mind, either.

As always, he came in through the kitchen entrance of the house. Originally, Nellie protested him doing that but soon saw the discretion of it once he explained he had no wish for any of her neighbors to see him. Donal had a fear that one of the other buildings might house someone of his acquaintance who'd glimpse him and question why he was skulking about, and from there— considering how loose-lipped some of his chums were— the story would spread to his father and spoil everything.

As far as Donal knew, Quinton was unaware of

Nellie, and he wanted to keep it that way.

It was possible his keeping a mistress might not be looked down upon by his father but simply accepted as a stage a young man of his position went through, and was expected, but that meant nothing to Donal. He preferred to have everyone, Quinton included, think he'd never stoop to such a practice, since he wanted no smudge to his image at all.

That Nellie had little to do with her neighbors and rarely, if ever, went outside, didn't bother him. In fact, he was pleased, because that meant she'd see and talk to no one to whom she might say the wrong thing. Donal had never forbidden her leaving the premises nor of having some of her Church judies come to visit. She definitely wasn't a prisoner. It was simply that Nellie had everything she wanted inside the Riverview Mews home and nothing outside its confines interested her.

That night, Donal tied his team to the hitching ring at the back of the house and made his way to the kitchen door. His discreet tug on the doorbell caused a single short, sharp jangle. In a few moments, he heard light footsteps approaching and the door swung open.

A young woman wearing a housemaid's uniform much like that of Lady Alistair's Judith, stood there. Because it was dark and the back entrance had no coach light, she was carrying a small lamp. She opened the door enough to peer out.

"Oh, it's you, Mr. Donal."

"Were you expecting someone else?" He laughed. "Come, Flossie. Who else would be ringing the bell at this time of night?"

"True, sir," she agreed, "but you can't never tell…sometimes thieves is bold an' will tap on the door an' then knock your 'ead when you answers." She nodded in emphasis. "Can't be too careful."

"Quite so," Donal agreed and gestured toward the interior. "Well? Am I allowed entry?"

"Of course, sir. Excuse me." Flossie stepped back, and he pulled the door fully open and walked in.

The kitchen was warm from the day's cooking, and the embers still glowed in the cast-iron stove. Flossie was employed both as cook and lady's maid, a veritable jill-of-all-work. A glance around the kitchen told him she'd cleaned it well and was now probably preparing to retire.

"Where's Nellie?" Donal asked.

"Where would you think…sir?" Flossie added that as if remembering he was her employer and therefore worthy of her respect even if he was a man keeping a Light Jane on the sly. "In her bedchamber, 'fore her mirror."

"In that case, set out a bottle of wine and a bit to eat. It doesn't have to be hot, a cold repast will do…and then you can go back to whatever you were doing. We'll retrieve it later."

"Yes, sir." Flossie dipped him a curtsey. "Does you need a light?"

"I think I know the way by now." He was already through the kitchen door as he spoke, walking down the corridor leading to the front foyer and the stairs going to the two upper bedchambers.

The sconces in the foyer and the front hallway, as well as those on the upper landing, were still lit. Donal made his way up the stairs, not attempting to be quiet. He was certain Nellie would hear his footsteps, differentiate them from Flossie's scurries, and fling herself into some artistic pose awaiting his entrance.

He wasn't disappointed.

Without knocking, he opened the door, standing framed a moment in the doorway.

"Donal. Darlin'." It was the greeting of a woman having long missed the man of her dreams.

****

Eleanor Nordin had been a member of the "congregation" of the Church since the age of sixteen when both her parents died in an epidemic engulfing her village and killing at least two in every household. Finding herself an orphan, she was also the sole surviving member of her family, since her younger brother and sister also succumbed. Having no skills at that point, other than domestic ones learned from her mother, she struck out for London in hope of being taken into service as a maid of some sort.

It took four days in the city to disabuse her of that dream. Within two more, Nell was attempting a living as a midinette, an independent prostitute. That lasted another two, her crude and awkward come-ons sending men scurrying instead of being enticed. Passing by in her carriage, the woman known as the Abbess saw the girl, thought there was potential in her looks if not her deportment, and invited her to take a ride with her.

Within three hours, Nellie was established as one of the novitiate of the Church, and within the month, she was a full-fledged worshipper at the shrine of Venus.

She was nearing thirty when Donal McCoy came to worship, six years older than he. The Abbess recommended her and they took a liking to each other, in spite of their differences in age, or perhaps because of it. Nellie had expertise; Donal had some but he was willing to learn more.

It didn't take long for him to become jealous at the thought of Nellie giving her favors to other men, while she encouraged that jealousy by comparing his performances to others, then always finding him better. The result was that, after six months, Donal paid the Abbess to release Nellie from her "vows." He set her up in the little house in Riverview Mews where he could have her lush charms all to himself.

Donal still came to the Church from time to time, however. For variety, as he told Joss. To keep the sparks between himself and Nellie alive and burning.

****

When Donal arrived, Nellie had been at her vanity, studying her image in the mirror. Hearing his voice below, she hurried to recline on a fainting couch of watered rose-colored satin, its alternating stripes of dark and light pinks complementing the burgundy silk wrapper she wore. She leaned against solid-colored rose cushions, the skirts of the wrapper tucked around her legs so only bare white feet were visible. Head tilted against the couch, her golden hair lay unbound and tousled about her shoulders as if she'd just awakened.

As the door opened, she blinked sleepily, widening her eyes in simulated surprise.

Donal always wondered how she managed to settle herself so quickly yet it appeared she'd been in the same spot for some length of time.

He took a step inside, giving the door a backward push to send it swinging shut. Then he slid off his coat, tossed it aside, and opened his arms.

"Darling? Is that all the greeting I get?"

"'Course not." She was on her feet in a flash, running to him.

The impact of her body against his wasn't as violent as Miss Bradley's had been, but Donal savored it a great deal more because there was nothing but the wrapper's thin fabric between her body and his vest…and he didn't need to restrain himself as he had with Araminta Bradley.

Wrapping his arms around Nellie, he engulfed her in a tight embrace, feeling the soft body through the filmy silk. It came to him he'd seen Nellie dressed only once in their association, and that was the day he took her from the Church and installed her in the Riverview Mews house.

It didn't matter. Naked or nearly so was the way he liked her best.

He gave her the kind of kiss he'd wished to give that eager girl. It deepened, his tongue claiming her own, which responded exactly as he wished. Donal pulled away, kissing just beneath her ear then running his tongue around its curve.

She was wearing diamond eardrops, a gift from Donal to celebrate his gaining sole possession of her charms. They were part of a set, consisting of the drops and a lavaliere necklace, on which Donal rather indiscreetly had inscribed "To my Eleanor, With All my Love, Donal."

He caught the one on that ear between his teeth. The post popped off, falling to the floor with a near-silent *ting.* He spat out the drop and began to nibble on the pale lobe.

"'ere now." Nellie pulled away. She stooped, scooping up the fallen eardrop and post. Holding them tightly in her fist, she returned to kiss Donal again. "Don't want that t' get lost. It were a gift."

"From one of your admirers?" Ignoring her less-than-educated pronunciation, he kissed down her throat, pressing his lips into the little hollow where her collarbones met.

Nell's diction hadn't improved, even with her change in status from brothel whore to mistress. Donal didn't let that bother him, however. If asked, he would've replied he didn't associate with her for her methods of elocution.

"From my *only* admirer…now." She allowed her head to fall back, giving him access to her bosom.

Donal needed no urging. After that brief skirmish with Araminta Bradley, he was more than ready for whatever was to come with Nellie. Pushing open the neck of the wrapper, he slid it off one pale shoulder, licking a trail from its curve across burgeoning breasts. He kissed the valley between them, letting their fullness nestle his cheeks in a warm embrace.

As he inhaled deeply, the titillating fragrance of rose-jasmine attar filled his nostrils. It was a scent he swore was an aphrodisiac whether it was true or not, for the smell always had the power to excite and arouse him, as it did now. With that first breath, he felt a stirring inside he was certain would soon burst into full-fledged lust.

"You're wearing that perfume I gave you," he said, unnecessarily.

"I was 'opin' you'd come by tonight," she answered, turning her head so she could speak, then doing so with difficulty as he seized one pert nipple between his teeth and sucked on it. "I've…missed…you."

She took a deep breath, sending the breast pressing against his mouth.

Donal took a good portion of it between his lips, giving its circumference a good laving.

"I've…been wearin' it…every night of this week…" She pushed away, out of his arms and out of reach. "Why've you stayed away?"

"We can talk about that later." He wasn't about to let what he *had* to do interfere with what he *wanted* just then. Sweeping Nellie off the floor and into his arms, he carried her to the bed. "Right now…"

"You've missed me?"

He placed her gently beside the bed. She didn't move as he pulled loose the ribbon bows holding the wrapper together.

"You can't imagine how much." Pushing the silk off her shoulders, he let it fall to the floor, then gathered the disarrayed ringlets in his hands and pressed them to his lips. "You…and Miss Laycock." His hand slid between her thighs, fingers probing gently.

"Not as much as me an' Miss Laycock has missed you an' Old Neb," Nell whispered and the low pitch of her voice sent a tremor down Donal's spine.

****

In spite of those pale tresses, Nellie was a false blonde. Donal learned this for a fact during their first encounter at the church.

"I say, Nell…your collar and cuffs don't exactly match."

"Disappointed?" She'd placed hand on hips and thrust her pelvis in his direction. Since Donal was kneeling at the time, the nether-part he was referring to struck him directly on the chin.

"Not in the least." He'd laughed. "It simply makes you much more interesting." With that, he wrapped his arms around her hips and nuzzled against that dark nest.

****

"So Miss Laycock has missed Old Neb? Shall we let him out to graze?" Donal reached for the front of his trousers.

"Stop right there." Nellie's hand slid under his, pulling open buttons. Fingers groped inside. "I think I'd best search you, m' lad."

"No need to fan me, officer." Donal took his mouth away from its task long enough to murmur, "I'll come quietly."

"You've never come quietly," Nell retorted. "I think you needs t' be searched thoroughly. Best make certain you ain't carrying an iron." She pushed past the tail of his tucked-in shirt, nudging through the plaquette of his drawers. "Aha…wot's this?"

"Damn, you found my concealed weapon."

Nell's fingers had indeed found what they sought. It attempted to meet those questing fingers, thrusting itself into them as it was drawn through the open fly.

"Ooh…ain't we eager tonight?" She looked down at the rampant organ attempting to leap from her grasp.

"Oh God, Nell, you just don't know," he groaned.

"Tell me." Nellie always liked to hear how much he wanted her, even when it was obvious.

"Later." Ripping the cravat from his neck, he pulled his shirt over his head and dropped both to the floor. Donal tugged open his trousers and the string-tie of his drawers, stepped out of them, and reached for Nellie again.

"Unh-uh." She stepped back, waggling a finger.

He stopped.

She pointed.

He looked down.

"No boots in bed."

The ankle-high Wellingtons sailed in opposite directions, one striking Nell's dresser, the other the wall.

"Careful. Don't break noffin'—" The rest of her warning was cut off as Donal's mouth came down on hers and he lunged.

They fell onto the bed, rolling over and over as they sank into its downy softness. Donal surfaced long enough to mutter, "I want you, Nell...now."

She wrapped her legs around his waist. He reached between them, fitting his member against that hot wet nest.

"I want to be as deep inside you as possible." That statement was accompanied by an inward plunge and a short cry from Nell as her body closed around his.

After that, there were no words spoken for quite some time, only moans and groans of pleasure. The latter were then stifled into brief whispers that died away to silence broken only by an occasional creak as the bedposts swayed in rhythm to Donal's thrusts. The one break in his movements was to retrieve the *préventif* from its place in the lamp table drawer. Then he was back to his target again. Not a moment too soon. Sometimes Donal liked to live dangerously, timing his climax and his donning of the sheath as closely as possible.

Tonight's dressing and finish were a bare hair's-breadth apart.

Later, they lay in each other's arms, munching on the raisin cake Flossie had baked that day.

Drawing circles with her forefinger on Donal's chest, Nell raised herself to take a sip of wine. "You said we'd speak o' wot's kept you from me for four days."

She replaced her glass on the lamp table and snuggled next to him, cheek on his chest, fingers returning to caressing, moving in a circle around one nipple. "Now then, tell me."

Briefly, Donal avoided looking at her. He drank more wine, ate another square of cake, before saying, with studied nonchalance, "It was nothing…a business matter."

"What kind o' business?" Nell asked, frowning. Her caresses slowed.

"Oh…just a chore I have to do for my father." He realized he didn't want to tell her, and also that his avoidance of a real answer was making her curious. Eventually, she was going to demand to know the truth.

"A chore wot took four days? What kind o' chore?"

Yes, there it was, asked in a tone brooking no more evasions.

"Your father ain't got no holdin's 'ere in London, 'as he?"

Donal didn't answer. He moved away slightly.

"Donal?" Now she was worried. She sat up, staring at him. "Donal, tell me." A hand went to his bare shoulder, gripping tightly.

"All right, if you must know." Gently but firmly, he removed her hand, dropping it into her sheet-covered lap. With a sigh, he said, "I've been courting."

"Courtin'?" Nell looked blank, then startled. "You mean…"

"As a prelude to marriage. Yes," Donal admitted. He raised his wine glass, guzzling its contents in frantic swallows, then lowered it to say, "How about pouring me some more? This is a very good vintage, don't you think?"

Nell didn't move.

"Nellie? I said…"

"How can you sit there talkin' 'bout wine when you just told me you're goin' t' be married?" she demanded.

"Quite easily." The cool demeanor Donal often employed to hide his true feelings fell into place. "I want more wine and I've a feeling I'm going to need it. Besides, there's nothing I can do about this marriage business. My father wishes it, so I have to, and that's all there is to it."

"If you've a wife, where does that leave me?" she wailed.

"Oh, I see…not concerned with my feelings in this matter, but thinking of your own sweet skin, eh?" The best way to prevent an argument, Donal had found, was to put the other person on the defensive.

"Why shouldn't I?" Nell wasn't to be manipulated. She was too much an expert at that herself. "After all, ain't I dependent on you now? I left a very good spot at th' Church t' be your mistress, an' if you're gettin' a wife…"

"Dearest," he managed a laugh. "Stop worrying. It won't affect our relationship."

"No?" She didn't relax, however.

"Not a bit. Hell's fire, Nellie…I'm not going to fall in love with her, whoever she is."

"You don't know her name?"

"I haven't picked her out yet," he explained. "After all, I only started making prospective choices three days ago."

The stare Nell now gave him held exasperation and perhaps a bit of accusation that he could be so cold-blooded about such an important step.

You and Joss, he thought.

"Look," he went on in a reasonable tone. "It's merely a business arrangement. I marry. I sire a child. My father gets the grandchild he wants and he'll continue supplying me with that very generous allowance so I can keep you in this lovely little house you like so much."

"You really mean that? We'll still be together, you an' me?"

Nell gave him that limpid look always making a quiver start in his belly and shoot straight to his groin.

"I'm going to want you more than ever," he promised. "To help me survive being a married man. I've a feeling doing the grind with someone I don't care for is definitely going to be a trial."

"You don't know th' 'alf o' it," Nell's mutter was so soft he didn't understand. She looked away.

"What was that?"

"Noffin', dearest." She reached for the bottle sitting on the tray. "'ere, let me pour you some wine. You did say you wanted more, didn't you?"

He held out his glass. "I daresay as soon as I'm back from my wedding trip, I'll be beating a path to your door every night." He laughed. "You'd better rest up while I'm gone."

"T' help you recover from pokin' th' old lady?" Nellie winked.

"Here, don't speak of my wife that way," he retorted, laughing. "She definitely won't be old, whoever she turns out to be. That'll be the only thing in her favor."

Briefly, Felicity Melton's piquant little face flared through his mind. He raised his glass, tapped it against Nell's, and drank away the vision.

"To us, Nellie…and a long and mutually sensual association. Give me a wine-flavored kiss, my dear."

Nell obeyed eagerly, leaning against him. She tilted her wine glass, dribbling the dark red liquid over his chest, then watched with satisfaction as it soaked through the coppery hair and trickled over his belly.

"Oh dear. I've spilled m' wine." She gave a mock sigh of exasperation. "I suppose now I shall 'ave t' clean it up."

"I suppose you shall." Hands behind his head, Donal leaned back against the pillows. "Be thorough. Don't leave a drop."

As Nell licked the wine off his left nipple, his body began to quiver and then visibly tremble.

"Enough of that. Come here, wench…and give me more of what I really want."

Seizing Nell by the arms, Donal sat up, flipped her onto her back and covered her body with his own.

Chapter 8

"You've deducted Araminta Bradley?" Joss picked up the list, staring at the line through Miss Bradley's name.

"Obviously." Donal's reply was a trifle short as he plucked the paper from his friend's hand and returned it to the desktop.

"She was at the top of your list," Joss argued. "Beautiful...baronet's daughter...dowry?" he reminded.

"She's all those things, but she's still out of the running. *Now.*"

"Excuse me for my ignorance." Joss affected a quizzical air, placing one hand thoughtfully against his chin. "Didn't you tell me the girl was...correct me if I'm wrong...quote, *hot as a live coal?* End quote?"

Donal had related the events of his morning tea with Miss Bradley and her aunt, and in vivid detail what occurred while Lady Alistair was out of the room. He didn't answer.

"Also, that you were *leaning favorably in her direction...*and that's also a quote, and a fairly accurate one, I believe."

"It is," Donal agreed. He realized he was gritting his teeth and forced his jaws to relax.

"Then, my dear fellow, I fail to understand why..."

"Perhaps I leaned too far when I should've stepped back and gotten the entire picture," he interrupted.

"Perhaps, after being inundated for an hour with the most inconsequential blather possible, I decided I couldn't endure a lifetime of that unless I were stricken deaf. I swear, Joss, I never realized a female could have such an obsession with clothing. I pray to God they aren't all so fanatically preoccupied with what they wear."

"Hm, wouldn't know myself," Joss murmured. "Most of the females I'm acquainted with don't bother with clothing all that much."

"Then you're a lucky dog. I don't remember my sister, or my mother, for that matter, carrying on so about the color of their gowns or what kind of ribbons adorned them. They certainly never saved a bit of icing from a cake to take to the seamstress to be duplicated." He fell silent, shaking his head as if he still couldn't believe the young lady had actually done that. "In answer to your question, Joss...yes, I have indeed cut Miss Bradley from my list, and I don't intend to see her again, except in the briefest of passings, if I can help it."

He shook with an exaggerated tremor.

"Gad, just thinking about it gives me the shivers."

"You're certain you won't change your mind?" Joss looked concerned. "From what you told me, with that much passion waiting to be unleashed, you probably wouldn't need Nell. That could save a bit of money," he added, helpfully.

"Not even for a moment. You weren't there, Joss. I couldn't."

"So, it's once more into the fray? That's not surprising, you know." As Donal gave him a questioning look, he continued, "You didn't expect Dame Fortune to smile upon you on your very first foray into the world of courtship, did you?"

Once more Joss held up the list, shaking it.

"So now it's down to Miss Smythe-Bolton—she of the giggles and rabbit's-teeth—and the Melton Mouse. Not much of a choice as far as I can see."

Joss gave a sarcastically consoling pat to Donal's shoulder while his friend glared. With a twist of his wrist, he sent the list spinning onto the desk.

"If I were you, old chum, I'd stick a pin into my eardrum and ask for Miss Bradley's hand, forget the clothing problem and think of those other passions. I understand a good deal can be conveyed through sign language."

"Oh, shut up," Donal growled.

****

Three hours later, having chased Joss from the house and dawdled over his *toilette* until Rollo chastised him with, "You can't delay any longer, sir. The message you had taken round to Miss Smythe-Bolton's did say you'll call by eleven, and it's ten-thirty now."

Donal regretted having sent that missive after returning from his visit to Miss Bradley. He'd simply been so appalled he'd wished to get the event out of his mind by moving quickly to the next on the list. Kind of like getting back on a horse after being thrown.

All that nattering about fabric and such had indeed unnerved him.

Act in haste, repent in leisure…wasn't that the way the old adage went?

He should've waited until the next morning, perhaps not even sent it at all. Perhaps he should've simply delayed until the coming Wednesday and returned to Almack's, found another lass whose name he could add to his list—hell, jotted down several more names—

before making another call.

Nevertheless, he *had* sent the note that afternoon, and then gone on his eager way to Nell's, where he'd eventually wiped the entire episode from his mind thanks to his light love's expertise. Oh Lord, he'd enjoyed that bit of rolling.

As Rollo pointed out, however, it was too late to back out now. He'd said he would call at eleven and he had to do so. He couldn't afford not to show up. That sort of thing would get around and wouldn't set well with any other mothers who had daughters he might wish to woo.

Deciding he'd go by carriage this time, he told Rollo to have the footman who acted as coachman to bring it round. He definitely wasn't going to drive himself. He had a feeling once he had the reins in his hands, he'd end up at some tavern guzzling bad ale in an attempt to bolster his courage, and would probably never reach the Smythe-Boltons' home at all.

Chapter 9

Three hours later, he was at Nell's, burrowing his face against her bosom as he groaned, "God, Nellie, what am I going to do?"

Arrival at the Smythe-Boltons' townhouse had been easy enough…inform the butler he'd earlier sent a note saying he would call at eleven, request the man inquire if Miss Smythe-Bolton would receive him, provide his card, and then be escorted inside. The entire family was present and all welcomed him graciously as they sat down to tea.

Amelia looked especially pretty in a light green morning dress complementing her blonde coloring. Donal was encouraged by that, but her giggles started as soon as she saw him, dashing all his hopeful expectations since that immediately grated on nerves already frazzled from anticipation.

Nevertheless, he forged on.

The conversation was much better than the previous one had been, probably because Mr. Smythe-Bolton was present. He dominated the subject matter while his wife was relatively quiet, managing a word here and there. At least there was no mention of clothing, ribbons, trimmings, or fabrics, but…

…Amelia's giggles continued, steadily gaining volume and momentum as the conversation progressed. Every sentence she spoke was prefaced by, and ended with, some form of edgy high-pitched nervous hilarity. They were of an irritating turn…giggles and titters, laughter, and an occasional chuckle. Donal told himself he might've tolerated the laughter—at least it sounded genuine and was quite melodious—and also the chuckles, but the titters and giggles… Then there were those abrupt harsh inhalations almost a gasp with breath expelled in a series of near-hiccoughs.

As if that wasn't bad enough, Mr. Smythe-Bolton also laughed the same way, though the sounds he produced were of a deeper variety. Apparently, Amelia came by her modes of mirth honestly. Her father was also possessed of an extremely large set of chompers, and as all three Smythe-Boltons sat munching on biscuits, Donal felt himself surrounded by rabbits…crunching loudly, prominent teeth flashing as they devoured those helpless crisp cakes. Amelia somehow managed to chuckle and chew at the same time.

The noise was deafening.

Donal struggled not to react, however, until a moment came when both Amelia and her father laughed simultaneously, he with a deep chortle delivered with the rapidity of a woodpecker's beak being driven against a sheet of tin and she with a high-pitched sound erupting through her nose as a snigger punctuated by a snort. The combination was so unnerving Donal bit his tongue instead of the biscuit he'd raised to his mouth.

The resultant pain as well as the blood he tasted did him in.

He set down his cup and saucer and leaped to his feet. Fumbling into his vest pocket for his watch, he explained, with a tongue thickening from the force with which he'd sunk his teeth into it, that a tardily remembered errand had to be done within the next twenty minutes. Not giving them time to make their goodbyes, he gave his own hasty farewells, then took his leave, snatching gloves and hat from the butler as he ran to the door. He stumbled into his carriage which, mercifully, was still before the house, crying out, "Take me to Nellie's, Charles, as fast as possible."

As the carriage sped away, he dabbed at his wounded tongue with his pocket handkerchief, then leaned back with a heartfelt sigh.

****

At Nell's, he jerked and jangled the kitchen doorbell until Flossie came running.

"My goodness, Mr. Donal," she cried as she opened the door. "Wot's happened? You're as white as a sheet."

He didn't answer, except to order, "Bring some of Grandfather's whiskey, Flossie," and dashed through the kitchen and to the stairs, taking them two at a time.

At Nell's door, he flung it wide and burst in. She was lying on the fainting couch, wrapped in a transparent teal-blue concoction whose many ruffles and flounces were sewn so close together it may as well have been opaque.

"Donal? Wot's th' matter?" She appeared startled by his pallor.

He didn't say a word, simply dropped to his knees before the couch and burrowed his face between those luscious, ripe breasts.

"I can't go on," he mumbled, words muffled against the comforting press of warm perfumed flesh. "I can't do this again."

"'Course you can," she replied, wrapping her arms

around him and holding him closer.

"I really can't." Donal raised his head, eyes meeting hers. "I can't and won't."

"Wot about your father? Wot are you goin' t' tell him?" The worry in Nell's voice wasn't feigned.

If Donal rebelled against Quinton's demands and had his allowance curtailed, or worse, got himself disinherited…it didn't bear thinking about.

"I'll tell him…" Donal's voice rose in defiance. "I'll tell him I hate women…yes…can't stand the creatures…that I'm a mandrake."

"Oh?" There was definite scorn in Nell's voice now. "In that case, who's goin' t' be your partner in crime?"

"Joss…" Donal didn't hesitate. "He's my best friend, he'll go along to help me out."

"'elp you both get thrown into gaol for unnatural crimes, you mean." She burst out laughing.

Donal stared at her, lower lip abruptly out-thrust at what he considered her unsympathetic attitude.

"Forget it, m' dear. You an' Joss are both too manly for anyone t' believe that o' you." Putting her hands on each side of his face, she kissed him, frowning as he winced. "Dear Donal, I'm afraid you'll 'ave t' keep tryin' until you find someone you can tolerate."

Nell pushed him away and Donal scrambled to his feet.

"I don't know why I'm encouragin' you," she said, fussing with a flounce on the sleeve of her wrapper and not looking at him. "I certainly ain't in no 'urry t' share you with nobody."

"I've told you," Donal assured her. "It won't be sharing. Not really. Well, twenty-eighty, anyway. Twenty per cent of my time will be with my wife, and that includes the thirty minutes or so I expend attempting to get her with child, and the other eighty percent will be spent in sheer pleasure with you, my dear."

"Well…" Nell was mollified. "If you put it that way…"

"I do." He dropped onto the couch beside her. "Nell, let's do something spectacular tonight, to drive this unpleasantness out of my mind."

"You mean…" She put her forefinger between her teeth as if thinking. "Somefing truly naughty?" She thought a moment. "Would you like t' tip m' velvet, p'rhaps? We ain't done *that* in a while."

There was a tap on the door.

"Just the thing," Donal replied, enthusiastically. He got to his feet, opening the door and taking the tray from Flossie. "That'll definitely take my mind off anything else."

He shut the door and set the tray on a nearby table. The maid had uncorked the bottle and poured some of the whiskey into two *apéritif* glasses. It was evidence of Donal's overwrought frame of mind that he needed something stronger than wine to fortify himself, and thought a bottle of his grandfather's whiskey, presented to him by Quinton on his twenty-first birthday, would do the trick.

He raised his glass, took a sip, and winced again.

"That's th' second time you done that," Nell observed. "Wot's th' matter with your mouth?"

"I bit my tongue, to keep from screaming in rage." He took a second sip and rolled the liquid around on the wounded appendage. It burned slightly as it soaked into the teeth-cuts.

"Oh, dear…" Nell looked worried. "Won't that

85

interfere with…" She gestured vaguely.

"Do you think I'm going to let a little thing like a cut tongue keep me from something so enjoyable?" Donal lowered the little glass and stalked back to her. "I don't think so." He held out the miniature wine goblet. "Don't you think your velvet would like a bit of a bath? An ablution with good Irish whiskey?"

As Nellie frowned and started to shake her head, he continued, in a wheedling tone, "It's Old Bushmills, the very best…thrice distilled and five years in the cask, corked the year I was born."

"Why didn't you say so?" Swinging her legs over the side of the couch, she pushed back the wrapper and spread her thighs.

Donal tilted the glass, pouring the whiskey into the dark curls. Setting the *apéritif* glass aside, he bent to finish his drink.

Chapter 10

He was with Nell all night, passing the Sabbath in a most irreligious way.

It was an unusual event for Donal to stay overnight, but he felt it was the only method of eradicating the episode with Amelia Smythe-Bolton from his mind. Nellie's lush charms, as well as what they did that night, certainly eradicated the memory…momentarily.

When Donal awoke with female warmth snuggled against his backside, it gave him a surge of peace so profound he nearly cried out in its serenity.

Is this how it would be if I had a wife?

Rolling over, he studied Nell's face. Relaxed in slumber, hair tumbled around her, that false but glorious golden brightness shining in the morning sunlight streaming through the window, she looked younger than her stated age.

How would it feel to awaken every morning and see the same face beside me? It wouldn't happen…when he married, he and his wife would occupy separate bedchambers, and he'd only be allowed into hers in order to attempt to create a child. He certainly wouldn't sleep there all night.

That made Donal begin thinking of other things, incidents occurring between his parents in his childhood that he'd witnessed but hadn't really taken note of, or so he thought. Now they came pouring back, like a flood.

His parents might've had separate chambers, but his father slept in his mother's room more often than in his own. Donal was aware of this because as a child he'd been an early riser and often saw his father emerging from Mama's room, clad in nightshirt and dressing gown. Upon seeing his son, Quinton would put a finger to his lips.

Walk softly, lad. Your ma's still sleeping.

In hindsight, Donal now wondered if Màiri-Caitlin's slumber had been the sleep of the exhausted, for three times over the years, after Quinton left her room, they announced Donal was to have another sibling.

Donal was certain his parents loved each other, whether it had originally been a love match or not, for he'd often spied Quinton steal a kiss in a hallway or reach out to touch Màiri's cheek. When he thought no one was looking, he might pat her on the bum in a gentle but proprietary way. His mother obviously liked that, if her giggle was any indication, a sound not in any way like Miss Smythe-Bolton's, either. It had been secretive but delighted.

As the children grew up, it seemed his father didn't go to her rooms as often, or at least it appeared that way to Donal when he visited home, but that fact notwithstanding, he was certain their love still glowed, even if the flames had dimmed a bit.

I want a marriage like that. He felt he had very little chance of finding it, however. Discovering someone compatible enough not to drive him to distraction would be blessing enough, if he could manage it.

At this point, Nell roused, murmured something unintelligible, and reached for him. Donal took that to be a sign she wanted an early morning bounce, and he eagerly complied.

He spent the entire day in bed with Nell, returning to his own dwelling only when the sun began to drop in the afternoon sky.

There, he was met by a waspish Rollo, who declared, "I was ready to send out a hue-and-cry, sir. Could you not have sent me word you wouldn't be returning, so I didn't have to wait up wondering if you were floating in the Thames or somewhere as terminal?"

"Wait up? Since when?" Donal gave him a disdainful stare. "You're usually asleep no matter what time I arrive home."

"Will you be calling on Miss Melton tomorrow, sir?"

Leave it to Rollo to change the subject by assuming he'd mizzled his chance with the Smythe-Bolton.

"Not tomorrow," Donal answered shortly. "I'm taking a holiday to recover."

The day after would be soon enough.

The valet didn't answer but there was much grumbling under his breath for the rest of the evening.

****

The next morning, with a glass of wine at his elbow, Donal stationed himself at his desk and set about doing what he termed *social chores*, those unpleasant but necessary tasks required of all gentlemen, such as paying various bills from Wellsby, the carriage maker who'd built his latest curricle, also the dealer supplying grain and hay for his horses, the greengrocer, Rollo and Charles's salaries, as well as the rentals on his home and Nell's, any gambling chits he might owe, and sending Rollo to the bank to deposit the coming month's allowance cheque from Quinton.

After that, he drank the wine, got out his very best grade of stationery, and penned a carefully constructed missive to Miss Felicity Melton, in which he reminded her of their introduction at Almack's the previous week. He then asked permission to call upon her on the morrow, preferably in the afternoon.

As he sat with quill in hand, composing the next line, a sudden superstitious feeling swept through him, warning that what he said and its significance were very important in his success with this particular young woman. The message had to be worded just so. Foolish, perhaps, but there it was…and he intended to heed that thought. It might be silly, but…hell, he was Irish under it all, and who knew but what he was receiving some signal from an ancient fey ancestor that how he couched his request was the key to his future marital happiness?

To that effect, Donal wrote and rewrote the note several times, as the crumpled sheets of paper littering the floor around the wastebasket attested.

Eventually, after numerous starts and stops, the finished product emerged.

My dear Miss Melton,

I was most struck with admiration upon being introduced to you by our mutual acquaintance Ashley Josslyn at Almack's last Wednesday night. I also appreciated your gracing me by allowing me to be your partner in a waltz that evening.

I respect that your household is still in mourning for the passing of your father and I wish to offer my belated condolences to you and your mother. Might I hope you would allow me to brighten your house of bereavement and call upon you tomorrow afternoon around three?

I anxiously await your reply, which may be sent by

the servant bearing my message.

> *Yours in most respectful anticipation,*
> *Donal Callum Seamus McCoy, Esquire*

Donal had pondered long and hard over adding that title after his name, wondering if he should use *Esquire* or *Gentleman*. He had the right to either, being a son of landed gentry of Ireland and also an *armiger*, since his family had a coat of arms, though they hadn't flaunted that since his great-grandfather's time. He vacillated back and forth briefly, then decided since he was an eldest son, received an allowance from his father as part of his legacy, and therefore could be considered independently wealthy and not needing to work, he would call himself *esquire* and hope he wasn't committing a social *faux pas*.

After reading and re-reading the letter three times, he decided the request was as good as it was going to get, rang for Rollo, and sent the valet via carriage to deliver the message as quickly as possible. Then he waited anxiously for Rollo to return.

It was two hours later before the valet reappeared.

In that time, Donal consoled himself with several more glasses of wine, so by the time Rollo again set foot inside, Donal was more than a little sloshed. He'd also taken it upon himself to discover the location of the dining room, as well as the kitchen and pantry, after hunger set in during his wait. That had involved several false starts and turns since Donal wasn't at all familiar with the downstairs of his own home.

"Sir?"

The door opened and he heard the valet's call.

"I'm back. Where are you?"

"In the parlor." The way he lurched from his chair

was a definite indication of how much wine he'd consumed, and the slices of bread and cheese he'd discovered in the pantry hadn't absorbed a drop of it.

"Sir?" Rollo came through the door, saw him wavering, and hurried to his side, grasping an arm. "Were you that worried?"

He eased Donal into the chair he'd vacated.

"About you? Of course not." Donal shook his head and it seemed to want to keep on shaking, doddling on his neck like a marionette with a broken string.

"I meant about whether or not your message would be kindly received." Rollo took no offense at Donal's dismissal of his welfare.

"And? Well?" Donal gave him an anxious look, thrusting out a hand, palm upward, and narrowly missing the full wineglass sitting by his chair.

"You went to the kitchen?" Rollo appeared distracted by seeing the plate of half-eaten bread and the nibbled-on slab of cheese sitting next to the wine decanter.

"What if I did?"

Donal didn't want to speak of food just then. He was anxious to know how his letter was received.

"Downstairs is an interesting place. I only got lost twice." He shook his head, waving the outstretched hand as if to dismiss the conversation. "That doesn't matter. Where's my reply?"

Rollo deftly moved the glass to safety before he spoke. "I believe the answer is favorable, sir."

"You didn't read it?" Donal's question was near plaintive as well as suspicious. He looked around for his glass.

"Of course not. Have I ever abused the servant-master bond?" Rollo's hand going to his inside breast pocket distracted his master and made him look back at the valet.

"Would I know if you had?" Donal retorted.

He waggled his fingers. Rollo placed a small folded square of creamy vellum on his palm. Donal stared at it.

"Aren't you going to open it?" Rollo prompted.

"In a moment." Donal didn't move. He wouldn't admit he was afraid to see the words Felicity Melton had penned.

"Would you like me to read it to you, sir?" Rollo's hand hovered.

"No." Donal's fingers closed around the letter and he jerked away from the valet, leaning back in the chair with the letter pressed to his chest. "I…"

He softened his tone. No need to let Rollo see how anxious he was. As if he could fool the manservant.

"I mean, no, thank you, Rollo, I'm quite capable of reading it myself. After all, I *am* a Cambridge graduate." He hiccoughed as if in emphasis and placed his hand against his lips, saying with extreme dignity. "Pardon me."

"Quite so, sir. No offense." Rollo managed to hide his smile by biting his lip and looking concerned. "I merely thought perhaps…"

Donal tore open the seal on the letter, unfolding it. He blinked several times to make the words come into focus.

My Dear Mr. McCoy,

Briefly, he had an image of Felicity sitting at a gilded secretary, holding a quill, perhaps nibbling daintily on a thumbnail as she composed her reply.

Thank you for your gracious letter, and also your

thoughtful concern for wishing to visit while our family is in mourning.

I have discussed the matter with my mother and uncle. They both were impressed with your demeanor when meeting you at Almack's and agree it would be permissible for you to join us for afternoon tea tomorrow.

We shall look forward to seeing you at that time.

With sincerest regards,

Felicity Honouria Augusta Melton

Donal looked up, dropping the letter into his lap. He seemed to be staring at nothing and didn't speak for so long Rollo finally asked in concern, "Sir? What…may I ask…what did she say?"

"She said…" Donal's answer was a bare wheeze, carried along on a sigh of relief. He retrieved the letter, waving it slightly. A faint smile touched his lips. "…I may come tomorrow for tea. Thank God."

With that, the wine got the better of him. The letter fluttered to the carpet as he passed out.

"Ah, master…" Picking up the letter, Rollo folded and placed it on the table next to the wine glass and the cheese plate. Then he caught Donal by the forearms, pulling him from the chair. "Come on, sir, up we go."

One arm around his master's waist and the other across his shoulders, he guided Donal up the stairs to his bedchamber.

Donal roused long enough to ask, "Where…we…going?"

"I'm putting you to bed," the valet answered, in the tone an adult might employ with a sleepy child. "You've a trying day coming up and I think you'll need all the rest you can get. Your bed is the best place to do it."

"Ri'…" Donal closed his eyes, walking carefully as they negotiated the stairs. "As usual…always looking out for me, Rollo…what…I do wi'out you?"

"I shudder to think, sir." Rollo's answer was both sarcastic and truthful.

They reached the top step and started down the hall.

Chapter 11

The next morning, Donal awoke surprisingly alert and eager, with an image of Felicity Melton's pretty face fading from an unremembered dream.

Perhaps that was what put him in such an optimistic mood. Whatever the reason, he found himself impatient for the afternoon to arrive, and when Rollo came through the door with his breakfast, he discovered his master not only awake but out of bed, wrapping himself in his dressing gown, and whistling.

"I'm eating downstairs today," he informed the astonished valet, waving a hand at the tray. "Take that to the dining room."

With that, he opened the door and stamped down the stairs, not bothering with his bedroom slippers, bare feet making a soft *slap-slap* on the carpeted steps.

Rollo followed silently, walking behind Donal as he made his way unerringly to the dining room. There, he went to the head of the table, waited while Rollo set the tray on the sideboard, then rushed to pull out his chair and push it under him as he sat. The manservant hurried back to retrieve Donal's plate of toast and place it before him.

"I hope it hasn't gotten cold, sir."

"I doubt that." He waited while Rollo removed the cover, then inspected the two slices of bread. "Looks all right. Let's see…" He glanced at the accompanying condiments. "Butter…jam… Good enough…and pour me some chocolate."

Supplied with a cup of frothy brown liquid, he nibbled on butter-drenched, jam-smeared toast alternating with sips of chocolate.

"May I ask why this sudden departure from routine?" Rollo hovered as if concerned for Donal's welfare.

"You may." Donal stopped munching long enough to reply, then bit into the second slice of toast.

"Will I get an answer?"

"Hm? Oh, of course." Donal set down the toast and reached for his cup. "I realized if I bring a wife here, I'll probably be dining in this room quite often so I should begin accustoming myself to that fact. What better way than to actually eat here?"

"I see." Rollo appeared to mull that over, then concede, "Very wise, sir."

"As you know," Donal continued, sipping chocolate, "I'm calling on Miss Melton this afternoon. For tea. Please have my best afternoon suit, shirt, and cravat readied. Are my other pair of Wellingtons polished?"

"Will you wish the silk shirt, then?" Rollo asked. "I always keep your boots ready."

Donal considered, lowering his cup. "Perhaps I should say my most acceptable shirt. Silk may be all right for evening wear, but I'm still a bit leery about wearing it in the daytime. My best *linen* shirt. After all, Miss Melton and her mother are still in some form of mourning, and I don't want to go against custom where that's concerned."

"Quite so, sir." Rollo could understand that, as well

as what Donal wasn't saying. That he didn't want any part of his wardrobe to raise any questions from Mrs. Melton any more than it might've at Almack's. "I'll get on it right away."

"I want to look sharp, Rollo, but not like a swell," Donal cautioned.

"Trust me. You'll be perfect."

"Good enough. Then pour me another cup and get to it." Donal held out the little china cup.

Rollo picked up the chocolate pot from the sideboard. As he turned back, there was a faint dinging. Someone was ringing the doorbell. He looked in that direction.

"Are we expecting anyone? Perhaps Mr. Joss?"

"Joss? Don't think so," Donal answered.

The doorbell sounded again. Rollo started through the dining room door, then remembered he still held the chocolate pot and looked back. Donal shook his cup.

The doorbell dinged a third time, as if whoever was outside was getting impatient.

Rollo again looked in that direction, then poured Donal's chocolate, hastily returned the pot to the buffet, and hurried through the door.

Donal leaned back in his chair, savoring his second cup as he listened to Rollo's footsteps gain momentum to a near-run as the doorbell's dings accelerated. He heard the door swung open.

"Yes, sir? May I help you?" It was the valet's standard greeting to a stranger.

"Thank goodness." A young man spoke. "I was beginnin' t' think I aithur had th' wrong house or e'er'one had scarpered when they learnt I was comin'."

That voice. Donal swallowed and nearly choked.

That all too familiar brogue.

Setting down his cup, he pushed back his chair and copied his valet's hasty exit from the dining room, following Rollo at a full gallop.

"Were you expected, sir?"

He heard the valet ask and saw Rollo's body change position as he looked down.

"Is that a suitcase?"

"Yes, I'm expected." The person on the other side of the door answered a bit sharply. "An', yes…if I'm a guest, surely I'd be bringin' at least a change o' clothin' with me. Why are you lookin' at me as if you're thinkin' o' sendin' me t' th' tradesmen's entrance?"

"Pardon me, sir," Rollo's voice changed to sheer confusion. "Who are you?"

"I'm…"

"Colin?" Donal swung the door wide. He stared at the youngster standing on the stoop.

The boy was dressed in traveling clothes, a dark coat and vest, gray trousers, and top hat from under whose brim fiery-red curls escaped.

"Hullo, Donal." His younger brother smiled at him. He looked extremely weary.

"What the hell are you doing here?" was all Donal could think to say.

"You didna get me letter?" He seemed taken aback by this greeting.

Unlike Donal, Colin switched his accent on and off according to whom he spoke. With his brother, it came out Irish.

"Letter?"

Vaguely, Donal remembered Rollo handing him a letter…no, *two* letters. He'd recognized the handwriting on one as Colin's, the other was from his father.

Oh no. What's happened?

"Oh, yes." He attempted to appear aware but feared he came across as merely bewildered. "I got your letter. Last Thursday…"

"…but you didn't read it," Colin finished, disappointment flooding his face. "If you did, you wouldna be askin'."

Instead of answering, Donal seized his arm and pulled him inside.

Colin resisted.

"Me bag…"

"Rollo will get it. By the way, this is my baby brother, Colin," he said by way of introduction as Rollo bent to retrieve the bag. He pushed the door shut, barely giving the valet time to step back inside.

"Master Colin." Rollo nodded a greeting. He held up the portmanteau. "What shall I do with…?"

"Just set it there." Donal nodded to a chair next to the mail table in the foyer. "Until we get this sorted out."

Still holding Colin's arm, he pulled the boy down the hallway to his study.

"You're still at breakfast?" Colin noticed the remnant of toast still clutched in his hand. "Donal, 'tis near eleven-thirty." He then realized Donal was barefoot. "Where are your bedroom slippers?"

"No, I'm not at breakfast." Donal stuffed the crust into his mouth, saying around it as he chewed. "I'm merely enjoying a leisurely morning."

Or I was, until you showed up.

Still chewing, he asked, "I never wear slippers when downstairs. Can I get you some coffee…or tea?"

"I'd prefer a good shot o' Grandda's whiskey if you

have it," Colin retorted.

"Whiskey? At this time of morning?" Donal blurted it out. "Good God, what's happened?"

"If you'd read me letter…"

"…I'd know. Yes, yes, you said that, but…"

They reached the study. Donal guided Colin to a chair near the hearth, fell into another, and gestured to Rollo to supply the requested whiskey.

Colin accepted his, slugging part of it with an expert ease that made Donal wince. The boy lowered the glass, studying the remains of its contents, running his finger around the rim.

Rollo offered Donal the other poured glass. He started to refuse, then decided he should keep it handy, just in case. He took the glass and set it on the table at his elbow.

"Aren't you supposed to be on your way to Cambridge?" Since Colin wasn't volunteering anything and seemed fascinated by the liquid in his glass, Donal decided he was elected to open their dialogue.

"After what happened, I felt I needed t' delay a bit…"

"You haven't been expelled?" Donal didn't give Colin time to finish. "You can't be. You haven't even registered yet."

"Didn't Da write you?" Colin looked up, frowning as if he couldn't understand his brother's continued ignorance of whatever it was that had occurred. "He said he was goin' ta."

"I got a letter," Donal admitted. "The same day as yours, in fact."

"…an' didn't read it aithur, I suppose?" There was a great deal of disillusionment in Colin's young voice.

"Colin, please tell me. What's happened?" Donal's own voice took on a note of urgency. "Has something happened to Father...or..." Abruptly, his acquired accent fell away as the worst thing imaginable shot into his mind. "Lord, nay! Naithin' happen t' Ma, has it?"

"Mama's fine, though a wee bit heart-wrung." Colin's faint smile at mention of their mother also acknowledged his brother's momentary lapse into the brogue he'd struggled to lose. "I wanted t' come here an' recover a bit afore goin' on t' school. I've still a bit o' time."

"If Father's all right and so is Mother," Donal recovered, all-British again. "Then what..." He stopped, shook his head, and said, with certainty, "Padraig."

"Aye, Padraig," Colin confirmed.

"What's he done this time?" Donal remembered he hadn't read Quinton's letter because he didn't want to hear of any more of his other brother's escapades just then. "Cheated someone else out of house and home in a card game?"

"Worse than that." Briefly, Colin's face primped, as if he wanted to burst into tears. He didn't, however, simply said, "The worst thing that could happen."

"Good Lord, he's not dead?" Donal remembered, a trifle jealously, how his younger brother looked up to Padraig.

Colin shook his head.

"Then it's not the worst thing."

"Donal!"

"What's happened, Col?" Donal forced himself to speak calmly when what he wanted to do was rail at his absent second brother, then seize Colin and shake him until he spilled whatever had happened.

Movement at his elbow made him look down. Rollo was quietly placing on the table the two letters he'd ignored. He picked up the first, tore open the seal, skipped the greeting, and read the first line. Then he sat there, staring at the letter.

"I don't believe it."

"Believe it," Colin muttered. "'Tis true."

He became aware he still held his drink and tossed it down, holding it out silently to Rollo, who hastily refilled it.

Donal forced himself to read the rest of the letter.

Mr. Donal Callum Seamus McCoy

7 Elm Tree Mews, Sedley House

Chesterfield, Mayfair

London, England

The United Kingdom of Great Britain

My dear son,

I have disinherited Padraig.

As much as it grieved me to do it, and even more pains me now to admit it, I had no choice. You're aware of your brother's propensity for trouble, as well as his eye for women. Recently, he combined the two in an escapade that has since become gossip upon every tongue in the county. It involved the wife of Lord Cornwell, and by extension, my employer, Lord Alisdaire, as well. Since Cornwell is a friend of His Lordship, I, as father of the miscreant, have also been dragged into the affair.

I felt I had to make some action before I was called upon to answer for my son's behavior.

I spoke to Padraig, reprimanding him and reminding him of the consequences to me as Lord Alisdaire's steward and estate manager. While I had hoped your brother would grow out of his womanizing ways, I see now this is not going to be the case.

Because of this, I had no choice but to send him away. Thus, I offered him a sizeable sum if he would leave not only my home but also Ireland, and agreed to pay him the same amount every month if he promised never to return. He accepted and is leaving today by packet.

Your mother is heartbroken, of course, but she will console herself that she still has two good sons. I will not forbid you to see your brother, should you wish, but do not allow him to cozen you into speaking to me on his behalf. No exhortation on your part will make me change my mind.

Your father, now minus one son bearing the McCoy name,

Quinton Aloysius Francis Xavier McCoy
McCoy Manor
Tipperary, Ireland

Donal reached blindly for the whiskey glass. Rollo pushed it into his waiting fingers. He raised it, drank, and inhaled a burning breath as he set it down.

"After seein' Padraig, I couldn't go directly t' school." Colin spoke now, though to Donal's startled senses, his voice seemed very far away. "I just couldn't face all those strangers."

"You saw Padraig?" Donal looked up. "At Eton?"

"He came up after arrivin' in England, wanted t' give me his side o' th' story, he said." Colin nodded. "Then he was goin' on t' London…"

"He's here?" Donal shot out of his chair as if stabbed in the haunch by a hatpin. "In London? Oh no, no, no." His hand clenched, crumpling Quinton's letter into a ball. "He can't be…he's going to ruin everything."

If anyone learned of Padraig's presence and tied Donal to him, his chances with Miss Melton, indeed with anyone, would be done for.

"Do you know where he's staying?" He spun around to find Colin staring at him as if he thought his brother had lost his wits.

"He didn't say. I don't think he knew. His main concern was getting' t' Da's bank an' depositin' th' money int' his account."

"He *would* be worried about that, wouldn't he?" Donal muttered. He returned to his chair. Rollo had refilled his glass, but he ignored it. "I've some things to do today, Colin. Actually, I'm calling on a young lady this afternoon, someone I'm hoping to become serious about."

"Congratulations." Colin sounded more automatic than sincere. "That ought t' make Da happy. If you get married, it might take his mind off Padraig for a bit."

"Providing Padraig doesn't do something…I swear, if he queers my chances, I'll kill him myself."

"Donal, you wouldn't?" The idea that one of his brothers might harm the other did bring tears to Colin's eyes.

"No." His voice softened as he placed a hand on the boy's shoulder. "I wouldn't, but I might give him such a thorough anointing he'd wish I had." He forced a smile, making Colin laugh. Donal picked up his glass. "Come now, let's drink to something good."

"How about…t' th' success o' your endeavor?" Colin raised his glass.

"Hear, hear." Donal tapped his own against it and

they both gulped down the whiskey, setting down their glasses together. "I'm going to go on the hopeful assumption, accompanied by many prayers, that Padraig will have an unheard-of moment of discretion and not make any jollies that'll cost me."

He got to his feet, throwing an arm across Colin's shoulders as his brother stood also.

"You say you needed to get away a bit before going on to university? I won't be late this afternoon. When I get back, we'll go out. I'll take you around to see a bit of London nightlife…would you like that?"

"I was hopin' you'd say that," Colin admitted. He looked down, as if suddenly stricken with shyness, lowering his voice so Rollo, standing behind them, couldn't hear. "I ain't had a chance t' see much in th' way o' dab-houses or…" He shrugged. "You know what I mean."

His voice changed, still quiet but with a desperate lilt.

"I want t' get drunk an' laid, Donal, an' not necessarily in that order."

"We'll talk about that when I come back," was all Donal could think to say to that bit of bluntness.

He told himself he shouldn't have been surprised that Colin would want to go to a brothel or expect his older brother to act as his guide, but he was. Shocked, in fact, mainly because it pointed out in no uncertain terms that his younger brother was no longer a child. He was eighteen now, and soon to be a man entering university life.

Donal told himself he and Colin would have a long talk about the boy's expectations and exactly how much experience he'd had so far, before he set foot in any place inhabited by a lady of the evening.

"Now, however," he continued. "I must begin my *toilette* for my afternoon engagement. Would you like to go to your room and rest, or sit with me and talk while I get dressed?"

"I'm not a baby who needs an afternoon nap," Colin exclaimed, insulted.

Donal made a mental note to start speaking to his brother as more of an equal, though that was going to be a chore. He'd been referring to Colin as *the baby* for eighteen years and the transition would be difficult.

"Perhaps I'll pick up a few pointers for me own *toilette*," the boy continued.

"Very well then." Donal was flattered by that remark, especially since Colin had always deferred to Padraig in such matters.

Flicking a glance at his brother's face, he wondered if those smooth cheeks had felt a razor yet. He steered the boy up the stairs toward his bedchamber.

"Though any expertise I have I owe to Rollo."

Chapter 12

Donal was so meticulous over this particular *toilette* both Rollo and Colin were driven to near-distraction, though Colin did more gibing than worry. That was left to Rollo, who supplied fresh shaving water and a second razor after Donal's initial shave was completed, and otherwise puttered around reminding his master how much time he was wasting.

From Donal's view, however, the time was anything but wasted, even if his second shave sent Rollo into a dither at what he considered a redundant and useless act.

Donal's stubble, being copper, wasn't quite as noticeable as it would be if darker. In fact, he could've probably gone with shaving only every other day, for the hairs were visible only when struck by light at the proper angle. He'd done that on occasion and no one even noticed.

Today, however, there had to be nothing about him, not in his wardrobe or on his person, that might detract in any way.

Therefore, he simply ignored Rollo's protests, asked for his second razor and more warm water, and proceeded to skim the blade over cheeks appearing completely bare.

Once finished, he inspected his chin in the shaving-glass, then asked, "I wonder...do you think I should apply a bit of that water from Cologne Father sent me for my birthday?"

"You mean, he actually did that?" Colin looked interested. His accent contrasted with Donal's precise tones. "When you requested it, after th' way he railed an' ranted about th' price, I was certain he'd refused."

"Hardly." Donal allowed himself a smug expression as Rollo disappeared into his dressing room and returned with an ornate but small vial whose brown label wrapped around it completely and also covered the corked mouth.

Eau de Cologne, the label read, with other words elaborately written in copperplate printing in French, and an ornate seal bearing more description. Rollo presented the vial as if it contained liquid gold.

Donal accepted and studied it intently.

"Joss mentioned it to me one day…you remember Joss, Colin?"

Colin nodded.

"He lamented how he wished he could afford even the smallest vial, but he hadn't the finns and his father wouldn't give him any more advances. I got the bright idea to ask for some—bit of one-upmanship, you know—but when Father told me what it cost, a civil servant's salary for half a year, he said, I decided I was out of luck." He shook the vial. "Then, a few days before my natal event, I was surprised to discover one of Father's footmen knocking at my door."

He turned an expression of sheer delight as well as astonishment, even at this late date, on his brother.

"Father had not only procured a vial for me but sent Colm all the way here to hand-deliver it because of its value." Donal laughed delightedly. "I suppose he thought for what he'd paid he didn't want to risk it being lost in the post, but… Can you believe it?"

"I guess that really does prove you're his favorite." Colin's remark held no envy, surprisingly.

Not only paying such a princely sum but buying a ticket for the footman on a packet as well as coach fare to take him from Tipperary to London... Quinton had never done anything like that for Padraig, and certainly not for Colin. It wasn't to be expected for second and third sons, only such deference for the eldest and precious heir.

"I've never used it." Donal's chuckle held a bit of embarrassment. "Kind of hated to break the seal and let even a bit of essence escape. Guess I was waiting for some special event to employ this miracle water."

He looked from Colin to Rollo.

"I suppose this may be the time."

He raised the vial, preparing to tear open the strip of paper around the mouth. Rollo caught his wrist.

"Sir, if you're planning on bathing, perhaps you should wait until afterwards. If that stuff's so expensive, it would be a tragedy to apply it and immediately wash it off."

"Hmm. You're right." Donal placed the vial on the tray holding the nickel-plated stand in which his badger-hair shaving brush and razor were air-drying above the little metal lather bowl. "Well? Let's get on with this. As you reminded me, Rollo, time is flying."

With that, Rollo enlisted Charles's aid in lugging the tin tub up the stairs, then hauled warm water from the kitchen so he could bathe. Rollo had gone downstairs during Donal's second shave, setting the kettles on the stove so that by the time he was finished, the water would be hot. He'd done this so often, he had it timed perfectly, the kettles beginning to whistle as Donal wiped the last bit of lather from his cheeks.

They were whistling merrily as he hurried to the kitchen.

When Donal doffed his dressing gown and stepped into the tub, rather gingerly for the water was very hot, he paused to ask, "You *are* still bathing daily?"

"O' course." Colin's answer held a bit of insulted air. "I long ago grew out o' havin' a fear o' water, Donal." He laughed. "No longer make mud pies, aithur."

"That's remarkable, if gratifying." Donal remembered how a dirt-covered Colin would always be hauled, fighting and protesting, into the nursery to be dunked into the tub by their nursemaid. "Cleanliness is next to godliness, you know."

Colin snorted. "At the moment, th' last thin' I want is t' be godly."

Donal let that pass. He mentally added it to the list of things he was going to discuss with his brother before their outing later.

Once bathed, he anointed his cheeks with the barest dash of the cologne, asking of Colin, "That's not too much, is it?"

His younger brother seemed to find his concern amusing though he leaned forward, sniffed sharply, and declared, "Barely detectable. Only th' faintest whiff o' somethin' absolutely…damn, Donal, I don't know how t' describe it. Makes me want t' get closer an' take anaithur breath or two. Is it suppose t' do that?"

"According to Joss…yes."

"Then it's definitely workin', but does it affect both men an' women, do you think?"

"Good God, I hope not," Donal looked alarmed. "That might become embarrassing."

"I doubt it." Colin took another deep breath. "I can't smell it now."

Donal relaxed and proceeded to dress with Rollo's assistance. As the valet picked up his cravat, however, he said, "I'm wondering if I should do something about my hair."

Colin shrugged. "Looks fine t' me."

"That's because you aren't a young lady," Donal shot back, giving a sideways glance at Colin's own hair, which he'd always compared to a bowl of carrot curls someone was preparing for a luncheon salad.

"Thank goodness for that." His brother gave him a crooked grin and a raised eyebrow. "Else I wouldn't be sittin' here while you splashed about in th' altogether."

Donal ignored that. "I mean…curls? Really? I'm thinking they need to be subdued a bit. Where's that bottle of Rowland's macassar oil, Rollo?"

The valet once more disappeared into the dressing room, returning this time with a small bottle. Rollo opened it, poured a bit onto his palm, and brushed it over the copper tangles.

In the mirror, Donal watched Colin's image shake its head.

"What?"

"I'm merely thinkin' how Mama always deplored Da usin' that stuff because it left stains on th' upholstery. She much preferred his hair lookin' like a red haystack t' having th' servants scrub th' chair backs once a week, she said."

"That's what antimacassars are for."

He remembered Quinton had foregone slicked-back hair rather than suffer the little crocheted doily-like protectors across each and every chair and couch in

McCoy Hall…a little eagerly, he thought. Could it be his father hadn't liked having his wild hair held captive in the grip of palm and coconut oil? Taking the hairbrush offered him, he smoothed the curls into a sleek mass, then set down the brush.

"There." He turned to Colin. "What do you think?"

"Egad!" Colin cowered dramatically, hands before his eyes. "Who is this magnificently clad example o' manhood I see before me?"

"Oh, shut up," Donal said, with the most good nature he'd ever displayed to his younger brother in his life.

****

Now Donal was on his way, utilizing his carriage again, but this time for elegance's sake and not because he didn't trust himself to drive. Though he wasn't sure why, he felt more secure, more in control, and definitely looking forward to this visit, even if anxiety continued hovering somewhere just out of sight. Felicity Melton's waif-like eyes floated in and out of his memory, along with the ash-pale ringlets and her very trim, doll-sized figure.

That also encouraged him. He wondered if he'd been in her thoughts since that night at Almack's. She'd certainly been in his—more than the other two, if he cared to admit it.

Why's that, I wonder?

Granted, it was as Joss said. The girl was a mouse, quiet, timid, shy as some woodland creature. Donal heartily agreed with his friend on that. Nevertheless, there was something about her…he could picture her as a faery-child, surrounded by bunnies, fawns, and chipmunks, the animals eating out of her hand as they gathered around her while she sat in a bluebell- and daffodil-covered glen and wove coronets out of flowers.

Since when do I wax so poetic? Egad.

He had to face it. The girl brought out a fanciful side of him.

The carriage slowed at a street corner, allowing a coach-and-four and a hansom to pass on the cross street. Donal looked around, seeing a young girl standing there, holding a basket…something in small purple bouquets? Violets? It was one of the few flowers, along with roses and buttercups, he recognized.

The other vehicles had passed now. Charles raised the reins…

"Hold up a moment, Charles," Donal called out, and the footman lowered the reins and waited.

Donal looked toward the flower girl again, gesturing. "You there."

She glanced around, saw the stopped carriage, and tapped herself on the chest with an inquisitive look.

"Flower girl. Come here."

She trotted to the carriage's side, a child of about twelve, dressed in a clean but patched dress with a pinafore over it. Her brown hair was braided into two long plaits, and briefly he was reminded of his sister Bridget. "Yes, sir?"

"What do you have there?" He waved a hand at her basket.

"Violet bouquets, sir." She looked eager, expecting a sale. "Would you like one t' take t' your lady?"

"How do you know I'm going to see a lady?" He laughed.

"Why else would a gent be so elegant at this time o' afternoon?"

"Well, you're right and I do want some flowers to take to her." He had a feeling Felicity would like any kind of flower.

She dug into the basket, producing a small nosegay of remarkably still unwilted violets, holding them out. "These 'uns is still fresh," she said, unnecessarily.

"How many do you have left?" he wanted to know.

"Only two more," she answered and brightened. "Then I can go home."

"I'll take them all." He dug into a vest pocket, finding the few coins he generally kept there. Receiving the three little bouquets, he dropped all the coins into her hand without asking her the price.

She studied them. "I ain't got no change t' give you back, sir."

"No problem. Keep it and hurry on home." Donal placed the flowers on the seat beside him and said, "Carry on, Charles."

The footman cracked the whip. Behind him, Donal heard the flower girl call out, "Thank 'ee, sir," as the carriage sped away.

Chapter 13

When he arrived at the Melton residence, it was the same routine as before…tell the butler who he was and his reason for calling, and present his card. This time, however, the man waved away the calling card.

"No need for that, Mr. McCoy. Miss Felicity's expecting you. Please come in."

Returning the card to its case, Donal stepped inside where his hat and gloves were taken. As the butler waited, he laid the little flowers on the credenza and pulled off his gloves, dropping them inside the hat the servant held. He picked up the three little bouquets again.

"Shall I take those and have them placed in water, sir?" the butler asked, holding out a hand.

"I'd like to present them myself, if I may." Donal actually drew back slightly as if he feared the man would snatch them from him.

"Certainly." The butler bowed and gestured. "If you'll come this way, please?"

He was led down a hall to an open door on the right. Donal expected the house to be shrouded in shadows, unlit and dark as befitted a domicile in mourning, so he was surprised to find it relatively well-lit, with drapes undrawn, its windows flung open to the sun. Then he remembered this was Felicity's uncle's home and decided the other Mr. Melton perhaps had certain ideas clashing with his widowed sister-in-law's in the matter

116

of how long mourning should be carried on and how far.

"Mr. McCoy, sir." The butler spoke into the doorway and then stepped back to let Donal enter.

Sir? Was he going to be interrogated by Felicity's uncle before being allowed to see her?

Donal's belly took a low lunge, then settled as he stepped inside and saw not only Mr. Melton but also Felicity and her mother. The uncle stood near the hearth, one elbow resting on the mantel. He looked as he had that night at Almack's, a tallish man, rather handsome, with dark hair touched at the temples with gray.

Vague as usual, Joss had told Donal he was *involved in some sort of manufacturing.* He appeared well-to-do, and since he'd been admitted to Almack's, Donal could only assume that, whatever his method of endeavor, it was legitimate, respectable, and profitable.

If this goes well, I'd best find out more, he told himself. He also realized he rather liked Felicity's uncle, from his looks alone. He wondered how much like his brother the late Mr. Melton had been.

There were two divans facing each other in a little grouping with two chairs, a tea table centering everything. Felicity sat on one of the divans, her mother on the other. They were both dressed in shades of lavender. He thought Felicity looked like one of those little wild violets called Johnny Jump-Ups, in her pale gown, while her mother was attired in a more somber purple almost black, an acceptable shade for later mourning. The severity of her gown was relieved by dark lilac bows on the sleeves and neckline.

"McCoy." Mr. Melton greeted him, coming forward and extending his hand. "Roger Melton. We met at Almack's the other night, but it never hurts to reintroduce one's self."

"Quite so," Donal had found that was always a safe phrase. He clasped Melton's hand, then released it, hoping his own was as firm as his host's.

"Are those for me?" Felicity asked.

Donal thought she looked lively, even eager, perhaps, since the moment he came through the door.

"I bought them on the spur of the moment," he admitted. "I must have had a premonition, for they'll match your gown perfectly."

That's damned lucky, too. He presented them with a bow.

She took them, murmured her thanks, and pressed one of the bouquets against her nose, inhaling gently. He thought she looked pleased as she let the three little nosegays rest in her lap.

"Thank you for receiving me, sir." Donal glanced around as he spoke, including the two women, in case Melton hadn't been the one giving the final vote in allowing him here.

"Think nothing of it," Melton rejoined, taking one of the chairs in the grouping. "I was very impressed by your deportment. Don't suppose I should've been, after all, you *are* a friend of young Joselyn."

That statement astounded Donal, that this man, who appeared so astute from the little he'd seen of him, could be so fooled by appearances.

"Please, sit." Melton gestured. Donal started to the other vacant chair, only to have Felicity say, "Please, Mr. McCoy, sit here."

She patted the cushion beside her. Donal hesitated only a moment. As he saw neither Melton nor her mother appeared about to protest, he sat, a bit gingerly, next to her. The brief vision of Araminta Bradley moving aside and hopefully expecting him to sit beside her flashed through his mind and was immediately extinguished. He was certain there was no way Felicity was going to act as that young lady had.

"Do you know Joss well?" Donal asked.

"His father and I were at university together," came the surprising answer.

"Uncle Roger is Joss' godfather," Felicity supplied.

She'd lost some of her timidity, though her voice was still soft and very quiet. Perhaps being in familiar surroundings brought about the change.

"He never told me," Donal managed, hiding his surprise by injecting a jocular note into his voice. "I suppose I'll have a bone to pick with him about that."

A bone? He'd have an entire skeleton. *Why didn't Joss tell me he and the Meltons were intimates?*

"Don't be too harsh," Mrs. Melton spoke up. She also appeared to have shed some of her gloomy demeanor. "Joss may not have spoken about us to you, but he's certainly said a great deal about you to us, on the occasions when we've seen him."

"Oh?" Donal tensed.

*What the hell have you said, Joss? If you've queered this for me…*the same words he'd said about Padraig, but if Joss knew the family, he might be more of a danger.

He affected a light air. "Nothing defaming, I hope?"

"To the contrary," Melton answered. "He sings your praises loudly. In fact, the day after our meeting at Almack's, he paid me a visit to inform me you had expressed an interest in seeing Felicity again."

"I…" Donal coughed to hide a brief quaver. "I hope that wasn't indiscreet."

"I didn't consider it so," Melton replied. "He said he wanted to let his little mouse know she had a possible suitor."

"Mouse?" Remember how Joss had characterized Felicity in just such a way, Donal was shocked. "I beg your pardon, sir?"

"That's Joss's pet name for me," Felicity explained. "Because I'm so small, you see. He says I'm as tiny as a mouse and almost as quiet."

Joss hadn't been using the term in a derogatory way? The things he'd said hadn't seemed exactly pleasant, however. Donal decided his friend's words had held meanings known only to himself.

The appearance of a maid bearing a tea tray prevented him from answering. She was given the violets to put in a vase and place in Felicity's chambers. He waited while tea was served and the cake plates passed around.

Melton led the conversation, with his sister-in-law and Felicity adding explanations here and there. In short order, Donal learned that Melton and his younger brother, Felicity's father, had been in business together. They were importers of wool, silk, and other fabrics, and had been for approximately ten years.

"Since Felicity was eight years old," her uncle said, giving his niece a fond smile that made her blush.

Donal decided he liked the color it brought to her face.

Melton continued explaining how, when his brother died five years before, he decided his niece and sister-in-law shouldn't live alone in the family home in the country. He'd packed them into his coach and brought them to town, planning to present Felicity to Society when she came of age.

"…and now she has, and here's her first gentleman caller," he finished, beaming at her.

"Oh, Uncle Roger…" Again. the blush bloomed, making Donal smile. She looked up, saw his expression and blushed more before smiling in return.

Donal was asked about his schooling. They already were aware he was a classmate of Joss and that Joss had been the "pig" he'd kept at Cambridge.

"Joss says you're his best friend," Felicity ventured. "*Pig* seems a horrid term for a friend."

"It's a school thing," Donal explained. "A way for a student renting out his spare room to save himself the embarrassment of admitting he needs extra money." He added, "Not that I needed any. I rented the room to Joss because he's a friend."

"What did you read?" Melton inquired.

"History. I've a tremendous interest in the history of our country…England, Scotland, and Ireland," he added as he thought he saw Melton about to ask which part.

It appeared Melton was a history buff, and for several minutes they chatted about that while Donal mentally chafed as he realized the uncle was monopolizing the conversation. He didn't dare say that aloud, however. Best to butter up the old man if it would further his suit.

"Well, now…" Melton abruptly drank the last of his tea and set his cup and saucer on the tray.

Donal leaped to his feet as his host arose.

"I must be going. I'm expecting a shipment and have to be at the docks when it's unloaded. Good to see you, McCoy." He nodded in Donal's direction, then went to the door. "Hope to do so again."

With that, he disappeared into the hallway, calling for the butler to bring his coach around.

"If you'll excuse me, Mr. McCoy…" Mrs. Melton also rose.

Donal, who'd just settled himself, once more scrambled to his feet.

"I've some crocheting I must tend to." She waved a hand in a sweep including the divans and chairs. "Antimacassars, you know."

It was only then Donal saw that each piece of furniture was fitted across the back with the protective coverings.

"I need a good deal of light, so I'll sit by the window."

Gathering her skirts, she walked over to a chair and lamp table near the open windows. Beneath the table was a yarn basket containing several balls of crochet thread and a good many hooks. Seating herself, she took out a ball of thread attached to an interwoven mass. She selected a hook, settled back, and began to thrust it through a loop in the thread.

"Well, now…" Feeling abruptly at a loss, though being more or less left alone with the object of his pursuit exactly as he desired, Donal now had no idea what to say.

"Thank you again for the flowers," Felicity said.

She spoke so softly he had to lean over to hear. He cast a glance in Mrs. Melton's direction, hoping she wasn't thinking him being forward. She was concentrating steadfastly on her crocheting.

"It was a mere whim, as I said, though I'm glad you like them."

"I think violets have such a sweet smell." She drew in a deep breath. "It lingers so…as if I can still smell them." She gave Donal a startlingly direct stare. "I shall always think of you when I smell violets, Mr. McCoy."

"I will be flattered, Miss Melton." He inclined his head slightly, wondering if she were detecting his cologne instead of violets.

They continued talking. The conversation veered from violets to her uncle's flower garden where Felicity admitted she liked to "dig in the dirt and plant bulbs and seeds."

"The first time I ventured into the garden, I didn't wear gloves." Felicity studied her hands.

Donal was struck by how small and slender her fingers were, with little oval pink nails.

"I got blisters on my palms and dirt under my nails. Mamma was very put out." She laughed and held up her hands. "I've learned always to wear gloves whenever I pick up a gardener's trowel now."

Donal's fingers twitched. His hand was halfway raised to seize one of her little ones before he caught himself.

"You must be careful," he agreed. "A blister can be extremely painful."

"Worth it, however, to make such beautiful things grow."

From there, the conversation wandered into other paths…various sites around London they'd both visited…people they knew in common, other than Joss, which were a surprising many…and eventually wound around to that night at Almack's.

"That was a most lovely dance I had with you," she admitted, looking away as if even saying such a thing was an embarrassment.

"For myself also," he said, thinking that wasn't so

much of a lie. "I suppose I was fortunate to be allowed that one."

"What do you mean?" Her eyes, of such a pale blue they appeared almost colorless, searched his face.

"Why, you surely had so many partners that night, I was glad you made space for me." He realized she wasn't colorless at all. When animated, she seemed to give off little sparks. It was simply that she was able to remain so still and silent others didn't notice her charm.

Donal decided he was going to have a talk with Joss about that nickname. He also would tell his friend never again to speak in even the faintest derogatory terms about Miss Melton.

That surprised him. He wasn't generally one to defend a female, mainly because most of those he knew didn't need defending.

At last, a sound interrupted their conversation, a familiar bonging.

"I say," Donal broke off in mid-word. "It can't be six o'clock."

He glanced to the window. The sun coming through had changed position and the sky seemed considerably darker. As he spoke, Felicity's mother stopped her crocheting to look at him. He saw then that the antimacassar she had been working on lay on the table, completed, and she was halfway finished with another.

"My dear Mrs. Melton, you should've spoken to me." He was apologetic though no one had chastised him. "I've overstayed my welcome."

"Nonsense," she said. Finishing off the last stitch and thrusting the hook through a loop, she dropped everything into the basket. "You and Felicity were having such a nice time, I had no wish to interrupt."

"It was enjoyable," Donal replied, and realized it was the truth.

He had enjoyed every moment, every word coming out of Felicity Mclton's rosebud mouth…and there hadn't been a single mention of fabric, colors, or fashions at all…except for his one brief allusion to the violets and her gown.

"However," he fumbled for his pocket watch. "I fear I must go. My younger brother, you see…" He hastened to explain, as he thought he saw disappointment on Felicity's face, as well as her mother's. "He's unexpectedly come to town and I don't dare leave him alone for long."

Realizing that made Colin sound as if he were incompetent, he added, "I promised to take him out to dinner tonight."

Dinner wasn't what Colin wanted, but it might be what he got if their talk didn't go as Donal wished.

"Then we'll say good afternoon and let you go," Mrs. Melton held out her hand. "Reluctantly," she added.

Donal took her hand, bowing over it. As he turned to Felicity, however, she slid her own hand around his arm.

"I'll walk you to the door, Mr. McCoy." She glanced at her mother as she said it and, receiving no opposition, turned him toward the hallway.

Mrs. Melton returned to her chair by the window as Felicity guided Donal up the hall.

"You made an impression on Mamma," she said quietly.

At first, Donal thought she was whispering to prevent her mother from hearing. It was going to take some time for him to accept that was her natural way of speaking.

I must help her learn to raise her voice.

"My uncle likes you, too," she added.

"Both of them? On such short notice?" he asked, smiling.

"I'm afraid so."

"Don't be afraid," he said. "What about you?"

"What about me?" She looked confused.

"I charmed your uncle and mother. Have I failed with you, Miss Melton?"

"I fear, Mr. McCoy…"

She paused for so long Donal felt his heart sink.

"You've succeeded only too well."

She blushed again, and that encouraged Donal to say something he hadn't planned, something he really shouldn't even have considered at that point in their burgeoning relationship.

"Miss Melton…Felicity…" His use of her first name made her colorless eyes widen. "Tomorrow night's Wednesday. Will you be at Almack's?"

"I believe so. My uncle seems intent on making certain I'm visible." She said it as if she didn't approve. "Perhaps I'll see you there?"

"You certainly will, if I've anything to say about it," he declared. "If you promise me a dance…no, three dances, all waltzes."

"I…if that's what you wish."

"I do," he declared. "I'd also like to take you riding in the park on Friday, if your mother will allow. She can come with us as chaperone," he hurried on. "Or bring your abigail…I'll bring Colin, too…we'll make a day of it…a family affair, a picnic."

He stopped, wondering if he was sounding too

eager, if he was spoiling everything. Would she think he didn't really care but was pushing it to make something not existing happen? Why was he rushing things, anyway?

"I'll have to speak to Mother about that," she answered, abruptly releasing his arm as if realizing her touching him might be considered a bold movement. "…and Uncle Roger, of course."

"Of course." His murmur was eagerly agreeable.

"As for the dances…" She gave him a brilliant smile. "I believe I may make that decision on my own, and I say…they are yours, Mr. McCoy, all three of them."

The butler appeared with his hat and gloves. He took them, bowed to Felicity, tapped the top hat onto his head, and walked through the door.

No…he *floated* through the door.

He was halfway to his carriage, automatically pulling on his gloves before he thought to himself how mooncalfed he must look. He wanted to glance back, to see if Felicity stood in the doorway, perhaps, watching him walk away.

He thought he heard the door click shut.

Donal continued staring straight ahead as he got into the carriage and told Charles to take him home. He felt odd and couldn't understand the sensation niggling at his insides…a feeling between the all-overish approach of impending illness and the similar sense of attaining some much-desired goal but fearing to hope lest it be snatched away…

…and then he knew.

I've done it. The feeling came over him in a wave of triumph so harsh it made him tremble. *She's the one.*

There was a brief moment when he wondered exactly how he meant that, and then his thoughts whirled away from the question, dazzled by his success.

He'd cornered his prey, captured her, and hadn't even realized it until that moment. He was euphoric with victory. He'd found the girl to marry. His father would be happy. So no doubt would her mother and uncle, since they'd received him favorably, thanks partially to his own disguised demeanor and Joss's good words. Felicity Melton was obviously smitten with him. She was pleasant enough, if not a raving beauty. They'd talked for some time and he'd not felt the least irritation in the conversation. She would be easily managed, and after he fulfilled his role as husband, doing what was necessary, he could be back at his old games nearly as free as he was before.

Feeling as if a great weight has been lifted, Donal relaxed against the carriage back.

They were nearly back to the mews house when he remembered Colin was waiting for him, eagerly expecting a night on the town with much collision of naked flesh and flowing of wine. Abruptly, he had no wish to deal with any of that. All he wanted was to revel in his success.

He tried to ignore that second niggle in his belly, the one more like a curl of guilt.

Chapter 14

Surprisingly, it was Colin and not Rollo who greeted him as he unlocked the door and came inside.

"How did things go?" he asked eagerly. "Did she inundate you with fashion stories or giggle you inta near-madness?"

Obviously, Rollo had filled him in on Donal's previous failures.

"Neither." Donal's answer was curt. He didn't want to think of Felicity just now, much less repeat any of his conversation with the Meltons. Hoping to change the subject, he asked, "Have you dined?"

"Rollo prepared high tea. I can see why you don't have a cook. It was excellent. Well?" It appeared Colin wasn't to be deterred.

"Well, what?" Donal turned away, placing his hat on the hall tree and removing his gloves before going to the study, his brother trailing.

"Do I have a prospective future sister-in-law, or…"

Donal didn't answer.

"Come on, Donal. I know Da was goin' t' write you about gettin' married."

"How do you know that?" Donal whirled to stare at Colin. "He didn't discuss it with you, did he?" *How dare Father do such a thing?*

"O' course not." He must've looked horrified because Colin chuckled as he said, "I overheard him talkin' t' Mama. When I went home for a visit."

"You'd better watch that," Donal warned, incensed that Colin had been aware of his father's plans before he himself learned of it. "Eavesdroppers never hear anything good."

"It didn't bother *me*," Colin pointed out.

"It may, if I ever again learn you've put your ear to a keyhole where my affairs are being discussed."

"Here now…" Colin made pacifying gestures, taking a step back as he saw Donal's hands ball into fists. "I didn't realize 'twas such a sensitive subject."

"Sensitive?" Donal blurted. "We're only talking about the rest of my life."

"Calm down, braithur." A hand went gingerly to his shoulder. Once assured it wasn't going to be slung away, Colin left it there. "I'm sorry, Don. I didn't think…"

"That's the trouble," Donal flared. "You don't think. Honestly, in that regard, you're as bad as Padraig."

"Nay!" Colin immediately defended his absent brother. "Don't compare me t' Padraig, an' don't traduce him, aithur, when he's nay here t' defend himself."

That stopped Donal's tirade before it began.

"You're right," he admitted. "I'm sorry, Col. This has been a distressing day. Sit down, and let's have a glass of wine and discuss our plans for tonight."

Colin accepted that apology by dropping into one of the chairs near the hearth and settling himself. He looked at Donal expectantly.

Not bothering to call Rollo, Donal busied himself with selecting and pouring wine, handing his brother one goblet and taking the other for himself. He sat in the chair facing Colin, waiting until his brother had taken the first sip before he spoke.

"I thought we'd go to a supper club and dine…"

"'Tisn't food so much I'm wantin'," Colin interrupted. "But some female companionship o' th' most carnal persuasion."

"Well. I must say you're forthright in stating your desires, aren't you?" Donal wasn't about to admit he was startled by this declaration.

Colin the freshman had been awkward and randy, but it appeared Colin the senior was definitely an adult in all areas.

"Why shouldn't I say what I want?" Colin answered. "We're both men o' th' world, ain't we?" He took another sip of wine, adding, "At least *you* are an' I've a desire t' be."

"As to that…" Donal drank from his own goblet, stalling to give himself time to compose what he wished to ask. "May I take that to mean you've been relatively active in the dalliance department?"

Colin gave him a slight glare.

"I haven't kept track of your conquests or lack of them," Donal mumbled, wondering if he should render an apology.

"I don't know that you'd call it *relatively active*," Colin frowned, not giving him a chance. "A student doesn't get much free time t' go t' toss-houses, an' those who do have t' be careful, as you very well know."

Donal nodded at that. He and Joss had been masters at being *careful.* Still were, for that matter.

"It cost more than me allowance could bear t' pay many visits t' that place you introduced me t'…thank you for that first visit, by th' way."

"Don't know if I should say *you're welcome*, or not," Donal muttered.

Abruptly, he didn't want to speak of the fact he'd been the one taking his sixteen-year-old brother to the brothel divesting him of his virginity. It was one of the few times he'd ever attempted to guide the boy as he'd promised his father he would.

Some guiding that was. I'm certain it wasn't what Father meant. At all. The thought gnawed. *Why am I ashamed now? I certainly wasn't then. What the hell is the matter with me?*

It had been on one of those rare occasions when Donal actually invited Colin to dine with him, prompted as it were by a letter from Quinton, reminding him he was expected to "look out for your brother."

They'd been accosted on a street corner by a ladybird who had eyes on Colin, though she offered to dab both for a sum shocking Donal in its low price. If he'd been alone, he might've taken her up on it, but he turned her away, dragging a loudly protesting Colin from the spot.

"All right. If you're in that much of a hurry to get yourself shucked," Donal snapped. "We'll do it properly."

With that, he hailed a passing cab, and shoved Colin inside.

That memory prompted him to ask, "Are you still using that *préventif?*"

"After you gave me holy hell about dabbin' barmaids?" Colin shook his head. "O' course."

****

"You idiot. Haven't you more sense than to let yourself get fucked by some tavern wench?"

Donal had shaken his head, voice rising in exasperation and a little concerned fear as Colin confessed he and a schoolmate had paid a barmaid at the students' snug they frequented to let both prong her in the tavern's storeroom.

"Next to forking a street bird, that's the best way to get the glim or something else as deadly." A hand went to Colin's shoulder, shaking him slightly. "Col, promise me you won't do that again. If you get the urge, just hail a cab, and say to the driver, *I need some rest and relaxation*. They all know what that means."

"But, Donal, I can't afford t'…"

That was as far as he got.

"I'll lend you the money."

That, coming from Donal, who was generally as tight with his own allowance as a Scot, shook Colin, for it proved how serious his brother was about his younger sibling's sexual welfare.

"Promise me that, will you, Col?"

He shook Colin's shoulder again in emphasis.

"All right, Donal," Colin nodded. "I promise."

"Good. Now then." Donal released him. "Watch your prick for the next month. If it turns red, you get a rash, or even a pimple, tell me. I know a doctor who's discreet."

****

"I thank you for steerin' me in that direction," Colin went on. He looked earnest. "Da also suggested it…a tad late."

"What do you mean?"

"This last time I went home on holiday afore graduation. He called me into th' study for what he called a *long-needed conversation*." Colin smiled, mouth twisting as he imitated Quinton's brogue. "Can you guess what 'twas about?"

"Not…" Donal shook his head. "Good God, Colin, you're eighteen. He didn't give you that Men-Women-and-Nature talk?" He'd gotten that lecture from Quinton when he was twelve, though it had been three years more before he acted on it.

"He did." Colin's nod mirrored his brother's. "Even recommended I visit a certain chemist when I returned t' school, one he said had been highly recommended."

"What did you do while Father was giving you this unnecessary information?"

"Don't worry. I didn't tell him I already knew more than he was sayin'," Colin reassured him. "Nor that me older braithur helped me get th' knowledge. I simply nodded an' thanked him an' assured him I'd follow his advice." He gave Donal an abruptly adult look. "Guess no man wants t' admit his baby's not that anymore."

"How much action have you seen so far?" Rephrasing his previous question, Donal unconsciously braced himself for Colin's answer.

"Not much. I'm been busy tryin' t' live *down* Padraig's reputation an' live *up* t' yours. Even this long after graduation, you're still highly respected at Eton, don't you know? I don't understand how e'er'one there an' at Cambridge learned o' Padraig's misdeeds when he was at Oxford," Colin replied. "Otherwise, I've been studying t' keep up me grades, an' that leaves blessed li'l time for much o' anythin' else."

He held up his right hand, flexing it.

"Most o' th' dallyin' I've done has been with Lady Five Fingers here."

The hand clamped into a fist.

"Damn it, I want somethin' else wrapped around me instead o' me own hand. Somethin' tight an' female."

"Then you shall have it," Donal promised.

After everything that had happened, especially that uncharacteristic feeling of guilt and the realization he'd been acccpted by the Meltons, he had a sudden yen to throw himself into some lascivious behavior, to forget it all by flinging himself into a pool of sensation and carnal delight. Not with Nell, however. What he wished tonight not even his mistress could provide. It had to be with one of the ladies at the Church.

He got to his feet, reaching for the bellpull. A single tug brought Rollo at a run.

"Sir?"

"Mr. Colin and I will be going out for dinner, Rollo. I imagine after that we'll stop at a couple of clubs for some wine and perhaps a few hands of cards, and then…" He held up a hand as Colin started to protest. "…we'll probably feel the need for some religious instruction. I believe we'll spend the rest of the evening at the Church."

Rollo's grin seemed to confuse Colin as much as did his brother's words.

"Donal, I really don't feel pious right now," he protested. "Especially when I'm thinkin' more along definitely profane lines. Th' last thin' I want is t' listen t' a sermon. Anyway, what church has services at night?"

"This one, dear brother."

Donal took Colin's glass from his hand and placed it by his own on the table. He threw an arm across his shoulders, aiming him at the study door.

"You'll like it." At Colin's skeptical look, he continued, "We need to change. Did you bring your evening clothes with you?"

Colin nodded.

"Good. Rollo, fetch my colombina, and that extra one also."

"Masks?" Colin looked more confused. "We're going t' a masquerade? I thought we were going t' church?"

"Just trust me." Releasing his brother, Donal started up the stairs. He heard Colin following. "If you need any assistance in dressing, I'll send Rollo to you as soon as he's finished helping me."

Chapter 15

Supper went well, though Donal noted Colin drank more than he ate. Afterwards, at another club, his brother surprised him by revealing he was a fairly good card player, though he didn't remember the boy showing the remotest interest in games of chance as a child. Was that something else he'd acquired at school? Donal's own gambling acumen had started long before then.

Though he played cautiously and not at all enthusiastically, Colin won several hands. It didn't take long for Donal to suggest they cash in their chits and go elsewhere. He found himself not enjoying cards as much as he usually did, nor was the wine as palatable. He felt an urgency to leave, probably triggered by his brother's own impatience.

"That should pay your tithe at the Church," he muttered as he gathered their winnings. That perked up Colin's expression considerably.

"Then may we go now so I can see this mysterious place o' worship?" Colin's confusion hadn't been dissipated by his brother's easy manner. "Would it be wrong o' me t' pray for someone t' deliver me from me lustful desires?"

"Come with me." Donal walked out, his brother running to catch up, like an eager puppy following its master.

****

"This ain't a church." Colin looked around, then up at the red brick mansion. "Where are we?"

Donal didn't answer, simply exited the carriage. He took the masks from his inside pocket, handing one to Colin.

"Put it on."

"You're serious?" He took the mask but held it.

"Never more so. Where we're going, it's best not to have your identity known. Dominos and full-face masks are *de rigueur*." He pressed his own against his face and began fastening the strings.

Colin's copper brows shot up. "Is this such a low place?"

"You can't possibly imagine, little brother…though fairly soon, you will. Go ahead, put on your mask." This time it was an order.

Colin obeyed, saying, "Well? How do I look? Would anyone knowin' me recognize me, do you think?"

"No, but if anyone you know also frequents such a place, I say you should reconsider your friendship."

"God, Donal…" He broke off as Donal made a sharp gesture.

"No names from here on."

"If we have t' be so secretive, what kind o' place is this?" Colin's voice dropped to a whisper, his tone saying he was getting a pretty good idea but wanted it stated plainly.

"You'll see." With that, Donal glanced at Charles. "You know where to take the carriage. We'll be back in a while."

He started to the steps. Halfway up, he stopped, looking back.

Colin was staring at the mansion.

It was four levels of red brick. All the windows on the ground, first, and second floors blazed with light. Those on the third were dimmed slightly, and the fourth story was completely dark because the drapes were tightly drawn. Occasionally a silhouette was glimpsed against the curtains but it was more or less a shapeless shadow and no discernible features could be detected.

"Why is that floor so dark?" Colin asked.

"That's the perversion level." Donal's answer was curt.

"Do you…are we goin' there?"

He couldn't tell if his brother's question was eager or fearful. The boy's next words, delivered in a tremulous whisper, said enough.

"D-Donal…w-we're nay goin'…?"

"Not while you're with *me* you won't." He gestured. "Come on."

Attached to the center of the door was a replica of a woman's hand, so lifelike it gave the illusion of someone having thrust her arm through the wood of the door. The hand held a bell with a red leather ribbon attached to the clapper.

Donal seized the ribbon and swung the clapper back and forth. It gave out a clear, loud *ding-ding* as it struck the inside of the bell.

The door opened. A man stood there. He was clad in a black robe, its cowled hood pulled forward, hiding his face.

"Welcome, worshippers." His voice was deep and sonorous.

Donal had always thought his appearance and his voice would've fit well in a dramatization of one of those popular Gothic novels.

Colin started to speak. Donal stopped him with a hand on his arm. Thus silenced, the boy stared instead.

There were other people in the room. Other gentlemen, at least one might assume so, but their attire told them nothing, since there was a singular lack of it. A couple of brocaded sofas and a chair or two held men, naked except for their dominos, with equally bare women on their laps. Apparently, they were so eager they couldn't wait to get to a room, for they were fondling and generally arousing themselves and being aroused by what they were doing. One man lifted the woman he held, revealing a spear of flesh protruding from between his thighs. He settled her upon it.

Hastily, Colin glanced away. Donal saw a crimson flush appear around the edges of the colombina, vivid against the mask's black silk.

The man in the doorway stepped back, with a grand gesture allowing them to enter. A woman walked up behind him.

"Abbot, thank you." Donal bowed to the man and drew Colin forward. The boy moved reluctantly, still caught in the shock of what he'd seen. "This is the Abbess."

Colin turned to her and reacted with a jerk.

She was wearing a coif secured by a white wimple of starched cotton, very proper and conventionally Catholic, tightly covering her cheeks and chin. Over the coif was stretched a black veil, but below that was a travesty of a nun's habit. Instead of the high-necked religious clothing one might expect, the neckline of her black velvet gown was so low-cut her nipples peeked out, pink against the dark fabric.

The boy swallowed loudly and stared.

Remembering his own initial reaction, Donal wondered how much was shock and how much pleasure at what he saw. The McCoys were Church of England, converting in the time of the eighth Henry to keep their lands and their lives, but to see the figure of a nun, whom they'd nevertheless been taught since childhood to revere, mocked in such a way…

Colin managed to convert his shock into a fairly formal bow.

"Pleased to meet you," the woman said. "Welcome to the Church." To Donal, she asked, "Your brother, is he, sir?"

"What makes you think that?" Donal was startled. *How could she guess?*

"The hair." She pointed. "One fox-haired man is rare. Two? They *have* to be kin."

"Most astute." Donal decided not to admit or deny but simply let it go at that.

"A bit of a novice, also?" She smiled as Colin actually winced. "Needs a bit of religious instructin', does he?"

"If you'd be so kind," Donal said.

"My pleasure." The woman took Colin by the arm. She winked. "Not really *my* pleasure, you understand, but…"

She didn't finish but turned, taking Colin with her so he faced the opposite wall. While Donal watched, she waved an arm at a nearby row of settees.

"There, lad…take your pick. Which one of the congregation would you like?"

Donal left Colin in what he considered good hands as he flicked a finger at not one, but two women, a blonde and an ash-brown beauty, who sprang off the divan eagerly. Each grasping an arm, they accompanied him up the stairs to the rooms on the first story, where lascivious but still rather mild activities were carried out.

For some reason, he didn't feel adventurous tonight.

****

Donal sighed and came abruptly awake. A heavy weight lay across his chest, another across his thighs. He opened his eyes and saw a wealth of tousled ash-brown hair about six inches from his chin.

"Felicity…"

The hair stirred, tickling his chin as its owner turned her head. He stared into brown eyes.

"Did you say something, luv?"

Why the hell did I say that?

He had no idea why Felicity Melton had come into his mind at the exact moment of his regaining consciousness, nor why he'd spoken her name aloud. Was it because the warm softness he felt made him want her lying against him? Surely he didn't wish she had been the one performing those decadent acts to his body.

"I said, *Felicitations*, my dear," he lied smoothly. "Your acute knowledge of the physical arts has been a most talented recital of sensuality."

She laughed. "I like the way you talk, Donnie, even if sometimes I don't understand what you say." She slid a hand beneath her, nails grazing his chest.

At his legs, the other whore, the blonde, came awake, causing Donal to grunt slightly as an elbow dug into a vital spot.

"Careful there. I was about to suggest another go, but if you drive that elbow any deeper…"

"Sorry, luv." Hastily, she changed position, removing the sharp point from his groin. "So, you wants another round, does you?"

"If you ladies are up for it."

"It's your fiver," the blonde said.

Even if they weren't ready, as long as he was paying, they'd put on a show and make certain he was satisfied again, in some form or another.

The girl on his chest shifted slightly. Donal stroked his fingers down her back, resting the palm of his hand on her broad but heavily dimpled buttocks. Before he could do more, the door opened.

He glanced in that direction, angry that someone would dare interrupt without even a knock. The Abbess always ensured that once a guest was in a room he had complete privacy unless he requested otherwise, as those in the open parlor obviously had. Donal preferred solo performances, if with multiple partners.

The person he saw gave him a shock.

Colin stood framed in the doorway. He was naked, body glowing in the combined light of the lamps and gleam of sweat, making his skin appear as if dusted with copper. Topped by a snug gray French glove, his cock thrust itself lance-like out of its wiry nest. He was alone.

"What the hell are you doing here?" Donal saw no need for politeness. It was a foolish question and he knew it the moment it was uttered.

"An' hello t' you, too." Colin ducked his head in greeting and stalked into the room. "I thought you might like a li'l company."

"I've all the company I want right here, thank you." Donal gripped a round buttock tightly, then gave it a resounding slap while he moved his legs, managing somehow to get one from under the blonde and wrapped over her so she was clasped between them.

"I was hopin' you might share." Colin came over to the bed.

The brown-eyed girl pushed herself onto her elbows, looking up at him. He tucked a finger under her chin, forcing her head up even further, then leaned down and kissed her.

"What say, braithur?" He straightened, one brow raised.

"I .don't know." Donal had a moment of panic as Colin said that, then realized the Abbess had already surmised they were brothers so that offered no new danger. Wondering what Colin intended, however, Donal was understandably doubtful. "One question."

"Which is?"

"From your earlier look when I mentioned the fourth floor, I'm guessing you aren't up for any perversion, are you?" He didn't try to keep either the disapproval or anxiety out of his voice. In that moment, he wondered if Colin had fallen into some deviation due to his big brother's early guidance.

The boy's frown told him he didn't understand.

"What I'm asking is…" Donal took a deep breath. "You want to share only the females? You don't want *us* to…"

"Good God, Don!" Colin actually went white. "*You* don't, do you?"

His question was also anxious and perhaps a bit frightened.

"That's all I wanted to know." Ignoring that use of his name, Donal relaxed, but thought of something else. "It's getting late."

"Is there sommers you need t' be?" Colin relaxed also.

"No, but…what time is it, anyway?" He glanced around.

No clocks in sight. When in meditation and worship, time was to be ignored.

"Don't know." Colin flicked a hand. "Left me watch in me aithur suit."

The Grandfather in the downstairs foyer obligingly chimed two o'clock.

"If we start anything now…you realize we're both going to feel like hell in the morning?" Donal cautioned, even as he slid over, making room.

"Do you have somethin' t' do tomorrow?" Colin wanted to know. He settled on the other side of the bed, pounding pillows.

"As a matter of fact, I do." He'd promised to see Felicity at Almack's Wednesday night.

I won't feel like doing that if I don't leave soon.

"In that case, I suggest we get started." Colin lifted the girl off Donal and settled her onto his own body.

She drew in her breath sharply as he slid inside her.

"There now, darlin', gives you a bit o' a thrill, does it?"

"Hell…why not?" Donal laughed. He maneuvered the blonde into the other girl's place as he spoke.

In two more minutes, they'd both forgotten about the urgency of time or anything else.

Chapter 16

"You're actually takin' me t' Almack's?" Colin was astounded if the way his voice wavered was any indication. He sounded as if Donal had offered him an impossible dream.

"Yes, and I'll warn you right now...I'm considered a gentleman there and you'd best act accordingly, or else." Donal warned.

"Or else what?" Colin shot back, challengingly.

"You don't want to know." Donal had no idea what he'd do if Colin decided to misbehave, and he hoped the mere threat of retribution would be enough.

"I think I know when t' be discreet." Colin's reply held affronted feelings. His lips pursed briefly in a pout, then relaxed as the expectation of the evening returned.

"Like you were last night...calling me 'brother' and using my name?" Donal didn't wait for an answer, but simply nodded and turned back to his mirror. "Best get to readying yourself, then. We're through here, aren't we?" he asked Rollo as the valet put a final fold into his cravat.

Rollo nodded and Donal waved him aside.

"Rollo will assist you." Donal ushered both brother and valet out the door, then shut it and dropped into his chair with a sigh.

Getting Colin ready would take a bit. That gave him time to compose himself and think of what he was going to say when he saw Felicity again.

Instead, memory of his brother's behavior the night before returned. Lord, he'd never realized the youngster had such *stamina*. Briefly, Donal felt old as he watched Colin. There were also a couple of maneuvers he'd performed that Donal had never seen before. He was astonished but also worried, for he felt if Colin continued with such behavior, their father might have an aspiring libertine on his hands….one who'd take Padraig's place.

I hope Colin's lack of funds prevent him from further explorations in that direction. Donal forced his thoughts onto more sublime subjects.

****

"Shut your mouth before something flies into it. God, Colin, don't gawp so. You'll have everyone staring at us." Donal was out of patience with his younger brother before they set foot inside the establishment.

"Sorry. Can't help it." Colin glanced around, blinking as if the glare of all the candles hurt his eyes. "I'm really here," he breathed. "Oh, Donal, 'tis much more wonderful than you said."

"Get your wonderment out of the way so we can move on," Donal instructed, torn for a moment between amusement at Colin's awe and likewise irritation. "I swear your eyes are as round as pocket watches."

Colin didn't answer. Instead, he glanced around a third time with those big green eyes, took a deep breath, and whispered, "You say you've a voucher?"

"Given to me by one of the Lady Patronesses herself." Donal couldn't keep a bit of pride out of his voice.

"At what cost?" Colin sent him a sideways glance holding more than a smirk of cynicism.

"It was a gift, and that's all." Donal's answer was curt. Not giving Colin time to say more, he strode forward. "Come on."

"Not so fast," came the command from behind him. "I want to see th' Assembly Rooms, an' th' supper rooms, an'…"

"All in due time." Donal didn't slow his pace, nodding to this person and that as they passed, and seeing the glances given the young man trying to keep pace with him and take it all in at the same time. "First, I need to see if…"

"Don?" Joss's familiar tones stopped him. "Who's this with you?"

He turned to see his friend studying Colin, who'd paused a few feet behind, staring through an open door at the people milling about inside.

"Is that Colin? Lord, the lad's grown. Almost as tall as you now, but what's he doing here?" Joss gave him a pitying stare. "Your father hasn't sent him to you for safekeeping until school starts again?"

"Worse than that," Donal answered. He drew Joss closer so no one would hear. "He came for consolation."

"No one's died?" Joss looked alarmed.

"Hardly." Donal drew in a deep sigh, releasing it slowly. "Padraig's gone and gotten himself disinherited." He explained about the letter he'd received from Quinton and of Colin arriving at near the same time.

"God." Joss was momentarily shaken, then rallied. "Guess it was expected sooner or later, but…as you say, he's a remittance man now, so the old man didn't just toss him out on his ear to become a full-time cony-catcher or worse."

"Father would never do that. I imagine it cost him a great deal of pain to do what he did," Donal agreed.

"Joss? Hullo." Colin caught up, joining his brother and recognizing Donal's old school friend. "How are you?"

"Surprised to see how much you've grown. How are your studies going at Eton?"

"You know I'm no longer at Eton," Colin answered. After all, Joss and Donal were in the same class, so he thought Joss should remember he was three years behind. "I'm on my way to Cambridge in a few weeks."

As usual, now that they were in Polite Society, his accent died away and he sounded more like his brother.

"Following in big brother's footsteps, eh?" Joss glanced at Donal, brows raised. "I'm impressed. Are you going into the ballroom?"

Donal nodded.

"I think there's someone Donal's looking for," Colin supplied helpfully.

Donal shot him a warning stare but Joss saw it.

"Wouldn't be a certain mouse, would it?" He looked amused.

"It would, and I'd like to speak to you about using that epithet from now on," Donal answered.

"Do I detect a slightly proprietary tone in that sentence?" Joss looked surprised. He fell in beside Donal as they entered the ballroom, so Donal was hemmed in by Joss on one side, Colin on the other. "From that, may I infer…"

"You may infer as much as you like," Donal snapped. "It's simply that I find Miss Melton a delightful companion and don't believe that word describes her."

"In that case, consider it stricken from my

vocabulary." Joss bowed slightly. He straightened, looking around. "In case you haven't seen her, she and her family are over there." He nodded.

Donal turned in that direction, spying Felicity seated by her mother. Tonight she was wearing a gown in a mauve so pale it was almost white, the only color about it little amethyst brilliants and velvet bows at the flounces of the skirt and the draping on her sleeves. Her mother was still in mourning but the shade of her dress was lighter than the one she'd worn before, so that was a bit of an improvement. Roger Melton stood behind the divan, speaking to someone.

The girl was looking around as if searching the crowd. She saw Donal and her little face lit up. Smiling, she half-rose. Donal shook his head, brushing a finger across his lips, and she sank back onto the divan. He nodded.

"Excuse me, Joss. Could I impose on you to tend the baby a bit? Perhaps introduce him around?"

"I say, I resent…" Colin took umbrage at Donal's remark. It fell on deaf ears as Donal hurried away.

"Be glad to." Seizing Colin's arm, Joss dragged him in the opposite direction. "Just look around," he whispered. "If you see a young lady you'd like to know, tell me, and I'll effect an introduction so you may ask her to dance. But…" He held up an admonishing finger. "Dancing is all. Understand?"

"God, Joss," Colin jerked his arm away. "We're not in the Church. I know how to act in public."

"What do you know about Church?" Joss looked startled.

"Enough to know not to take off my mask while there." Giving his brother's friend a knowing smirk,

Colin looked around. He spied a young woman sitting nearby. "That's a pretty lass. Do you know her?"

"I know almost every family here," Joss replied.

****

"Mr. McCoy, how pleasant to see you again." Mrs. Melton smiled as she saw Donal approaching.

"Mrs. Melton." He nodded and addressed Felicity's uncle, who turned at the sound of his voice. "Mr. Melton, good evening. Did your cargo arrive in good shape?"

"Fine condition," Melton replied. "Thanks for asking. One hundred bolts of China silk plus other assorted fine fabrics."

"Uncle Roger let me choose a bolt," Felicity spoke up.

Donal tensed slightly, *If she begins extolling the virtues of silk or compares it to some kaleidoscope of color…no, please…*

"He seems to think I've a need for more ball gowns." That was all she said.

Donal relaxed. "You don't?"

She shrugged. "Who'd notice me? Amid such a glamorous crowd as this?"

Behind them, the music started and couples began filling the dance floor.

Donal held out his hand. "This dance is mine, I believe? The first of three?" He glanced at Mrs. Melton. "With your permission?"

She nodded and Felicity placed her hand in his and was pulled to her feet. He escorted her onto the floor and practically swung her into his arms. She laughed as she spun around and was clasped tightly.

"If I had my way, you'd need a dozen new gowns," he said as they started the first set.

"Oh?" She was still smiling. "Why?"

"Because I'd take you to every ball this city held." He knew that sounded reckless, but in that moment, it was the way he felt. His arms tightened, drawing her perhaps a little closer than was proper.

"I'd love to go to all of them, providing I was with you, Mr. McCoy." She didn't protest his embrace, the fingers clasping his seeming to cling. She looked away. "I suppose you think that forward of me."

"Miss Melton, I don't think you have it in you to be forward." Immediately he realized that might be the wrong thing to say. Hastily, he corrected, "I mean, you're too much a lady to ever say or do the wrong thing."

"Thank you." She blushed.

They continued dancing, not speaking for several minutes. After the first set had been completed, Felicity said, "You seem tired, Mr. McCoy."

"I didn't sleep well last night," he admitted. *Not at all, as a matter of fact.*

"You're not ill?" She looked alarmed.

She's concerned? That gave him a contented feeling.

"Just all-overish, I suppose. I kept thinking of dancing with you tonight, and that prevented me from sleeping."

"Oh dear. Perhaps you should go home and to bed."

"Is that an…" He was so accustomed to innuendo he nearly asked if that was an invitation before he caught himself, changing it to, "Are you trying to rid yourself of my company?"

"Oh no." She was earnest. "It's just…you look so weary."

"I assure you, Miss Melton, I'd be wearier if I didn't see you, but if it will reassure you, as soon as I've been given my allotted three waltzes, I'll hurry home and get a good night's sleep."

She thought about that. "Are we still going on our picnic tomorrow?"

That she called it *our picnic* registered with delight. She was already thinking in terms of being solely with him. That sent a tingle of warmth through Donal.

"I was about to dare ask you the same thing," he replied. "Will your mother or your abigail be accompanying us?"

"Mamma, of course." She frowned as if not particularly liking that. "She said Amy isn't old enough to be a chaperone."

"Well, Mamma does know best," Donal said.

They both laughed.

"We'll have another member of our little outing also," he continued. As she gave him an inquisitive glance, he explained, "My younger brother, Colin. I said I'd bring him, if you remember. He's up for a few days before going to Cambridge and I have to watch out for him."

At that moment, he saw Colin guiding some young woman over the dance floor and frowned slightly. Joss was nowhere in sight.

"I'm sure he'll be a welcome addition."

In spite of her comment, he thought she didn't look too happy about that, either, and that cheered him considerably.

As the dance ended, Donal escorted her back to her mother. He hovered nearby, chatting with Mr. Melton, occasionally nodding and speaking to others, allowing someone else to dance with Felicity between claiming his other turns. As he led her back after their third and final waltz, he saw Joss and Colin speaking to her uncle.

"Hullo, brother." Colin spoke before Donal had time to say anything. "Is this Miss Melton?"

His green eyes were sparkling. Donal silently prayed that sparkle didn't herald mischief.

"Please, introduce me. Joss has already done the honors here," he added, nodding to Mr. Melton and Felicity's mother.

Reluctantly, Donal complied. "Felicity, this is my younger brother, Colin, of whom I've already spoken. Colin, this is Miss Felicity Melton."

"I hope he didn't traduce me too badly," Colin smiled, displaying charm Donal hadn't known he possessed.

It worked, if Felicity's expression was anything to go by. She appeared enchanted.

What the hell's he trying to do? Donal felt anger rising. *He's too young to be courting anyone, or fascinating them, either. He's leaving for school in a few days, even sooner if he continues looking at Felicity that way. He...*

"Mrs. Melton," Colin broke into his thoughts by turning to Felicity's mother. "Will you permit me to have the next dance with your daughter? If you agree, Miss Melton?"

He glanced back at Felicity. To Donal's chagrin, she nodded. To his further discomfort, her mother agreed.

"Brother...Joss..." With a bow to each, Colin walked Felicity to the dance floor, took her in his arms, and swung her into the dance.

"Your brother's a handsome young man," Mrs.

Melton said.

"Thank you." Donal wasn't certain what else to say.

"He's a charmer. He mentioned something about going to Cambridge?"

"He'll enter this fall." This time Donal bowed slightly. "Colin's eighteen," he added.

Why did I say that?

"The same age as Felicity."

Again, Donal stiffened.

Is she thinking of pairing Colin with Felicity? Is my own brother about to become my rival for the woman I lo…

His mind went blank as he realized what he'd almost thought.

Can it be?

"I'm certain when he attains as much maturity as you, he'll be an outstanding young gentleman."

At that moment, Colin stumbled, nearly treading on one of Felicity's little toes. She winced but laughed. He apologized profusely, reddening all the way to his tightly wrapped collar.

"…but it appears he has several years to go before attaining that state," she added. "Thank goodness you've already reached it."

Donal relaxed.

Colin spoke, earnestly. Felicity smiled and nodded.

What is he saying? Why is she agreeing?

Filled with anxiety, Donal watched, hands clenched at his sides. Joss put a hand on his shoulder. When Donal looked at him, he shook his head slightly.

"Three dances, old boy?" he whispered, mock disapproval in his voice. "What are you thinking? By tomorrow they'll be posting the banns. The Meltons are friends, and I like Felicity, but heed my warning...best slow it down a bit."

"I don't think I can."

There. Let him interpret that any way he wishes.

Donal was still trying to untangle that confused word he'd nearly allowed himself to think.

****

In the carriage on the way home, Colin was a chatterbox, talking of the dances, being at Almack's in general, and of Felicity in particular...*Felicity, Felicity, Felicity*...the conversation centered around her and stayed there....how well she danced, how charming she was, what a good conversationalist...

"You noticed it, too?" Donal tried to sound nonchalant. "What did you speak of, pray?"

"Oh, various subjects."

"All in the space of one dance? It must have been quite interesting for you to remember it so. Care to elucidate?"

Colin started to answer, then grasped what his brother wasn't saying. "I say, you're not jealous, are you, Don?"

"Jealous? I?" Donal allowed himself a scoffing laugh.

Yes, damn it, I'm seething with that emotion.

"Of course not," he denied and felt it was blatantly obvious he lied. "Why should I be?"

"Because Miss Melton is quite taken with *you*. If you want t' know th' truth, that's all she wanted t' speak of. *You*. I must say I got quite tired o' thinking up good things t' say..."

"But you *did* say them," Donal blurted anxiously. "You didn't disparage me?"

"According t' me, you may sprout wings an' a halo by tomorrow mornin'," Colin assured him.

"I hope you didn't overdo it."

"Make up your mind. She was also gracious in sayin' she looked forward t' th' drive and picnic we're goin' on tomorrow." Colin showed surprise. "I didn't know I was invited. Almack's tonight, picnic tomorrow. Well!"

"Can't very well leave you alone, can I? You're my guest."

"Thanks for not sayin' I'm merely your braithur. That might make it sound as if you're me nursemaid." Colin laughed and assured him, "Don't worry. I plan t' be on me best behavior tomorrow. I'll speak t' Mrs. Melton, monopolize her so you an' Felicity can be more or less alone. Besides, I'm goin' t' be all agog because we'll be ridin' through Hyde Park. Will we get a glimpse at Kensington Gardens, do you think? See th' Serpentine? Or Rotten Row? Why such a name for what I imagine is a lovely piece o' land, anyway?"

"It's a corruption of *Route du Roi*, and used to be the king's private road to Kensington Palace," Donal explained patiently, selecting one of his brother's questions to answer. "Since it's a carriage track, we'll be driving it, though I imagine there'll be more on horseback than not. As to seeing the Serpentine, I don't believe we'll be going that far."

Colin looked disappointed.

"Nor will we be going through Kensington Gardens. This is to be a leisurely drive and a quiet picnic, not a sightseeing tour."

"I suppose I shall have t' come back some other time for that, then."

"Tell you what." Donal immediately realized Colin hadn't expected him to show interest in some young woman but that his younger brother's entire visit would monopolize his time. He also saw that Colin had actually wanted to see some sights other than risqué ones. "On your first school holiday, come back and we'll go sightseeing, just the two of us. We'll play the tourists."

"Really?" Colin looked childishly delighted.

"Big brother's promise." Donal placed one hand on his heart and raised the other.

Chapter 17

"I must say you look extremely well today, Mr. McCoy." Felicity's pale eyes studied Donal as he assisted her into the carriage.

Was that a twinkle he saw?

"May I assume your slumbers have been undisturbed of late?"

"They've been completely serene, Miss Melton. Last night, I thought of our outing today and drifted directly off to sleep."

"Should I be affronted?"

Yes, her eyes were sparkling—with mischief. He was certain of it.

As he gave her an inquisitive look, she continued, "Only last night you said thinking of me kept you awake. Now the same subject puts you to sleep?"

He laughed quietly. "One carried anxiety, my dear Miss Melton. The other, anticipation."

"Ah…which night held which?"

Donal managed to hide his surprise. So his Felicity had a wit about her, and a slightly sharp one at that.

His Felicity? Wasn't he a little premature in being so proprietary? He was rescued from answering as Colin leaned forward and took Felicity's hand.

"Dear Miss Melton, how good to see you again. Please, sit here." He guided her to the seat opposite in the rear quarter of the carriage, the proper place since she shouldn't sit beside him. He turned back to Mrs. Melton, whom Donal was now helping up the folding step. "Mrs. Melton, good morning."

He aided Felicity's mother into the carriage, pulling her down beside him on the front quarter seat. Since he was clasping her hand tightly, she had no choice but to sit there instead of by her daughter as was proper.

Before she could protest, he said, "I wish to thank you, dear lady, for allowing me to come with you on this outing."

Donal climbed into the carriage and settled himself beside Felicity, making certain they didn't sit too close. With her voluminous skirts, that wasn't too difficult. He nodded to Charles, who folded the step, shut the carriage door, and climbed onto the driver's seat.

"How could I not?" Mrs. Melton answered, not by any quaver revealing she had nothing to say in Colin's being there, since she hadn't been told of his presence until she'd seen him sitting in the carriage. "You were so mannerly last night, I found your company appealing, though you were with us such a short time."

"Donal was good enough to invite me along this morning," Colin confided. He glanced at his brother, who was meeting a sidelong glance from Felicity. "My arrival was a surprise, I'm afraid. I came for an unannounced visit before I go on to Cambridge."

"Oh?"

There was a note of interest in Mrs. Melton's voice that made Donal scowl slightly. He noticed Felicity raised her head, looking in Colin's direction as he said that.

"What year will you be, Mr. McCoy?" Felicity asked.

Donal's scowl tightened. Surely she could've figured that out from what he'd told her mother. As much as he hated to think it, he was certain she and Mrs. Melton had discussed both of them after returning from Almack's, perhaps comparing him to Colin and vice versa. He hoped he hadn't been found lacking.

"I'll be a first-termer, Miss Melton." Colin turned to answer her question, then directed his next words at her mother. "I'll be reading math."

Donal thought he saw his brother's intention. He remembered what Colin had said to him as they got into the coach earlier.

Don't worry about th' maithur. I'll keep her distracted while you whisper sweet nothin's t' Miss Felicity. At least he knew he didn't have to worry about his brother being after the girl.

"Math?" murmured Mrs. Melton, looking impressed. "That seems such a weighty subject. All those numbers."

"I suppose." Colin's answer was nonchalant. "To some, but I've a head for numbers. I thought originally to read History. I've a great memory for dates, also. 1066…1215…1605…"

With aplomb, he rattled off the years of the Norman Invasion, the signing of the Magna Carta, and the Gunpowder Plot.

"Then I realized Donal had already tied up History, and, after all, the most notable philosophers and mathematicians of any time have come from Cambridge…Newton, Bacon…so I chose to follow in their footsteps…"

Here, Donal gave a slight snort, warning Colin not to pour it on too thick, then managed to convert the sound to a cough.

"I'll be leaving in a couple of days." Colin shot him a quiet glance and continued smoothly, "I daresay I probably won't be back for a while. Have to dig into the old textbooks and make good, you know."

"Cambridge isn't that far away," Donal put in. "Only fifty miles or so. You should be able to come for a visit on a long holiday weekend."

"Yes, Mr. McCoy," Mrs. Melton agreed. "I imagine you'll be able to see your brother often. He's your only family here in England, isn't he?"

"Uh...that's right." Colin's look told Donal he wasn't going to mention Padraig, who was, as far as either knew, still somewhere in London, but carefully not making appearances anywhere he might meet his elder brother or anyone Donal was acquainted with.

By that time, they had arrived at Hyde Park Corner. Charles guided the team through the Apsley Gate.

The entrance, with huge Ionic columns, held three carriage archways and two pedestrian accesses. The iron gates were bronzed and affixed to piers by gunmetal rings decorated in a Greek honeysuckle design. To each side of the central entrance was a frieze of a military victory.

Nearby stood Apsley House, giving its name to the gates.

"How lovely," Felicity exclaimed, with a hurried glimpse at the friezes as they rode through. "I would love someday to simply walk beside the gates and study those in more detail."

"Perhaps we might." Donal glanced at Mrs. Melton. "Would you care to look more closely at Apsley Gate?" As she nodded, he continued, "I understand the Grand

Entrance was designed by Decimus Burton and the frieze by Mr. Henning, Junior."

"Henning? I say," Colin spoke up. "Is he the chap who did the models of the Elgin marbles?"

"That was his father," Felicity answered. As Donal turned to her as if surprised, she murmured, "I try to keep up with art and such."

By now, they were on the carriageway and being passed by several riders on horseback.

Colin heaved a loud sigh. "What I wouldn't give to be riding with them on one of my hunters."

"You like to ride, Mr. McCoy?" Felicity asked.

"Most assuredly. I've several horses, though I had to leave them all at home. If I want to get around now, it's either hire a cab or coach, or…" He patted his thigh. "Go about on good old shank's mare." He laughed. "Donal here's the one with the animals."

"You keep a stable, Mr. McCoy?" Felicity looked at him.

"Only a small one."

Donal became aware he wasn't holding up his end of the conversation very well. Colin was doing most of the talking and was entrancing Mrs. Melton, at least, if not Felicity, also. He decided he'd best get himself into the game with some sort of chitchat on a hopefully not inane subject.

"I only have the carriage team and a single saddle horse in town. Back in Tipperary, my father has a large stable, and he kindly agreed to board my horses."

"Did you bring those you now have from Tipperary?" Mrs. Melton asked.

"Indeed, no. It would've been too much of an ordeal for the poor creatures, bringing them on board a ship. I bought this team," he nodded toward the animals pulling the carriage. "Plus my own mount, after I arrived here."

"Tipperary…" Mrs. Melton interrupted, in a musing tone. "I know dear Joss said you're from Ireland, but I must say, neither you nor your brother sound Irish."

"Received Pronunciation, ma'am," Donal replied. "An educated Irishman should speak like an Englishman."

At that, Colin cleared his throat slightly. He met his brother's eyes. *Only in public*, his gaze declared. Donal was thankful Colin didn't say that aloud.

"I hadn't realized…" Mrs. Melton murmured.

Donal hoped she never heard Colin as he spoke away from English ears. With a bit of astonishment, he wondered if he could actually affect an Irish accent after his determination to lose it.

They were approaching one of the smaller ponds. He called out, "This should do, Charles. Let's stop here."

There were stone benches under the trees for the ladies to sit upon. After Charles carefully spread the ground-covering tablecloth and laid out the contents of the hamper, Colin and Donal sat on its edges while Felicity and her mother occupied the benches.

When Charles had finished arranging the picnic fare, Donal said, "Make yourself a plate, Charles, and take it back to the carriage with you."

"Thank you, sir." Charles did so quickly, taking two of the dainty sandwiches Rollo had gotten up early that morning to prepare and two sugar biscuits, placing them on one of the delicate china sandwich plates. He poured a cup of liquid from a small carafe, then retired to where the horses stood, held stationary by carriage weights resting on the ground and attached to their bits by hooks on leather leads.

"That was thoughtful," Felicity noted. "I've often felt the driver on a picnic must get terribly hungry, watching others eating while he sits with the team."

"I try to be good to my employees." Donal attempted to look modest.

He was surprised Colin didn't comment on that.

"May we serve?" Donal selected sandwiches and little delicacies, offering the little plate to Felicity while Colin did the same for Mrs. Melton.

The sandwiches were truly tiny, little more than a man might eat in one bite, and he felt a bit foolish, nibbling on them so he wouldn't appear to be wolfing them down. He wondered if he looked as silly as his brother did, taking such small bites.

Rollo had also supplied a carafe of lemonade, which was now open, thanks to Charles.

"Goodness, you must give your cook my compliments," Felicity commented, after finishing one miniscule treat. "This watercress sandwich is the best I've ever tasted."

"I'm afraid I don't have a cook," Donal replied, swallowing.

What I wouldn't give for a trencher of beef right now.

Rollo had convinced him not to eat a large breakfast, to "*leave room for the delights I'm preparing,*" and he feared the hollow left by its absence was going to produce screaming hunger sounds. He'd already gobbled, in a most refined way, three sandwiches in an attempt to forestall the outcry.

"I only have a manservant and Charles, who doubles as footman and driver."

"Then your valet prepared this lovely repast?" Mrs. Melton asked.

Donal nodded.

"Why, the man's a gem," she exclaimed. "You must make certain you don't lose him, Mr. McCoy."

"I daresay someday I'll be forced to hire a cook, as well as a couple of maidservants," Donal replied.

"Why?" Felicity asked.

"When I marry, I can't expect my wife to cook three meals a day, or dust and sweep, or do housework…" He allowed his voice to trail away as he left the rest of that image, of how considerate he'd be, settling into their minds. "…after all, a gentlewoman will be too delicate to handle such heavy chores."

He thought Felicity looked thoughtful at that. Wondering if he considered her delicate, perhaps?

"Why don't we go for a walk?" Colin set down his plate and practically leaped to his feet. "I feel the need for a bit of exercise after that fine repast." He bowed, offering Mrs. Melton his arm. "My lady?"

That made her smile as she accepted and stood, placing her hand on his sleeve. Colin led her to the pond's shore. Donal and Felicity followed. Colin kept up an incessant chatter. It floated back to them in a steady stream, with an occasional answer or laugh from Mrs. Melton.

Neither Donal nor Felicity spoke much. They didn't need to, Donal realized. They were too comfortable in each other's company.

Yes, I feel comfortable with her. That surprised him. It also made him a bit uneasy. *Why? Is it because I can envision myself in the future with Felicity by my side…sitting in the parlor before the fire, my hair white, a shawl over my shoulders, as I adjust my spectacles to read the newspaper while Felicity sits nearby, sewing a garment for a grandchild? White hair? Grandchild? Oh God...*

That startled him so, he stopped abruptly.

"What is it?" Felicity frowned, looking up at him.

"It's getting on toward afternoon. I think we should start back." He spoke decisively.

Colin must've heard. He also stopped, turned, and guided Felicity's mother back to them. She looked disappointed, Donal noted.

When they arrived back at the carriage, Charles had gathered the picnic gear and repacked it, lashing it to the mudguard on the back of the carriage. They assisted the ladies into the carriage, and Charles turned the horses toward the entrance.

Donal was quiet on the way back and Felicity noted that, if the way she continued glancing at him was any indication. She didn't question him, however. As if to compensate, Colin kept up a running commentary until the carriage pulled up in front of the Melton home.

"It's been a lovely afternoon, Mrs. Melton. Thank you," he said as Donal got out to help her alight.

"Thank you, Mr. McCoy. The feeling is mutual. I must say, for one so young, you're very attentive to an old lady."

As Colin protested that she mustn't consider herself *old,* she continued to the door, while Donal walked Felicity behind her at a slower pace.

"Thank you for a wonderful outing, Mr. McCoy." At the door, Mrs. Melton stopped. "Perhaps you could come for tea again sometime soon...or luncheon...perhaps supper." Without waiting for an answer, she went into the house.

Standing on the stoop, Felicity held out her hand. "Thank you for a wonderful day, Mr. McCoy." She looked away, then whispered. "I hope to see you again soon."

"I daresay you shall," Donal answered. Gently, he clasped her hand in his. "Since it appears I've been invited to the meal of my choice."

"I wish it were to be a breakfast." She looked up at him and the sun seemed to focus solely on her, lighting her eyes to a pale blue, tinting her hair under its little pillbox bonnet with gold highlights. It also added a deeper rose to the blush touching her cheeks.

For a moment he was dazzled, actually couldn't speak, not only by the boldness of those words but by the visions they conjured.

"Miss Melton…Felicity…"

Something seemed to block his air. He felt as if he were choking. He took a deep breath.

"Donal…" she whispered.

He lifted her hand, seized it in both his own and pressed his lips against her fingers, so strongly their imprint was left on the leather of her glove. Her eyes widened. He was certain his did also, by the audacity of that act, as well as speaking her name.

Donal released her hand and stepped back, performing a short, curt bow. "I'll see you again. Soon."

He whirled and nearly ran to the carriage, repeating his previous retreat with a word to Charles. Felicity stayed on the stoop, watching the carriage ride away, returning Colin's wave though Donal didn't look back.

"What's th' matter?" Colin asked. "You've gone pale."

"What?" The look he gave his brother was preoccupied. "Hungry," he lied. "Those little sandwiches weren't enough to feed a lapdog. I hope Rollo's got a true dinner waiting."

When they reached the mews house, however, Donal ushered Colin inside, telling him, "I'm going out again."

He headed back to the door as he spoke, ignoring Colin's protests.

"Have Rollo prepare you some supper, then read a book or go to bed. I'll be back later."

Back in the carriage, he directed Charles to Nell's, where he was greeted by Flossie and made his way up the stairs to his mistress's boudoir.

She was on the fainting couch, as usual. Donal had a fleeting wonder if she ever left it.

"Donnie!" Her greeting was joyous.

She'd been reading. He saw the title *Northanger Abbey* and was surprised Nell might read such a novel. In fact, he was surprised she could read at all. The book fell to the floor as she held out her arms.

"No small talk tonight." He unwrapped his cravat as he spoke. "I want action, not words. Get into bed."

He slung his coat onto a chair.

He definitely wanted something to drive that image of Felicity Melton, wrapped in a dressing gown startlingly resembling Nell's transparent teal delicacy, from his mind.

Chapter 18

Three day later, Colin left for Cambridge.

With assurance he'd be welcome for his first holiday, and at Christmastime, when they'd meet and go home together, Donal saw him off on a post coach. Before the vehicle was out of sight, he realized he missed his brother.

Padraig hadn't been spotted and he'd heard no gossip of his being in town. He hoped that meant his errant brother had decided London was too quiet and chose instead to plague the Continent. Perhaps he'd even gone farther east into Egypt or possibly China.

God help those poor heathens, if that were the case.

Perhaps that wasn't such a good idea. Padraig might start some kind of war the British would have to finish.

Now, however, Donal had things other than his second brother to think about.

More than ever, Felicity was on his mind. His little slip of the tongue, saying her Christian name aloud, actually kissing her hand in full view of any passerby...both were severe deviations from the accepted procedure of courtship at this stage of their acquaintance. That vision he'd had of her in delicious dishabille, and harking back even further, the night he'd called her name when awakening beside that whore at the Church...

All those things told him he was more serious about

the girl than he'd believed. Indeed, thinking of both of them in that domestic little mental scene, he was certain he was envisioning a life with her.

Damn it, I love her. That was it, plain and simple. How had it happened? He considered himself a rake, a rogue, and here he was thinking of hearth and home instead of gambling dens and dolly-mops.

In a flash, Donal understood, as, in one of those wild mental quirks the brain will have, he remembered a lecture from one of his literature classes at Cambridge. They had been studying the so-called Restoration Comedies, and the instructor pointed out that one of the main characters in those dramatizations was the Rake.

"Pay heed and be forewarned, young gentlemen…" the instructor said, looking out over the heads bowed over their notebooks, as the young men in their student gowns scribbled rapidly.

"…if you're planning to become one of the well-educated but lascivious men we call a Rakehell. There are two types of those rogues prominent in our literature as well as our society."

He went on to explain. While both were characterized by drinking, whoring, and gaming, they differed from that point on. The Falsewit or the Hypocritical Rake was one who abandoned his chosen way of life in order to secure financial gain, such as marrying for money, while the Truewit or Honest Rake met his match in, and succumbed to, the charms of the heroine and actually settled happily into matrimony.

My God, I'm a Truewit.

Donal had never considered himself an honest rake, he'd thought surely he was the hypocritical kind, but now it was as plain as could be that indeed he was the latter.

He'd unconsciously followed that dramatic description all the way. It was he who had become the prey, falling under the spell of clear blue eyes and gilded ashen hair.

He hadn't planned it, didn't intend for it to happen, but it had, and there was only one thing he could do about it.

Well, in the long run, wouldn't that make his father happy? *While I*—Donal admitted it only to himself—*I'll be ecstatic.*

Nevertheless, he forced himself to proceed cautiously. He still attended Almack's on Wednesday nights, where he made certain he saw Felicity with her uncle and mother. As soon as she came into sight however, he threw caution to the winds and monopolized her for nearly every dance, not caring at her protests that, "Really, Mr. McCoy, you should give someone else a chance."

He was invited for tea, returned for luncheon, came back for a small dinner party, and thought he'd nearly stifle with joy when Roger Melton announced he was planning a house party in the near future and wished Donal to be one of the guests.

To be in the same house with Felicity, overnight, to see her at breakfast... Donal didn't know if he could resist the temptation. He decided there would be only one way to find out, and if he failed...either a duel or a wedding would appear in his near future.

During this turmoil, he sought Nell's company every night. She was overjoyed, of course, ignorant of the fact he was attempting to prevent his growing lust for Felicity from becoming full-blooming passion, to control it by assuaging it with a feast of Nellie's overblown charms.

At last, the night came when Donal rose from Nellie's bed, dressed himself, and walked out with the realization he could delay no longer. The last three visits had been disasters as far as he was concerned, though Nell was replete and near exhausted from his misdirected passion. He'd carried through but was unsatisfied, unfulfilled, and wishing the woman in his arms was small, slender, and ashen-haired and not a plump, full-bosomed false blonde.

That was the night Donal decided he was going to make Felicity Melton his wife.

****

The next day, he had been invited for tea. He dressed with that same care he had on his first foray to the Melton home. Since his visits were by now commonplace, Rollo didn't note his half-abstracted air, though Donal thought it so blatant he expected the valet to comment. He was sincerely grateful Colin was no longer around. Joss had also been absent for several days. Donal decided he couldn't have borne it if either were present to point out his anxiety.

On the way, he bought another bouquet of violets from the flower girl. By now, she was so accustomed to be called over to his carriage, she automatically started toward it as soon as it appeared. He always paid her more than she asked. Today, he did the same, sending the child dancing back to the curb.

He wasn't going to wait for that house party. He was going to act now.

At the Melton home, upon relinquishing his hat and gloves to the butler, he said, "I wonder if I might have a word with Mr. Melton, if he's available."

"The master's in his study, Mr. Donal. He asked me

to say he'd like to speak with you before you see Miss Felicity today," the man replied.

"Oh?" That sent the wrong kind of jangle down Donal's spine. He nodded, and held out the nosegay. "In that case, would you see that Miss Melton gets these?"

"Certainly, sir." The butler took the flowers and gestured down the hall. "This way, please."

****

Melton greeted Donal amiably enough, saying, "Mr. McCoy, come in. Shut the doors, Sheldon, if you would."

The butler, who'd gone into the study ahead of Donal, speaking to his master before announcing him, nodded and pulled the doors closed. They seemed to clang with the weight of a gaol cell's gate slamming shut.

This isn't good, if he's going to say something he wants no one else to hear.

"Sheldon tells me you wished to see me," Melton said, walking to the fireplace and standing with his back to it. The weather being that of a summer's day, the fire was unlit.

Donal felt his stance might have been merely habit, though he looked a little confrontational.

"That I did, sir." He spoke lightly and hoped the unease he felt wasn't evident. "By some remarkable coincidence, you also requested speaking to me." He affected a slight laugh. "Perhaps our minds are running along similar lines."

"That depends on what those lines are." Melton's expression took on a serious cast.

"Sir?" Donal sounded, and truly felt, confused.

Oh God, has he somehow found out about Nell, or the Church, or...

"I shan't patter around the subject," Melton said.

"You've been much in my niece's company this past month, Mr. McCoy, both in my home and in public. In fact, you've been so close at Almack's no one's able to ask her to dance or even speak to her. Soon, I fear, it may lead to gossip if some declaration isn't made, so I believe it's time to ask you…"

"Indeed, we do think along the same lines," Donal's exclamation didn't let Melton finish. "It came to me rather abruptly I was paying Miss Melton too much attention and my conscience attacked me for it. I have no wish to cause any untoward opinions to form about our association, so therefore, I've decided I should…"

"I see." Melton didn't allow him to finish. "I'll truthfully say I'm disappointed, but I do thank you for showing the proper concern. Felicity likes you but she's young and will recover…"

"I don't think you understand." Donal felt his heartbeat speed up. He put a hand to his chest. *Slow down, damn it*. "In the absence of her father…I wish your permission to ask Felicity to become my wife."

The silence following that declaration was almost deafening.

"I…well…this is…" Melton mumbled about a moment, then caught Donal's hand between his own, shaking it rapidly.

"Does this mean, you…"

"Yes, yes…you have my blessing and more." Melton released his hand, gesturing. "She's in the parlor…go…"

He must've run from the study though he didn't remember opening the doors, closing them, or reaching the open parlor door.

As her uncle had said, Felicity was waiting, holding

the violets. She looked up as he entered.

"Mr. McCoy? Sheldon said you were speaking with my uncle. I hope nothing's wrong? Uncle Roger's seemed distracted today."

"Nothing's wrong, Felicity. In fact, everything's as right as it can be."

He wanted to seize her, dance her around the parlor, leap into the air and click his heels in joy. He told himself not to act the fool but get control of his emotions. With an inner struggle, he managed.

"That's the second time you've called me by my name," She caught that slip immediately. "You must be more discreet. Though I do like its sound on your lips."

"I'll say it as much as I want," he declared recklessly. "Felicity, Felicity…Felicity…" He laughed. "There's something else I want on my lips… Yours."

"Mr. McCoy!"

"Call me Donal…after all, a husband and wife should call each other by their Christian names, shouldn't they?"

"Husband?"

"Felicity, I've spoken with your uncle and he's of an obliging frame of mind, so now I'm asking you…will you consent to be my wife?" He felt shocked as he spoke words he'd never expected to say to any woman.

"Your…" She didn't finish, simply sat there, staring at him with those wide pale eyes.

"I love you, Felicity. You do love *me*, don't you?" He didn't think she looked as a young woman being proposed to should.

Doubt rushed in, thundering over him.

"I knew Uncle Roger was going to ask you your intentions, since you've made no mention of them." She spoke so quietly he had to lean forward to hear. "I was certain you'd say you merely enjoyed my company but if he were to push things, you'd bow out. I…"

She shook her head, and dropped the nosegay into her lap, hands going to her face.

"Here now." He pulled her hands away, dropping beside her onto the settee. "There's nothing to cry about. Either you want me or you don't, and if it's the latter, I'll take it like a man."

"Want you? Of course I do."

"Then shall I do it properly…on the knee, hands to my heart, and all that?" He realized he sounded as sarcastic as Colin and didn't care. For once, he was going to let himself be as carefree as his younger brother.

"Don't you dare."

"Well, then?" As she frowned, he prompted, "What's your answer?"

"Yes, Mr. McCoy…Donal…I'll marry you."

"In that case, Felicity…" Donal released her hands, "May I kiss you? To celebrate the honor you've done me?"

She raised her face. Donal pressed his lips to hers, feeling soft but hesitant pressure. There was an abrupt surrender as that warm mouth yielded to his insistent one. It was an innocent kiss and he didn't push it further.

She'll learn, he told himself. He sensed within Felicity a fire that might match his own passion if properly ignited. *I'll teach her.*

He released her and sat back, not allowing himself to prolong that kiss, else he'd want to do more, and that would spoil the perfectly beautiful moment. Donal smiled and kissed Felicity's fingers.

"Shall we tell your mother?"

Chapter 19

Mr. Quinton Aloysius Francis Xavier McCoy
McCoy Manor
Tipperary, Ireland
The United Kingdom of Great Britain
My Dear Father,
This is my notice to you that I have at last fulfilled the requirements of the letter you sent me concerning my seeking a bride for the purpose of continuing the McCoy lineage.

You will be pleased to know I am now betrothed. Her name is Miss Felicity Melton. She is of good parentage and her family well-to-do. Though her father is now deceased, she has been raised by her uncle and her mother. Her uncle is owner of Melton & Melton, Importers, in which he was in business with his late brother. I imagine you've heard of them.

In order to proceed with furthering the McCoy name as soon as possible, I have requested of Felicity's uncle that our engagement be as short as can be arranged without arousing gossip. Believing me to be so enamored of his niece I am impatient, he has agreed to a three-month betrothal.

There will be many celebrations and parties in the coming months and I regret your being in Ireland will prevent the formal meeting of our families beforehand as wedding etiquette requires. I do hope you and Mother can be present for at least some of the festivities before the wedding. Otherwise, it may appear you disapprove of the match.

I do hope you are pleased with my choice, Father, but let me say here and now, whether you are or not, I will be wed to Felicity and she will become your daughter-in-law, for she is the woman I choose.

Your obedient son,
Donal Callum Seamus McCoy
#3 Elm Tree Mews, Sedley House
London, England
The United Kingdom of Great Britain

The days and nights seemed to fuse together, a jumble of dinner parties and dances, toasts and well-wishes. Donal was soon tired of all of it, but he understood the necessity, as well as the rules concerning such events, so didn't complain.

On Sundays, he obediently attended church services with the Melton family, where the banns were read, and no one objected.

No surprise there.

Joss was present to moan and groan over the loss of his partner in seeking clandestine passions, though Donal assured him nothing would change in that respect, even as he was dressing to go to yet another betrothal celebration given in his and Felicity's honor.

Donal had tried to explain about hypocritical and honest rogues to Joss and how his being an honest one meant nothing since that gentleman often merely went through the *motions* of fidelity, which was what he planned to do. Joss simply shook his head.

"That so-called *honest rake* is a dramatic fiction, Don, made up by someone with a flair for words. What happens to him is manipulated to bring about the ending the author wants. This is real life and there's no guarantee there'll be a Happily Ever After or whatever outcome you're expecting. Did you think of that? I certainly hope so."

He promptly buried his nose in a wine goblet as if he could drink away the problem, then loudly decided he'd better begin looking for someone else to accompany him to the Church and other places. Aloud, he wondered if Colin might be available.

"No, absolutely not. I may have taken Colin to the Church, but no one else is going to. You're my friend, Joss, but I will look at you over the barrel of a dueling pistol if you so much as point my brother in that direction. Understand?"

"Perfectly." Joss' reply sounded surprised that Donal was so adamant, since he'd been vehement in not having much to do with Colin when they were at Eton. "Now that you're about to take the thorny path of matrimony, you're becoming protective of everyone you deem even slightly innocent…and that, unfortunately, includes little Colin, though I wonder how innocent he may be if he's already set foot inside those unhallowed surroundings?"

He poured himself another goblet of wine, drinking half of it before continuing.

"It frightens me to admit I can see your point. I think. I suppose if I had a brother Colin's age, I might be the same way. Perhaps. Anyway, you have my word, as your friend, Colin will get no help from me in becoming a rake. If it happens, it'll be his own fault."

Donal thanked him, requesting they drop the subject. He was relieved to discover everything proceeding calmly. He'd written his father, and Quinton had replied that he and Donal's mother would come for the later parties and stay for the wedding. To show their approval, they would also give a dinner party at Donal's home, where they would be staying.

Donal wasn't happy about that last statement. He'd planned to have the wedding breakfast in his own home, spend his first night with Felicity there, and leave for their wedding trip in the morning. He certainly didn't want to enjoy his first intimacy with his wife with his parents only a door away. He decided then and there they'd leave for their trip directly after the reception and breakfast.

Life seemed to be steady at the moment. He spent his mornings and middays in the usual routine, then arrived at the Meltons' to go with Felicity, her mother, and uncle to whatever *fête* was happening that night.

Not that he disliked the parties, but the continuous toasts of well-wishers, as well as the innuendos of his friends, even Joss, who was still a bit resentful and disbelieving that Donal could continue his old, secret life, soon began to wear thin. He rarely saw Felicity after they arrived at a gathering. She was immediately whisked away to be inundated in a whirl of crinolines and hoopskirts by young ladies gathering around her and chattering incessantly, with many glances in his direction followed by giggles and whispers.

Donal wondered what they were saying, imagined he knew, and thought, *Oh my dear little innocents, if only you were really aware of what your friend is going to learn from me.*

The idea and the images forming in his mind gave him a lascivious pleasure, though he continued telling himself they were of the purest form a future bridegroom could have for his intended. Then his mind, the traitor, would ask, *If that's so, why do those thoughts make the ol' Neb stiffen so readily you have to march about a bit to calm him down? Hmm?*

Unable to give himself a satisfying answer, Donal inevitably found himself at Nell's, shaking off the weariness those celebrations brought on as well as pacifying the urges continuing to surface. Nell was such a soothing shelter in the storm of his emotions, he abandoned the Church altogether, seeking refuge in her passionate arms. Getting more and more panicky as the fateful date approached, he found losing his inhibitions made him momentarily forget the rapidly arriving marital deadline.

He hadn't said anything to Nell of his engagement, not seeing the necessity since, as with Joss, he expected nothing in their relationship to be affected. Also as with Joss, he was soon enough disabused regarding his mistake in that fact.

Chapter 20

"You bastard!"

A cushion sailed past Donal's head, striking the wall next to the door as he walked through. It was satin, its reverse side alternating dark and pale stripes, one from the fainting couch. Rebounding off the wall, it fell to the floor.

"I resent that." He bent to pick up the cushion, feeling another buffet his back as he straightened.

It followed its fellow to the carpet.

"You'll do more than resent it when I get through wiv you," Nell threatened, searching on the couch for another cushion and preparing to throw it also.

"Here now, what is this?" Donal scooped up the second cushion, replaced both on the couch, and plucked the third from Nellie's hands. "What, pray, have I done to deserve such disapprobation, as well as becoming a target for these less-than-lethal missiles?"

"Damn it, Donnie." Nell glared at him, eyes swimming in tears. "You know I don't understand half you say when you use them big words."

"Nellie…" Setting the third cushion beside the others, Donal dropped onto the couch and caught Nell's hand to prevent her from seizing anything else to throw. The other, he saw, was tightly clutching a newspaper. "What have I done to anger you?"

"You know very well," she declared.

"If I did, I wouldn't be asking, would I?" He made his tone reasonable.

That stopped her briefly. She wavered, pulled her hand from his, then thrust the newspaper at him.

"Is that a copy of the *Illustrated News*?" Donal was startled that Nell would have a copy since he'd never seen her read a newspaper before. Then he remembered he'd never seen her read a novel, either, until a few weeks previously. Still…she would've had to pay sixpence for it and he didn't give her an allowance, so… "Where'd you get that?"

"That delivery o' fish you purchased came wrapped in it."

Donal remembered. Nell had stated she'd like some fish to vary her diet. He'd promised to have a fishmonger make a delivery, then promptly forgot. Only the day before had he remembered and made the purchase. She shook the newspaper again and he took a step back. By now the scent of flounder was quite redolent, wafting upward with each movement of the paper.

"Flossie brought it t' me."

"Flossie can read?" Well, he'd learned several things tonight, as well as understanding why the maid gave him such a glare when she opened the door…something in the paper had riled both her and Nell.

Rather gingerly, Donal took the paper, being careful not to touch the damp spots. It was folded to an article in the center of the third page. Though the print had run from contact with damp fish scales, it was still quite readable. He studied it silently.

Mrs. Stella Melton
Of 120 Willingham Place, London,

Announces the Betrothal
Of her Daughter
Felicity Honouria Augusta
to Mr. Donal Callum Seamus McCoy
of #3 Elm Tree Mews, Sedley House, London.
Miss Melton is the daughter of the late Mr. Stephen Melton, part owner of Melton & Melton, Importers. She is the ward of Roger Melton, current owner of Melton & Melton.

An autumn wedding is planned.

"Oh." Donal let the paper fall to the coach. "I see."

"I should hope you do. Why didn't you tell me?" Nell demanded.

"Truly, Nell." Donal fell back on the same explanation he'd given Joss. "I didn't think it necessary."

"Not necess'ry?" She looked around, as if seeking another weapon to heave at him.

Someone, Flossie, Donal hoped, had removed all vases and bric-a-brac from arm's reach. He wished she'd removed the cushions also.

"That's your engagement announcement." She flapped a hand at the fallen paper.

"Which you've known about since before it happened," he reminded her. "Why all this to-do?"

"To-do?" Her voice hit a treble note making his ears ring.

Donal was certain any dogs in the neighborhood were howling in misery at that shrill sound.

"You call it a to-do when th' man I love takes a wife?"

"Nell…" Donal marveled how he could maintain calm in the face of such high-pitched female fury.

Nellie was visibly trembling. He put his arms around

her, feeling the tremors transfer themselves to his own body. He wondered if that was how the early stages of an earthquake felt.

"Sweetheart, we've gone over this. My marriage is merely to appease my father. It won't affect us in any way."

"No?" Though she leaned against him and seemed to calm, she was still doubtful.

"Didn't I say so?" As far as Donal was concerned, that settled the matter. He cradled Nellie's head against his shoulder stroking the tousled blonde curls. "Earlier?"

"I know, Donnie, but..." Nell heaved a loud and tear-filled sigh, and Donal stiffened in expectation of another tirade. Fortunately, it didn't come. Instead, there was a torrent of tears. "I'm so afraid."

"Afraid?" He hadn't expected that. "Of what?"

"That she'll learn o' us an' make you leave me. She'll force you t' choose, an'..."

"Eleanor..." Donal's use of her real name was an indication of his seriousness. He pushed her away, taking out his handkerchief and blotting her eyes, making her blink. "She isn't going to find out, and if she does, she can't give me an ultimatum. After all, she's only going to be my wife...not my gaoler."

"But..."

"What if she knows? If she asks where I'm going, I'll simply say, *Out*. If she wants to know where, I'll say, *It's my business*, and if she demands to know anyway, I'll display my husbandly wrath and send her to bed without supper."

"Really?" Nell gave him the look of a child talked out of a nightmare by an adult.

"Have I ever lied to you?" Donal gave her a

reproachful stare.

"If 'twas a lie, how would I know?" She laughed slightly.

He laughed also and patted her hands. "That's my girl. Really, Nell, I don't understand why you're so upset."

She didn't answer, merely burrowed her head against his shirtfront.

"Anyway," he continued. "Felicity has taken to her bed with a bad case of the megrims and a summer cold. The result of too many parties, too much exposure to night air, and the struggle of writing all those individual wedding invitations, I presume."

Donal hadn't bothered with a guest list. He'd simply written his father when a date was settled upon and informed him, telling him to bring the entire family. He'd been surprised when Felicity chided him and sent a letter to his parents, one to Colin, and a separate one to Brigid. As far as he was concerned, it was expected his family would be there, and the only other person he wished present was Joss, whom he'd decided to burden with the onus of being his marital witness.

"She expects to be indisposed for at least a week, so until such time as I'm informed she's recovered, I'm all yours."

"For as long as I want?" The words were muffled against his chest.

"All day and night for seven days," he promised.

There was a long, drawn-out sigh.

"I'm sorry, Donnie." She leaned against him again, trailing a finger around and around the knot in his cravat, then slowly tracing down the delicate embroidery on the placket of his shirt. "It's just that…I've give you th' best years o' me life, an t' know some girl barely out o' pinafores may steal you away…"

"Nell." Donal's tone became patronizing with a touch of sarcasm. "You're barely thirty-three years old. Have years thirty, thirty-one, and thirty-two really been your best?" He tutted slightly, shaking his head. "I was truly expecting perhaps thirty-four onward would be slightly more spectacular."

"Oh, you!" She struck his chest playfully, immediately back in good humor again.

"All better?" he asked.

She nodded. Donal carefully dropped the newspaper to the floor, kicking it under the couch.

"In that case, why don't we go to bed, and let you prove my assessment correct?" He got up from the couch and began unwinding his cravat.

"Before we do that…"

"Yes?" He stopped in the act of pulling his shirt from his trousers, looking around inquiringly.

"There's somefing else."

"Oh?" Unconsciously, he stiffened, though he continued his movement with the shirt, letting the tail fall around his thighs as he worked the pearl studs out of his cuffs. "What? Exactly?"

"There." She pointed to the lamp table by the bed.

Walking over, Donal looked at the tabletop. He didn't see anything out of order. He shook his head.

"In th' drawer." Nell gestured.

He opened the drawer. There was nothing inside but the *préventif*, resting on its dowel. He took it out. "This?"

"'Tis wearin' thin. I checked it yesterday. Donnie, you need a new one."

Donal turned the dowel over in his hands. Sure

enough, there were several spots near the tip with lighter areas, the stretched membrane worn so the wood pattern of the dowel could be seen plainly.

"You're right." He remembered his statement months before to Joss, and how he'd forgotten. "I'll stop by the chemist's tomorrow and get a new one."

"You'll get one t'night." Nell's voice brooked no argument.

"I'll do it tomorrow." Neither did Donal's. He replaced the dowel in the drawer. "I'm not going back out tonight, Nelly. I'm already half-undressed."

"You can re-tuck your shirt."

"The chemist's closed, so it doesn't matter whether I redress or not. Come on now." He walked back around the bed to the couch, lifting her off it and into his arms. He began to nuzzle her neck, making Nell laugh even as she attempted to stay stern. "I'll get one tomorrow, I promise. This one's good for another night or two…Oh Nelly, I want you so, and I don't want to spill myself into a towel…" He planted a kiss on her ear. "You're a much better place."

"Damn it, Donal…" Putting her arms around his neck, she kissed him as he carried her to the bed.

Chapter 21

After Felicity recovered from her bit of exhaustion and megrim attack, several more parties strictly for females were held. During those times they were apart, Donal managed to convince himself he felt nothing for her but a mild fondness. He told himself he'd merely been caught up in the emotion of the moment, that slight euphoria following the accomplishment of something demanded but at the same not wanted. Though they'd exchanged little missives while apart, a fortnight in Nellie's arms made him think someone as gently bred as his betrothed could never perform for him the acts the talented Nell did, nor would she want to.

He returned to the Melton residence fairly reluctantly, and was surprised to discover Felicity had acquired a near-boldness during his absence. In the presence of her family, she allowed him to hold her hand. Neither her uncle nor Mrs. Melton objected, but they were now left alone quite a bit, and then he was not only permitted to kiss her fingers, and once, her bare palm, but also her cheeks.

He had a brief moment of wondering how far she'd let him go. Remembering the thought he had that Felicity might possess wells of untapped passion waiting to be plumbed, Donal wavered on whether to pursue that course or not. Discretion told him he'd best play it safe and act the prudent swain, for now.

So, he did.

Chapter 22

"Do you, Donal Callum Seamus McCoy, take Felicity Honouria Augusta Melton to be your wife, following the rite of holy Mother Church?"

"I…" He knew he looked like a fish stranded on a beach, mouth working, no sound coming out. *I can't say it. I can't!*

Joss leaned forward and rather ungently struck Donal's arm with his shoulder, breaking the spell.

"I…do."

****

There had been a final party the night before, with the entire wedding party present—his parents, Joss, Mr. and Mrs. Melton, the cousin who was to be Felicity's bridesmaid, Colin, and the Anglican priest, Mr. Atherton, who was to perform the ceremony.

Afterward, Joss whisked him away for "one last night of glorious debauchery before you become enslaved in the chains of matrimony." That speech had been delivered so heavy with sarcasm it made Donal wonder how his friend managed to speak the words.

Joss's attempts were an apparent success.

The last thing Donal remembered was being at the Church and settling onto a bed with three lovelies, his mask firmly in place. His next conscious thought was marred by a splitting headache, the morning sun glaring through his bedroom window, and Rollo's hand offering a cup of coffee while Joss peered over his shoulder, saying, "Up and at them, old chum. Today's the day."

Both valet and best friend looked much too cheerful, and Donal told them frankly and succinctly what they could do with the day. In spite of that, he was hauled from the bed and, while Joss poured black coffee down him, Rollo got him bathed and shaved and dressed in the evening suit from Wellsby's.

The next thing he knew, he was being hustled into his carriage while Rollo stood at the door, welcoming a group of strangers whom he explained were caterers. "You can't expect me to prepare a wedding breakfast, can you, sir?"

Donal had no chance to answer as the carriage sped away, carrying him and Joss to the church, where they waited for what seemed an eternity in the choir room before the priest sent an acolyte to conduct them to the altar. Wondering if the hollow feeling in his belly was the same a prisoner felt when being ushered into the dock, Donal followed the altar boy into the church. His headache was still raging as he saw his parents, his sister, and Colin, seated on one side of the church, Mrs. Melton and a female friend or two on the other. Behind them, on both sides, were a scattering of relatives and some school friends.

From somewhere, an organ struck a chord sounding like the scream of a lost soul in Hell. Felicity appeared in the church doorway, her arm wrapped through her uncle's.

Donal went pale, swallowed loudly, and was certain if Joss hadn't stepped up to bar his way back into the choir room, he'd have turned and bolted…

****

193

The priest nodded. "Then repeat after me…I do take you, Felicity, to be my spouse…"

Dutifully, Donal spoke the phrase without a stammer. Behind him, he felt Joss relax slightly, saw Mr. Melton, who'd also tensed, visibly ease his posture.

"…I pledge to you loyalty in all things…in the faithfulness of my body to yours, as God commands, forsaking all others for you, the loyalty of my goods to keep you in plenty…"

It took him a moment to get past that *faithfulness* bit without choking, but he managed.

"…I will honor you in illness, good health, or whatever condition the Good Lord visits upon you…"

Though he repeated the words, Donal's mind begged frantically, *Good God…please no. I don't want an invalid to wait upon,* and was immediately ashamed of that thought.

The priest turned to Felicity and Donal forced himself to concentrate.

She was beautiful, in a pale blue gown of satin and Chantilly lace, a pert little bonnet with blue feathers and velvet ribbons adorning the crown. Her left hand held a little white prayer book with a spray of stephanotis attached. Her right hand, in its blue glove, lay clasped in his left. Donal grasped it tightly, lest she detect the tremors going through it.

She repeated her part of the vows calmly, neither stumbling nor stuttering, and definitely didn't blush when it came to the part about being *obedient and compliant according to the duties of a wife to her husband.* The direct stare she gave Donal as she said it, made him frown.

Is she sending me a message of some kind? He

didn't know whether to fear its meaning or rejoice.

The priest said something else. Joss stepped forward, holding out his hand. Donal stared at it dumbly, then realized he was offering the wedding ring, the ring he'd gone to a jeweler's and chosen, the ring he hoped matched the other he'd given her as a sign of their betrothal and his love.

Silently, he took it, placing it on the priest's palm, barely listening as it was blessed, and then…he slid it onto Felicity's finger.

"I place this ring upon your finger, and declare to all here present you are my wife." As he said that, he thanked God men weren't required to wear wedding rings.

I'd be forever taking the thing off and probably lose it somewhere between home and the Church or Nell's.

"Let us pray."

He held Felicity's hand as she knelt, then went to his knees also, still not hearing the words as the priest entreated God to look kindly on and bless their union. As he got to his feet, assisting his wife—*Dear Lord, she's now my wife*—to rise also, the priest spoke softly.

"You may kiss your bride, Mr. McCoy."

Eyes closed, Felicity pursed her lips for a kiss. Donal froze.

Frowning, she opened her eyes.

He leaned forward, his own mouth barely grazing hers, the kiss the barest adolescent peck of lips, nothing erotic about it in the least. He thought Felicity looked disappointed and wondered what she'd expected. Mouths and tongues and bodies grinding together? His mind veered away from that like a runaway horse.

In that moment, Donal felt he'd never kiss anyone

again. His entire mind held only one thought, jarring around in his head like the clanging of a brass bell.

Oh God, it's done.

****

The breakfast was probably delicious, since it had been catered by one of the best restaurants in London, a generous meal of ham and eggs, crusty loaves and whipped butter and jams, white soup, a small wedding cake frosted with buttered crème, and negus, a wine flavored with nutmeg and lemon.

Mr. Melton had spared no expense for his niece's wedding breakfast. He'd originally planned to have the reception at his home, with Donal and Felicity spending the night there, but Donal had immediately nixed that idea. To have his wedding night in Felicity's uncle's home was almost as bad as spending it within a few feet of where his parents slept.

Now, thinking of that, and what was to come, he used his fork to stir the morsels on his plate but didn't taste them.

"Is there something wrong with the food?" Felicity whispered.

"What?" He looked up.

"You aren't eating," she continued. "Are you all right?"

"Of course." He forced himself to smile and caught her hand, squeezing it. "I'm married to the most beautiful girl in London. Why shouldn't I be all right?"

"That's good." Her voice sank even lower. "Because I don't want anything to keep us from our wedding night. Donal? You're as white as milk."

"It's nothing."

He ran a hand over his face. God, he felt cold, then

196

abruptly hot, and welcomed the thought of incipient sickness.

Can I possibly plead illness and postpone this ordeal another day?

That could only work for perhaps one day or, at the most, two, and no doubt would be something enabling Joss to rain ridicule upon him at a future date, and conceivably cause both his father and Mr. Melton wondering if he had some problem or other.

Donal took a deep breath and forced himself to rally.

"I'm…the truth is, Felicity, I'm afraid I've been thinking of our wedding night, also, and…" He hesitated, wondering why he'd said that and what he could follow it with.

"Yes?" she encouraged, forehead puckering in a little frown Donal found abruptly delightful in spite of the way his stomach was coiling.

"…and I hope you'll be gentle with me," he ended, making his lips quirk slightly.

"Oh, you darling." It also made her laugh. "I promise." Her voice went so incredibly soft it shocked him. She cupped his cheek, fingers warm through her glove.

He lifted her other hand, kissing her fingers.

"Here now, none of that. Not at the table." Joss had to turn at that moment, of course.

"Felicity, are you packed?" Donal ignored his best friend who shrugged and turned back to the young lady who'd been Felicity's attendant at the wedding. Suddenly, all he wanted was to get away from here.

Run away, yes…leave everything and everyone he knew, but…and here was the startling part, he wanted to take Felicity with him. *Why would I wish that?*

"Of course. My bags were taken to the church and loaded onto the coach this morning. Then it was driven here. Didn't you notice it when you left earlier?"

"I suppose Rollo has loaded my luggage also." He'd seen nothing that morning, didn't remembered much of it at all. "Does that mean…"

"Before you ask," Felicity seemed to anticipate his question. "When we arrived, Rollo whispered to me that he and Amy would be following us in the carriage. They're probably sitting in it even now."

"In that case, let's go. *Now*."

"Donal, we can't."

"I think we can."

"I need to change." She indicated her gown. "I can't get on a ship wearing this."

"Yes, you can." Getting to his feet, he dropped his napkin onto the table, and seized a spoon, tapping it against the goblet holding the negus.

At the first tinkle, everyone looked his way.

"Thank you all for coming to celebrate our marriage. Now, however…" He turned to give his new wife an abruptly burning stare that surprised him as much as it did her. "It's time for us to make it a marriage in fact and start on our wedding journey…to Paris, and then…through life. My dear?"

Dropping the spoon, Donal pulled Felicity to her feet. He looked down the table at Quinton.

"Father, I know you're planning to stay on a few days here, so enjoy your visit. My home is at your disposal during that time. You and Mother have a safe journey back to Tipperary. Mr. Melton…Mrs. Melton…" He bowed and nodded to his new mother-in-law and uncle. "Colin, don't forget…that holiday trip's still on." Colin nodded eagerly. "Joss…" He had no idea what to say to his best friend. "I suppose…"

"Exactly," Joss murmured and took a too-casual swallow of negus.

With that, and a final nod, Donal swept Felicity from the room, nearly running for the front door. His top hat and gloves were available. Releasing his wife's hand long enough to snatch them up and put them on, he pulled open the door and was relieved to see the coach directly in front of the walkway to the street. Behind it was the carriage in which Rollo was sitting with a very excited-looking Amy.

Donal nearly dragged Felicity down the walk, pausing only long enough for Charles, acting in his capacity as footman this time, to pull down the steps and open the door. He handed her inside. Felicity had barely settled herself and her many skirts before he was beside her and the door slammed shut. He heard Charles scramble onto his place at the back top of the coach. The driver, loaned by Roger Melton, cracked the whip and the coach rolled forward.

In the semi-darkness inside the coach, they stared at each other in a silence threatening to become awkward and embarrassing.

"Donal," Felicity breathed his name. "At last." Leaning toward him, she caught his face in her hands, kissing him on the lips.

He actually recoiled.

"What is it?" She was startled, not expecting her bridegroom to act in such a way, not after those stolen little kisses to her fingers and cheeks, and every indication he was restraining himself from doing more.

Donal asked himself the same thing. *What the hell's*

the matter with me? I'm alone in a coach with a woman who appears quite ready for a roll... Here he momentarily chastised himself for using that term in relation to his wife....*and I want nothing to do with her. That's not true. I want to do quite a lot. No, I don't. I...*

In truth, he was in a turmoil, excited but reluctant, teetering on full arousal and at the same time refusing to act, and just plain...confused.

"Felicity...please...not here...in the coach..." God, he sounded like the most dried-up prude imaginable. "I..." He pushed her away, gently, not wanting to insult her more than he believed he already had. "Be patient... We have to wait..."

Damn it, that wasn't what he wanted to say at all. He leaned against the seat, then drew in a deep breath, thought, *to hell with niceties,* and blurted his desire and inner chaos in one wild sentence.

"I wish you weren't wearing all those petticoats."

"What?" She looked startled. "Why?"

"Because if you weren't, I swear I'd act on my impulses and celebrate our wedding night here and now, instead of waiting for Paris." There, he'd said it, committed himself and reinforced in no uncertain terms those wedding vows.

"Why wait for Paris?" She gave him a look startling in its clarity. "Won't we have a cabin on the boat?" Her gaze met his in the boldest look he'd ever seen, speaking her desire for him without a single word.

"It's not a passenger ship," he explained, quelling the lurch in his heart. "It's mainly for ferrying passengers from one shore to the other."

At his explanation, Felicity looked as frustrated as he felt.

My God, she's disappointed. Donal marveled that a few words by a priest and a ring on her finger could work such a startling transformation. "We can't do what you're so very unsubtly hinting at, my dear wife."

It almost hurt to see the way her face glowed as he used those three words. He felt his own cheek warm and wondered if he reflected that radiance. His next words were heartfelt and gentle.

"That's not what I want for us, not for our first time together, Felicity." He leaned in to press a kiss against her cheek, then brushed his lips across her earlobe. She shivered and he told himself he read anticipation in that tremor. He whispered, "Be patient, and afterward…we'll have world enough, and time…to do whatever we wish, I promise."

Chapter 23

It was evening when they reached the wharfs, and late into the night upon docking at the French shore. There were several others making the crossing and many stared at the sight of a young woman in what was obviously a wedding gown, as well as the young man with her in similar finery. Felicity might be shivering slightly in the cold spray splashed from the ship's prow but she bravely stood at the rail with Donal and looked happy in spite of the damage done to her clothing and her flimsy slippers by the salty water and damp air. Nevertheless, she did appear relieved when land came into view.

Engaging one of the coaches loitering around the wharves in hopes of picking up passengers, Donal assisted Felicity and Amy inside, then supervised Rollo and the coachman in unloading their trunks from the ferry and placing them on the cargo area of the coach top, with the servants' bags stowed in the rear boot.

Donal had suggested to Felicity she not pack so heavily since he'd overheard Mrs. Melton telling her she simply had to buy a few Parisian frocks while in the city. He'd also packed accordingly, thinking to purchase a couple of suits of his own. That meant there were only two large trunks with a smaller case each for the abigail and his valet.

They went straightaway from the ferry to a nearby

inn Felicity's uncle had recommended, a place where he stayed when traveling to France on business.

Le Repos du Voyageur was a good-sized brick building of three stories, with a white round-tiled roof and white wood embellishments.

It had begun as a coaching inn, where travelers might disembark and rest the night before boarding the ferry. The establishment had prospered since being built in the seventeenth century and was still owned by the same family. There were stables where the horses could be cared for and smaller quarters at the back for servants. The inn had always done a thriving business, especially during *La Terreur* of the Revolution when so many nobles and their families fled across the Channel to be received as *émigrés,* although still treated somewhat with contempt by the English.

The place was fairly well known and extremely respectable. Melton's endorsement silenced a good portion of Quinton's objections when he learned Donal was making France part of his wedding excursion. Like a good many of his generation, the elder McCoy still harbored prejudices surviving the Napoleonic Wars, and seemed to expect both Donal and his bride would be murdered in their beds by vengeance-seeking Frenchmen.

Melton had offered to pay for all the arrangements of the wedding trip. At first, Donal protested that, not wanting there to be any action on his part making either Felicity's mother or her uncle think him merely interested in whatever fortune his new wife might inherit. He'd brought up mention of her dowry with great hesitation, assuring Roger Melton it was only curiosity in how transfer of the portion would be made.

Once Roger assured him paying for the trip would be considered part of his wedding gift to the newlyweds, Donal accepted graciously.

Though Felicity was practically ecstatic at the notion of traveling to Paris, Donal wasn't all that enthralled since he'd seen it as part of his Grand Tour upon leaving Cambridge some three years previously. He supposed seeing it all again with someone viewing it anew might make a difference. As far as he was concerned, the country hadn't changed much. Except for contrasts in architecture and the fact that everyone spoke French, the town and the people appeared much as an English one and its inhabitants might.

Felicity's uncle told Donal to mention his name and that fact garnered them a hearty welcome. Duchaine, the *aubergiste*, spouted a wealth of terms about Roger Melton, most of which Donal, as prolific as he'd thought himself to be in French, couldn't translate. He supposed it was flattering, at least he hoped it was, and, when the man bowed, and ushered them inside with a "*S'il vous plaît, entrer, neveu de mon bon patron, M'sieur Melton,*" he was certain of it.

With Amy and Rollo sequestered in a small servants' room toward the back of the inn, they were ushered into the dining room where they were given supper…an *apéritif* of fresh-baked *baguette* served with a slightly pungent but very creamy brie that M. Duchaine assured them had been aged for seven weeks. The cheese had a soft *pâte* of a suitably grayish tinge, covered with a perfect rind of white mold. Donal enjoyed it but was very surprised when Felicity declared she did also.

"Uncle Roger was always bringing back wedges from his trips," she explained.

The *entrée* was *poulet a l'orange* and butter-roasted vegetables, served with a *sauvignon blanc*. Waxing expansive after his second serving, Donal invited M. Duchaine to share a glass with them, in thanks for being such a good host.

When they were alone again, Donal said, "You haven't eaten much." He'd noted how Felicity was copying his earlier behavior at breakfast, pushing food around her plate and stabbing at it with her fork. "You should, you know. You're going to need your strength."

At the sharp look she gave him, he added, "For all that shopping you're going to do. Paris frocks, remember? As well as the sightseeing?"

"In that case, you should also," she retorted. "You've as much lack of appetite as I."

He realized that was true. Though he had eaten hardly any breakfast and there had been no luncheon for either of them, he barely felt hungry.

Donal sighed. "Why don't we admit it? We're both anxious about tonight. Aren't we?"

Felicity didn't answer. She got very interested in crumbling the remaining rind of the brie into even smaller bits. It clung to her fingertips. She brushed her hands together.

"I daresay I should be more anxious than you," she said quietly, not looking at him. "After all, you're not going into this marriage unarmed."

"What does that mean?" he asked, rather sharply.

"It means…" She raised her head, eyes meeting his, not defiantly, but almost pathetically. "You're a man, and…"

"…and therefore I've no right to anxiety of any kind?" He laughed.

"…and you've already gained more knowledge of…certain aspects of life than I." She paused, then added, in a surprisingly sardonic tone, "No doubt many times over."

Briefly, Donal felt as if he were being challenged somehow. *Does she wish me to deny it?*

"Does that prevent me from feeling even a jot of nervousness?" This time, his laugh was a trifle too high and definitely ironic. "I promise you, Felicity, whatever I may have done before I met you—and I'm not going to elaborate on that—I've never had a wife before, so I hope I may be as apprehensive because of that as I please."

He raised his glass, practically gulping the wine.

"I love you, Donal."

"If you really do, you'll eat a bit more." He tapped the rim of her plate with his forefinger. He knew she wanted him to return her statement, but he couldn't. Not yet.

"Then you must, also," she replied. If she was disappointed in his refusal to reciprocate, she didn't show it.

"Agreed." He picked up his fork and stabbed it into the sliced chicken on his plate.

They ate in silence a few moments more before Felicity again set down her fork. Donal finished eating his portion, then pulled the napkin from his collar, blotting his lips.

Immediately, M. Duchaine was there. "Sir? You have finished your meal?"

"A fine meal, it was, too," Donal replied. "Would you tell my wife's maid Mrs. McCoy is ready to retire?" He had to admit a thrill shot through him as he said those two words for the very first time. *Mrs. McCoy...*

With a nod, the innkeeper disappeared down a short hallway. There was the sound of a door opening, words being spoken, and a young female voice replying. In a few moments, he reappeared with Amy and Rollo following.

"Yes, ma'am?" Amy bobbed a curtsey as she approached the table.

Out of habit, Donal got to his feet at the approach of a female, even one in service. He quickly sat down again.

Amy was a plump little lass of about sixteen, pink-cheeked and looking as if she'd have been more at home milking cows and feeding chickens than being a lady's maid. Her gown was a suitable blue broadcloth, high-cut in the neck, with a white collar. It was simple and serviceable and definitely not detracting from her employer when they were together, as was the way her blonde hair was twisted into a psyche knot at the back of her head.

"Help your mistress prepare for the night." Donal felt his words were curt when he didn't intend them to be. Perhaps it was the way Rollo, standing behind Amy, was looking at him, with one brow cocked in a slightly sardonic attitude, or so he thought. "Then you may go to your own room."

"Yes, sir." Amy bobbed again and stood back for Felicity to leave the table and precede her out the dining room door. They met Madame Duchaine in the hall. She led them up the stairs.

"Will you be needing me to prepare you, sir?" Rollo's tone was deferential.

Donal found himself straining his ears to detect sarcasm.

He was relieved when the valet added, "Not that you need it."

"Thank you, Rollo."

"For what?" The valet appeared confused.

"For not disappointing me in making some mocking comment. Since Joss isn't here, I suppose you think you have to take up his position."

"I assure you, sir, I meant…"

"No, don't do that. You and I both know you're only saying what I'm certain my best friend would be voicing if he were here, so I can't fault you. However, now that you've done your duty, I'll hear no more about it." Donal looked directly into the valet's eyes, raising one hand in emphasis. "Heed me in this, Rollo. From this moment forward, I will brook no innuendo or mockery in regard to my relationship with my wife. Understood?"

"Certainly." The valet's expression held surprise, quickly veiled. He nodded. "I assure you I'll treat the mistress with the utmost respect, though…" He paused, then added, "Though it seems she may need my pity more, being married to you."

"You had to say that. You can't help it, can you?" Donal sighed. "Damn it, Rollo. You can no longer speak to me that way. Today's events have brought that part of this employer-employee relationship to an end. From now on, be discreet…and prudent."

"Yes, sir." It was evidence of Rollo's training that he didn't flinch as Donal said that but simply became a little more staid in his reply, just as Donal didn't raise his voice as he gave his manservant that ultimatum.

"Good. Now then…I've something to ask you."

"Which is, sir?"

"The abigail. I notice you kept up a running

commentary while we were on the ferry. Not moving in for the kill, I hope? I mean, you may be my servant and she may be my wife's, but the relationship between the two of you isn't the same as ours."

"I'll tell you the truth, Mr. Donal." Rollo relaxed as if this wasn't what he'd been expecting Donal to say. "When I heard Mrs. McCoy's abigail was coming along, I'd hoped she might be a sprightly bit. Well, the girl's pert enough, and good company. This is her first time away from home, so to speak, and I was hoping I'd be called upon to soothe a spate of homesickness, but… To tell the truth, she's a bit on the young side for me. I'm no cradle-robber, so I'm thinking the big brother attitude would be more proper than anything else."

"Good. That takes considerable off my mind."

"Leaving you to think of more pleasant things, I hope."

Though Donal gave him a bit of a glare, he could detect nothing in Rollo's expression saying that sentiment was anything other than as it sounded.

"Mr. Donal?"

Amy was back.

"Yes, Amy?"

"I've finished helpin' Miss Felicity…I mean, Mrs. McCoy, an' that Madame Duchaine says she'll show Rollo an' me where we's to sleep now."

"Thank you, Amy. You go with Madame Duchaine. Get some rest. We'll see you in the morning."

"Thank 'ee, sir." There was another of those bobbing curtseys and Amy turned to where Mme. Duchaine waited in the doorway.

"Good night, sir." Rollo followed Amy from the room.

As they walked behind the innkeeper's wife, Donal heard the valet say, "I know you're probably going to be nervous, sleeping in a strange place, especially a foreign one, but remember…I'll be next door and the master and mistress are one floor above. The innkeeper's a trusty sort, and you're completely safe."

Donal waited until the sound of Rollo's voice and Amy's answering murmurs died away. Then, he tossed down the last of his wine and left the dining room, going up the stairs.

At the door to the room they'd been given, he paused, knocking gently.

"Who is it?" Felicity's question sounded puzzled. Undoubtedly, she didn't think it was he.

"It's Donal. May I come in?"

What will I do if she denies me entry?

"Of course." As if it would be otherwise. "Come in."

Donal opened the door and went inside.

Felicity was sitting in a chair by the fireplace though no fire was lit at this time of year. She was clad in a white muslin nightgown, all-covering but somehow its fine fabric still translucent enough to reveal a curve of slender limb, hip, and bosom. In spite of that, she looked so innocent and fragile, her appearance made Donal tremble. Her hair had been brushed free of its ringlets and lay on her shoulders like an ashen cloud, Amy's handiwork, no doubt.

The room was dim. Only a bedside lamp, a coal-oil affair, was lit, casting shadows from under the bed's canopy onto the hearth and their figures.

"Why did you knock?" she asked.

"Habit, I suppose," he managed, seeking some unspoken chastisement in her tone. It was as good as any other excuse he might give. He found he didn't want to speak above a whisper, the lamp's flickering flame giving the room and everything in it an odd, intimate air.

"Why did you take so long to come up?" She stood, the gown wrapping her in its semi-transparent folds.

"You look tired." He ignored her question. "Get into bed." He stepped aside and gently pushed her toward it.

She went hesitantly, looking back at him, a question in her gaze.

"I'll be there shortly."

He waited until she pulled back the covers and climbed into bed, settling with the sheets and summer quilt draped around her. Someone had placed his overnight valise on the chest at the foot of the bed, next to Felicity's. Hers sat locked, the tip of some lacy feminine *accoutrement* caught as the lid was snapped shut. He flipped his case open, taking out the nightshirt he'd purchased at Wellsby's.

Briefly, he was acutely aware of Felicity watching him from the shadow of the bed's hangings. Looking around, he saw a dressing screen in the corner by the hearth and hurried behind it.

He thought he heard a faint sigh follow him.

He took time in undressing, removing his cravat and refolding it meticulously, inserting the gold stickpin through the black silk. His coat, vest, and shirt were taken off with as much extreme care, smoothed, and placed on a chair, the cravat atop them.

"Donal?" There was impatience and confusion in her call.

"I'll be there in a moment, sweetheart." He pulled off his boots, setting them by the chair, slid off his trousers and small clothes, and dropped the nightshirt over his head. It fell as heavy as a downpour of cotton rain, an uncomfortable sensation, and seemed to wrap around his legs and encumber his gait as he emerged from behind the screen. Feeling as though he were swathed in some kind of cloth sack, he hoped it wouldn't trip him and send him nosing against the floor.

He stopped, waiting for some comment on his appearance, perhaps a cringe at sight of his bare legs, long and hairy under the nightshirt's tail, an affront to maidenly modesty.

There was no sound.

Donal took a step forward, peering into the shadows.

Felicity was curled on her side, eyes closed, one hand cradling her cheek. Her soft, even breathing told Donal she'd fallen asleep, no doubt exhausted from all the day's excitement and travel as well as in waiting for him. Gently raising the quilt, he gingerly slid into the bed. Making certain their bodies didn't touch, he'd just settled himself when Felicity spoke.

"Why are you avoiding me?"

The question was so sudden and sharp Donal barely controlled a start.

She turned her head, eyes dark in the shadows. "Why are you acting this way? I thought you loved me…with all those kisses and those little…liberties…and what you said in the coach…" She rolled over, facing him. "What happened, Donal?"

She raised a hand as if to touch his cheek, then stopped.

"I'm not avoiding you, sweetheart." He caught the hand, pressing a kiss into its palm. "I…the truth is…" He thought frantically. "I was attempting to be mindful of your sensibilities…"

"My sensibilities?" She frowned as if unaware of the word's meaning.

"You've been so sheltered, Felicity, and now things are so different. Being married, accepting another person into your life, especially in such a complete way. I thought to perhaps allow you to become accustomed to my presence…in your company…my body in your bed…before attempting any intimacy."

"Oh. I see."

He'd swear he felt her eyes search his face, the brush of her gaze skimming over his skin. It seemed to burn. She pulled her hands from his.

"That's kind of you, and as thoughtful as I've always found you to be. Would you hold me, at least?"

"Gladly." He put his arms around her, cuddling her close. Surprisingly, she didn't resist but snuggled against him. Like a child, he told himself, a child seeking an adult's comfort.

"You're so warm," she whispered. "I know it's summer, but you feel so good."

She moved slightly, as if trying to get even closer. He thought she fit against him as if she were fashioned to be there.

Eve was Adam's missing rib, and Felicity is mine. He mentally laughed at such a fanciful thought, and realized every whimsical one he'd had always involved a thought of Felicity. The fabric of her nightgown seemed to disappear as her body touched his, the fine cotton of his own shirt dissolving under the heat of their bodies.

Donal suppressed a shiver and tightened his embrace.

"This is a lovely nightshirt."

Fingers traced the bordering plaquette around the buttons at the neck and midway down his chest. The front was smocked and decorated with white silk embroidery. He'd thought that a poncy, insultingly feminine adornment, but Wellsby had assured him even the most masculine of men wore some fanciment on his nightclothes, especially those destined for a wedding night. Nevertheless, Donal had purchased the nightshirt with severe misgivings. Felicity's comment made him glad he had.

"I bought it especially for tonight," he murmured, wondering what she'd say to that.

She didn't answer. He realized she'd gone back to sleep. He lay there, enjoying her warmth cradled in his arms, the rise and fall of her breasts against his chest. Soon, lulled by the soft sound of her breathing, he also slid into sleep.

When he awoke a short time later, it was because Felicity moved. Missing her warmth, he touched her shoulder, intending to draw her back. She woke also and again rolled over so they lay face-to-face, so close together they both shared his pillow.

"Come back here." He drew her closer, wanting her lying close to him again.

She surprised him by drawing back, then putting her arms around his neck.

"What is it?" He thought he sensed a slight stiffening of her body to his touch.

"I've a confession," she whispered.

"What could you have to confess?" He smiled.

"I'm not as sheltered as you think," she replied. "Nor am I as ignorant of what tonight should've brought as you expect."

"What does that mean?" Either it was too late at night or it was too early in the morning because he couldn't make sense of that statement.

"It means, I know more than you believe, my husband."

"Felicity, don't say things like that." He was damned certain no one had done more than kiss Felicity's hand, if that much. He was sure he'd been the only man granted that liberty and that pleasure.

"Don't misunderstand." She didn't raise her voice, still speaking in a whisper, and the sound was so intimate and secret, it sent chills across his skin. "You wouldn't think it to look at her, but my mother loved my father passionately. When I reached the age to know, she explained to me what she called the *delights of the marriage bed*, of the things my husband would do to physically satisfy me and what I could do to pleasure him."

"God." Donal was shaken, completely unable to envision plump Mrs. Melton actually speaking such things to her daughter, much less performing those acts herself.

So that's why she's prolonging her mourning. She truly must've loved Felicity's father.

"I want to do those things with you, Donal." Felicity inched closer, so close he could feel the warmth of her breath on his cheek. "Don't be concerned with my sensibilities. I assure you I'm prepared to toss them aside. I love you, my husband, and I wish to show you how much, as I want you to show me."

With that, she pulled his head down, kissing him full on the lips. Not expecting that, Donal's mouth opened in surprise. Felicity deepened the kiss, tongue flicking

215

against his and before he recovered from that, she pulled away, her hands sliding down his chest.

"Take off this lovely shirt, Donal."

While he slept, the tail of the shirt had become hiked up. Her fingers walked up his bare knee, circled around his thigh, caught at the hem and pulled it upward. Without a protest, he helped her slide it over his head, tossing it over the side of the bed to the floor.

Donal lay back against the pillows. Felicity kissed his chest, fingers trailing down his body, mouth following, placing nibbling little butterfly kisses against his bare skin. At his groin, those fingers hesitated, then slid between his thighs, cupping gently. He couldn't believe it as her hand continued on, stroking down his shaft. When she pushed back the enfolding flesh and kissed the bared tip of his member, he gave a stifled groan.

Good God.

His Felicity, his little Felicity whom he thought so shy and untouched, had just committed an act he thought only Nell and other whores performed. How could he think she would do that, or that she'd been taught such by her mother? Donal gave himself up to a haze of overwhelming sensual delight. Through it came the astonishing thought, *I'm being seduced...by my wife.*

Then he surrendered to whatever else she might do to him, feeling weak and powerless in this newly born temptress's lure. When she rolled onto her back and pulled him atop her, he went willingly.

"I want you, husband." Her whisper was so fierce and insistent, Donal had no wish to deny her whatever she demanded. "I want you upon me and in me. *Now.*"

Felicity's nightgown was swept away, finding itself

on the floor atop his own. He kissed her, was on her and in her, his desire matching hers. In a burst of unbelievably searing passion, Donald made Felicity his wife.

Later, spent and exhausted, he lay awake in the dark, holding his sleeping wife in his arms. In that moment, being so close to Felicity, alone with her, knowing no one had any right to keep them apart or prevent him from acting on the emotions wafting through him, he knew the things he'd told himself in the past weeks had been a lie.

I do love her…and no one else.

Any doubt completely fled, leaving in its place only impatient eagerness—for her to again awaken so they might renew their lust, for the morning to come so they could continue their journey together.

Why couldn't I admit it before?

He was impatient for their arrival in Paris and their travels to Rome and Venice. Donal was not only ready for whatever life with Felicity would bring, but eagerly looking forward to it.

The "honest rogue" was truly tamed.

Chapter 24

In Paris, Donal and Felicity sequestered themselves in their suite, leaving Rollo and Amy to their own devices. Giving the valet a small wallet, Donal told him to take the maid sightseeing. Neither was to return to their master's suite unless summoned.

For a week, he and Felicity saw only each other. They wanted no one else. Meals were brought in via room service. They ate with gusto, each feeding the other. They even dressed each other…when they put on clothes, that is, for they spent most of their time in bed, Donal making vigorous love to his wife and she returning the favor. By the third day, Felicity was quite willing to scamper about the suite naked, making Donal marvel at the delicious and loving wantonness he'd released.

My God, are all women like this? Underneath all those well-bred ruffles and petticoats, do all their hearts beat with such well-controlled passion? He didn't know or care. He'd found the one woman for him and that was all that mattered. His delight in that discovery was hitherto unimaginable.

After a week, however, practicality set in, and they ventured forth into Paris. They patronized several restaurants and attended the theatre enough to be able, when they returned, to tell everyone what they thought of French cuisine and speak intelligently of several plays. Felicity bought the frocks she wished and Donal even took time to have three suits made. Then, it was on to Rome and Venice, where Felicity revealed more of her daring by actually allowing Donal to make love to her in a gondola as it floated on one of the canals.

During that time, Donal realized decisions had to be made concerning his life. He'd thought to continue that division of personality, to be staid and reserved in public for the rest of his life, allowing himself freedom of emotion only in the wild embrace of Nell's arms and the Church's confines. After the past seven days, he knew he could never again go to any woman other than his wife, or set foot in a brothel again. Felicity was all he wanted. She fulfilled his every desire.

To that end, there would be changes upon his return to London, as he admitted he'd lied to Nell when he said his marriage wouldn't change their relationship, and to Joss as well. Now he would have to face both his friend and his mistress as he recanted that statement.

Donal put those thoughts aside, living in the moment and the pleasure of his wedding trip. Soon, however, that voyage of discovery came to an end. England and London loomed on the horizon, along with a confrontation he anticipated but fervently hoped would not occur.

Chapter 25

The small insertion in the *News* was short and succinct:

Mr. and Mrs. Donal McCoy have returned from their wedding trip to Paris, Venice, and Rome and have taken up residence at #3 Elm Tree Mews, Sedley House. They are at home to relatives and friends wishing to call.

****

A few days after returning from Paris, Donal wrote his father.

Mr. Patrick Aloysius Francis Xavier McCoy
McCoy Manor
Tipperary, Ireland
The United Kingdom of Great Britain
My Dear Father,

Felicity and I have returned from our trip and are now setting up housekeeping at Sedley House where I am currently in the midst of hiring a cook, a maidservant, and a butler. Once the uproar has settled, I hope you and Mother will come for a visit.

I have discussed matters with Felicity's uncle and plan to buy a partnership in his importing business. I will use some of the funds from Grandfather's inheritance placed in Trust for me. This is to ensure there is a continuous income so you may soon be notified I no longer need your financial support. I also wish to provide for Felicity should something untoward happen to me. I trust that is not too morbid a thought since I am newly wed. I also hope you approve my farsightedness.

Please give my love to Mother. Felicity also sends her regards.

Your affectionate son,
Donal Callum Seamus McCoy
#3 Elm Tree Mews, Sedley House
London, England
The United Kingdom of Great Britain
****

It was nearly six weeks after his return before Donal saw Nell again. Not because he was avoiding her, he simply was enjoying married life too much to think about such an entity as a soon-to-be-discarded mistress. At last, he decided not to delay any longer. Telling Felicity he had a bit of business to attend to, he ordered the curricle hitched and brought round. As he climbed into it, he wondered if perhaps he should see to selling the little carriage. Such a sporty vehicle might not be considered proper for a settled, married man.

At Nell's residence, he was met by an unusually glum Flossie, who greeted him with the rather enigmatic statement, "Welcome back, sir, though I don't know if that's the right term to use."

The girl looked harassed and tearful. Deciding she had developed a few vagaries in his absence, Donal let the remark pass. He hurried up the stairs to where Nell waited.

She wasn't on the fainting couch this time, but lying on the bed, wrapped in yet another diaphanous robe. She didn't move as he came through the door.

"So…you finally condescendin' to pay me a call?"

Granted he hadn't been around for some time, but

that wasn't exactly the welcome Donal expected. In view of what he planned to say, he decided perhaps a less than affectionate greeting might be best.

Seeing her appearance, he wondered if Nell's attitude had anything to do with Flossie's gloomy expression. Truly she looked to be in a bad way…pale, her lack of cosmetics making her appear even more washed out and colorless. Her eyes were red, as if she'd indulged in a month-long bout of tears. Indeed, there were very obvious tear tracks on her cheeks.

"God, you look awful." The words were out before Donal could stop them. "Nellie, are you ill?"

"Ill?" Her laugh was scornful with a watery echo. "Not me. 'ealthy as a 'orse, the sawbones says."

The way she said that worried Donal, who thought her lying, and yet… Nell was never ill. In all the years he'd known her, she'd never shown signs of any indisposition, not even during her Time, as she delicately called it.

"I'm glad of that, for I've something important to tell you."

"I've somefing important to say to you, too," she retorted, sitting up a bit straighter but not getting off the bed. "You said your weddin' trip would last four weeks. That was more than a month ago. Why ain't you been to see me before now?"

"That's what I wish to talk about." He stopped, waiting. When she didn't respond, he continued, "I know I said things between us wouldn't change, Nell, but…well, the truth is…they *have*."

"Oh God!" She screamed, body stiffening as if she'd been struck. "You've fallen in love with that…that…whey-faced chit!"

"Here now, there's no need to insult Felicity," he retorted.

"So, this is the end for us? You've come 'ere to give me the mitten? Where am I to go? Back to the Church?"

"Of course not. Don't think I'm simply going to abandon you," he assured her. "I'd never do that."

Her expression didn't change.

"I'll help you find another patron," Donal continued, meeting her glare with one of his own.

This wasn't going exactly the way he expected. Nell's reactions weren't the ones he thought she'd give.

"Joss, perhaps. He's always fancied you…" Donal felt he was making a generous offer. Randy old Joss would be cooperative. Nell could go from his arms to his friend's without a word being said.

"I don't want Ashley Joselyn," she flared. "I want *you*."

"I'm afraid you can't have me," he said coldly. "Not anymore."

"Oh, no?" Her expression changed, coming calculating, almost sly.

"No." He made it a dogmatic and very short statement of fact.

The expression hardened. "That's where you're wrong, Mr. Donal McCoy, I…"

She stopped abruptly. She was holding a handkerchief in one hand, wadded into a sodden ball. Now, she pressed it against her mouth, gagged, and bent over, free hand scrambling under the dust ruffle adorning the bed. Nell pulled out a chamber pot, leaned over and vomited copiously into it, body heaving.

Without thinking, Donal rushed to her side, preventing her from toppling off the bed. He took the chamber from her and, with a hand on her shoulder, held it. As the spasms ceased, he shoved it out of sight and brushed her hair out of her face.

"You *are* ill, Nell." Even if he was putting her aside, his voice held concern.

"I ain't ill." She leaned back against the pillow. "I'm knackered."

"What?" Surely, he'd misunderstood.

"You 'eard me."

When he shook his head, she sprang off the bed with surprising speed, flinging herself at him. Donal didn't have a chance to step back.

"I'm knocked, you bastard!" Her fists hammered his chest, each finding a painful mark. "You've got me with child."

"That's impossible." He pushed her away.

She fell back onto the bed. Instead of bursting into tears as he expected, however, Nell lay there glaring at him, eyes filled with anger, and something else…hatred.

"I was care…"

"You were careful all right. That damned French glove failed. I told you to get a new one, but no…you couldn't be bothered. Well, bother with this!" She struck her belly, such a resounding blow Donal winced. "The bloody thing sprang a leak."

"If it did, it's because you took a pin to it," he accused. "What kind of trick is this, Nell? Do you think to bind me with such a lie?"

"I didn't do noffin'. See for yourself." She gestured to the lamp table.

Donal opened the drawer, taking out the dowel. He turned it over, inspecting it more carefully than he had since the initial time he'd used one of the things. At first, he thought the *préventif* intact. Then, his fingertip found a tiny scuff, a minute tear, where the strained and worn fibers had simply pulled apart. *Oh God...*

"Flossie found it when she was cleanin' the thing the last time you was 'ere…two nights before your weddin'." She made it an accusation.

Donal dropped the dowel back into the drawer. He felt numb, as if his mind had completely stopped working, all sensation gone from his body. He actually couldn't feel the edges of the drawer with his fingertips as he pushed it shut. He turned to look at Nell, forcing bloodless lips to ask, "What are you going to do?"

"What am *I* goin' to do?" She shrieked the words. "What are *you* goin' to do, you mean. I swear, Donal…"

"Quiet." He turned away, hand to his mouth. "I need to think."

"No, you don't." She sat up, scrambling to all fours and crawling to the foot of the bed, where she got to her knees, holding onto the bedpost as she stared at him. "Listen…there's a doctor…not a 'arley Street one, disgraced, he's been, but he tends the girls at the Church and other places when one gets caught. He says he can get rid of it and make sure I don't die…" She paused, staring at him. "Donal, are you listenin'?

The look he gave her was dazed. Truly, he felt as if he'd been struck both in the belly and between the eyes at the same time.

"You seem to have it all thought out." He forced his tone steady and a little callous. "What is it I'm supposed to do, then?"

"I need money. Them things cost."

"How much?"

She named what he thought an exorbitant sum,

nearly the cost of the curricle and the horse pulling it. When he frowned, she said, "These procedures ain't cheap. He's breakin' the law so he has to charge a lot…to pay for the barrister if he's caught."

When Donal still didn't speak, she slid off the bed, seizing his arm and placing a hand on his cheek.

"You'll 'elp me, won't you, Donnie?" The hand slid to his chin, making little circles with the nail of her forefinger, her voice dropping to a low, cozening whisper. "You'll get the money. In cash. I'll go round to the doc… It'll only take a hour or so, and I'll be good as new afterward."

"No." He managed to get the word out.

"No?" She took a deep breath as if preparing for another scream, then seemed to think better of it. "It's the least you can do. God knows I've put up with you all these years. Poppin' in 'ere at all hours, expectin' me to be amorous and do whatever you want, no matter when. Listenin' to you pule and blubber about 'avin' to get married, and now givin' me the swat after you've gotten shackled. You owe me, Donal."

"Thanks for telling me you didn't really care." His own tone was abruptly cold. "May I say you're a very fine actress, Nell. You certainly had me fooled. I guess I couldn't expect more from someone I had to pay for sex, could I?"

She didn't even flinch. "I don't want this baby…you certainly don't. We can be rid of it and…then…"

"I don't have that much money lying around." He moved away from her touch, struggling to make a coherent thought form in his mind. The only one taking hold was, *Nell's pregnant with my child and she wants to kill it. Oh God.* "It…it'll take me a few days to liquidate some assets. I'll have to do it secretly."

"Do it quick," she ordered. "Else I might get impatient and give your new little wife a visit. I'm sure she wouldn't appreciate being told her 'usband's got a bastard on the way."

She screamed as he turned on her, catching her by the wrist and slinging her toward the bed. Nell struck the four-poster's frame and rebounded, landing on the floor. Donal made no move to help her get up.

"Don't you dare come near Felicity." There was nothing dazed in his voice now, nor anything gentle, all his father's teachings of treating females kindly disappearing. "If you do…"

"Wot'll you do?" She scrambled to her feet, pulling herself up by grasping the bedpost. A large bruise was forming on her wrist. She rubbed it ostentatiously, moaning softly. "Damn, I think you broke my wrist."

"No, I didn't, but I will break your neck if you tell anyone of this."

"And be 'auled up for murder?" She smirked. "I don't think so."

"The only way for you to be certain is to try it." Abruptly, he loomed over her, hand raised threateningly.

Afraid, realizing she'd tried a bluff that failed, Nell cowered. "I'm sorry, Donnie…please…I didn't mean it. It's just…I'm so worried…"

"Let me do the worrying," he snapped, and turned to the door. "I have to go. I need to think and I can't do it here. In the meantime, you'll stay here, and take care of yourself. Rest and stay calm. Getting excited won't be good for the baby."

"What does it matter, if we're goin' to…?"

"Don't do anything until you've heard from me." He

didn't let her finish. "Promise me that, Nell." He made certain that didn't sound like a plea.

"All right." Thinking he was agreeing, she added, "I love you, Donnie."

He didn't respond to that, simply opened the door and walked out.

****

He drove slowly, thoughts colliding and banging around in his brain like marbles dropped to skitter and roll wherever they might. Luckily the horse knew its way home, for he barely guided the creature at all. Once back at Sedley House, he hurried to his study, poured himself a brandy, and threw himself into a chair.

Now his thoughts coalesced, and they weren't pretty.

My God, what am I going to do? His very careful life was about to be ruined forever because he'd been careless. There would be a scandal. Felicity would probably forbid him ever touching her again. She might even leave him. His father would possibly disinherit him. He'd join Padraig among the disowned, without the solace of a remittance.

With Nell's words, all appearance of a rake disappeared. Now Donal was merely a young man faced with a dilemma. He told himself other men might have risen above it with reputations intact, but he was certain that, in his case, there would be no reprieve. He'd been too scrupulous in keeping his private life secret. The public Donal McCoy was spotless. This revelation would spread through the gossip mills like wildfire and he'd be finished as everyone realized how he'd fooled them.

Common sense told him it would be easy enough to

228

solve the problem. Simply sell off a bit of that land his grandfather had left him, hand over the money, and that disgraced surgeon's knife would rid him of the problem fast enough.

Donal's basic humanity quailed at the thought.

I can't do it. I can't. His upbringing as well as his Church of England teachings rose, opposing any thoughts he might have of agreeing to Nell's plan. *I can't destroy an unborn life. I don't want this child but I can't kill it. Whether I love its mother or not, I can't do that.*

His mind argued it would be so easy, might even be for the best.

What kind of life can it have? A bastard, unwanted, with a whore for a mother…

His heart made a different thought intrude.

What if it's destined for greatness…and I kill it? What if Mankind suffers because I helped snuff out that barely budding life? It could become a monster, but it could also be good. It's my child, too. Surely, I couldn't sire someone evil.

He fought to calm his wild thoughts. There was an answer, one that wouldn't make him a murderer. He simply had to find it.

I need to speak to someone. I need advice. There were only a few men he would dare trust with such information.

Telling Joss was out of the question. He'd say, *Do it and be done.* There was Roger Melton. *I can't speak of this to him. How could he understand? His niece's husband asking his advice on how to dispose of a bastard?* The other was Quinton. *It's his grandchild. Surely, he has a right in deciding whether it lives or dies.*

That was the answer.

Yes, I have to tell Father. He'll be greatly disappointed, of course. It may break his heart to learn I've acted so irresponsibly, but…I'll tell him…that his first grandchild may be born on the wrong side of the blanket. I admit it's cowardly. I'm a grown man and should be able to handle a problem of my own making, but…he has a right to know. I'll tell him, and his reaction will decide what I should do.

Tossing down the brandy, he got to his feet, catching his breath as the liquor seared its way down his throat. When he emerged from the study, he saw Felicity on the stairs.

"Rollo told me you'd returned." She gave him a gentle kiss on the cheek.

Donal nearly flinched. *Would you want to kiss me if you knew what I may be about to do?*

"You look worried. Didn't your business go as you expected?"

"Not really," he answered and looked away. "I'll have to seek advice on how to handle it, I'm afraid."

"I'm certain Uncle Roger would be glad to…"

"No!" He forced himself to smile, easing the sharpness in his voice. *Roger Melton must never know.* "I'm afraid this is something requiring my father's assistance, and to do that…" He swung her around, forcing a jocular note into his voice. "Pack, Felicity, I'm going home and you're coming with me."

"We're going to Ireland?" She sounded delighted. "Another trip so soon? Oh, Donal!"

"I need to see Father. We'll make this into a combination business and pleasure trip."

"I'd love to see your parents again."

"Then you shall visit with Mother while Father and

I figure this out."

Father will know what to do, and it'll be the right thing. Donal was certain of it.

Chapter 26

"Now then...what's th' problem?"

Quinton and Donal were in the elder McCoy's study. He and Felicity had arrived that morning, surprising the entire household. The day had been whiled away with harmless conversation. After supper that night, father and son retired to the study, Felicity and Mrs. McCoy going into the parlor.

Donal remained silent while Cormac poured whiskey and served each man, then withdrew, shutting the study doors behind him. He didn't drink from his goblet but simply studied it as Quinton selected a pipe, filled it with tobacco from the humidor on the mantel, tamped it, and lit it with a taper thrust into the fire.

"Well?" He puffed a few moments before looking at his son.

"What makes you think there's a problem, sir?" Donal didn't look up as he spoke.

"The fact you're avoidin' lookin' at me, for one thin'," Quinton answered, sharply. "Felicity told your maithur you had a business problem needin' me advice, for anaithur. *You* told me you'd merely come for a visit."

He laughed slightly and shook the taper, dousing the flame. He returned it to the brass case on the mantel.

"Since when do you make visits without a reason, son?"

"Father, how long has it been since you've heard

from Padraig?"

"Padraig?" Because that wasn't what Quinton was expecting him to say, his father frowned. "Has *he* gotten himself into anaithur predicament?"

"No, sir, I was merely curious."

"I haven't heard from Padraig since he left here. Th' bank tells me he's drawin' on th' funds placed in his account monthly, but where he is…" Quinton shook his head and seated himself in a chair opposite Donal. He puffed a moment, then admitted, "All right…I received a letter recently. He's somewhere in America, but not settled yet. He said he was thinkin' o' travelin' t' what's called th' Great Plains, where'er that is, an' would send me his bank's address when he arrived." He shook his head.

"Great Plains?" Donal raised his goblet, taking a careful sip. He needn't have. Quinton only drank Bushmills and it was always smooth. "Where those wild Indians live? And those undisciplined cowboys? I understand that's a rough place…people getting shot and scalped all the time."

"Then it ought t' suit Padraig," Quinton muttered. He puffed even more, briefly enveloping himself in white smoke. As it cleared, he said, "I've thanked God a thousand times you turned out so well, Donal." The look he gave his son was fond and surprisingly grateful. "You've done e'erythin' I've asked o' you an' fulfilled me e'ery expectation, given me no grief, an'…"

"You may change your opinion when you hear what I have to say, sir." Donal rose, staring into the fire.

"Why?" Quinton looked up. "What's happened?"

"I fear I've let you down, Father."

"What do you mean?" When there was no answer,

Quinton, prompted, "Son?"

Donal took a large swallow of whiskey, then set the glass on the mantel. He didn't turn to look at his father...couldn't, and say what he had to. "I'm afraid I've bested Padraig in vile behavior, sir. I've betrayed your trust in me."

He heard Quinton set his pipe in its ceramic holder on a nearby table, and get up. A hand rested on his shoulder. Donal turned but couldn't meet his father's eyes. He studied the floor, feeling like a child again, caught with crumbs on his face while denying he'd been the one stealing cookies from the plate Cook set in the window to cool.

"Tell me," was all his father said.

Donal took a deep breath. Pulling away from Quinton's encouraging touch, he retrieved the glass from the mantel and pretended to study the books on the shelf behind his chair.

"You weren't aware, but for three years now, I've had a mistress..."

It took several minutes for him to get the entire story out. Afterward, Quinton didn't speak. He simply returned to his chair, picked up his own glass and took a long, slow swallow. For several moments more, he sat studying the amber contents while Donal waited.

At last Donal ventured, "I suppose I should've broken off with her *before* my marriage..."

"If you'd done that, then she could accuse you o' abandonin' her."

"That doesn't matter now, does it?" Donal answered. "I know I'm a disappointment to you. In all Padraig ever did, he never was unfortunate enough to manage something like this. I've truly bested my brother in licentious behavior. All I can do now is ask your forgiveness."

"Me forgiveness can wait," Quinton answered. "At present, what I wish t' know is why you're tellin' me this? You could've taken care o' it yourself an' I'd have never known. Why make a special trip t' confess t' me?"

Donal didn't answer, unable to tell whether his father's tone was accusing or pleading.

"Well? Do you expect me t' extricate you from this matter?"

"No." That brought Donal out of his muteness, thinking Quinton's reaction no harsher than he deserved and at the same time, rather unfeeling. "I don't wish to become more like my brother than I am by having you buy me out of my offenses as you did him. I'm man enough to handle this myself. I simply—"

"Yes?"

Donal shook his head.

"Th' solution would seem t' offer itself simple enough," his father continued. "I understand there are back-street doctors specializin' in removin such…problems…"

"That answer has been offered to me, sir, but I…" Again, he hesitated, then forced himself to continue. "I not only find it distasteful, I hesitate to end an unborn life, as unwanted as it may be. You know God teaches that's a sin."

Donal was certain he saw his father relax slightly.

"Then what do you propose? Do you plan t' acknowledge th' child? Provide for it? Does Felicity know, by the way?"

"No, she doesn't. No one, other than myself and now you, have been made aware."

"Then why…?"

"I felt you had a right to know that a kept woman is carrying your first grandchild. Can you accept there will be a bastard with McCoy blood? I'm fully prepared to admit my sin if you say *yes*."

Now it was Quinton's turn not to answer. He drained his glass, set it down, and picked up his pipe. Drawing on it, he sat smoking in silence. Then he got to his feet and walked past his son to the hearth, where he tapped the pipe against the stone, dislodging the ashes into the firebox. Replacing it in the stand on the mantel, he turned to face Donal.

"When you return t' London, I shall go with you. I'll handle everythin'."

"No, Father, I told you, I don't want that. I know you're disappointed in me, but I'll face this. Alone. I simply wished you to be aware…"

"I don't think it wise for you to see that woman again," Quinton said decisively. "You may be an adult now, son…as evidenced by this fix you've gotten yourself inta, but in this you must listen t' me. *I* will confront her, tell her what's t' happen, an' pay out o' me own account. That way nothing can be traced back t' you an' your reputation will stand."

He put a hand on Donal's shoulder, feeling it sag slightly as if in relief, not knowing it was in despair.

"After this, I'll expect you t' toe th' line an' ne'er again exhibit such untoward behavior, however. Is that clear?"

"Yes, sir," Donal answered with reluctance. This wasn't going the way he expected. He shuddered and bowed his head. In that moment all he wished was to shed bitter tears. "Father, I'm so ashamed."

"You told Felicity you came askin' me for business advice?" Quinton ignored his statement.

Donal nodded.

"We'll tell your mother an' Felicity th' problem requires me presence in London." There was a gentle slap to his back. "Come now, buck up, lad. Put on a happier face as we again face th' ladies."

Donal closed his eyes briefly before nodding.

"It's not as if I haven't done this before," Quinton continued, not making his son feel a bit better. "Payin' for me son's mistakes, I mean. Before God, I hope this is th' last time," he muttered.

Donal didn't answer, wondering if he would ever forgive himself. In that moment, he hated himself.

I'm a weakling, a coward, a papa's pet, relying on my father's money to buy off my sins. I can never look down on Padraig again. Pot and kettle, that's what we are, and I'm the blacker of the two. Will I ever outlive this shame?

****

If anyone noticed how quiet Donal was during the week of their stay, no one commented on it. He was generally so reserved and serious when at home, especially when compared to Master Padraig's shenanigans, everyone simply put to it down to his usual nature.

At that moment, not knowing what Quinton intended, for his father refused to speak of his plan, Donal wondered if he would ever again be without a feeling of guilt.

Chapter 27

Quinton had cautioned they shouldn't return to London too soon, so Donal managed to contain his anxiety for a week, after which time he decided he'd best get back to London. Greatly fearing Nell would become impatient and do some mischief while he was gone, he said to Felicity on the eighth day of their visit, "I fear we shall have to begin thinking of returning home, sweetheart."

There was sincere regret in his voice because, in spite of his worry, he'd enjoyed being with his parents again.

"Oh, Donal," she immediately made a little *moue* of disappointment. "I was expecting to stay at last another two weeks."

"I'd dearly like to," he replied. They were in the parlor, and he truly hated spoiling the calming atmosphere by thinking of returning to what awaited him. "Now that Father has given me a solution to that problem I brought to him…" Here he managed to keep his voice from trembling, making it as firm as usual. "…I really must get back and put it into action."

At that, as if this were some well-rehearsed play script, Quinton spoke up. "An' I shall have t' come with you. The solution requires me presence, I'm afraid." He looked at Màiri, whose expression mirrored her daughter-in-law's. "Don't worry, me dear, you're comin' with me."

"I'm glad of that." Màiri smiled. "I was about to protest having such a short visit with Felicity and then my husband running off to London also."

"I'm truly sorry this has been so unexpected and brief, Mother," Donal apologized.

He was dismayed to think his mother was going to be there while his father was doing whatever he was going to do, fearing somehow she'd discover her eldest's shame. At the same time, he was also pleased she would be able to witness what a fine job Felicity was doing of running his home.

"You and Father will be our first guests." He forced his voice into a brighter tone as he looked at Felicity. "Won't that be exciting, dearest?"

Her smile told him she was looking forward to entertaining her mother-in-law.

"When will we be leaving?" Màiri asked.

"Day after tomorrow," he decided. "That should give you time to decide what to pack for…how long will you be staying, Father?" He looked at Quinton.

"A fortnight," Quinton said decisively. "I don't believe our business plans will have any complications. I'll get it out o' th' way as soon as we arrive an' then we can spend th' next thirteen days enjoyin' our visit."

He took a glass of wine from the tray Cormac was passing around, gesturing with it in Donal's direction.

"Here's t' a pleasant visit."

"Hear, hear." Donal accepted a glass and drank.

He still had no idea what Quinton planned. A few days before, finding himself again alone with his father, he'd tried to broach the subject but Quinton waved him away. He very obviously didn't want his son aware of how he was going to handle things.

Much as if he's committing some crime and wants me kept ignorant so I can't be guilty by association, Donal decided. On the heels of that thought came another, more startling one. *Good God, perhaps he is. He's going to give Nell the money to...*

His mind refused to finish the sentence.

Donal didn't want to believe it, not after the way Quinton had acted when he admitted he couldn't bring himself to have the child destroyed. This current attitude, however, treating the whole thing as a pleasure jaunt... Could a man do that if he were planning what could be called nothing but murder? He didn't believe his father could be so cold-blooded. Kept in the dark as he was, his mind conjured up horrid but unsubstantiated notions he forced himself to disbelieve, while wondering what was actually going to happen, then telling himself it was better if he didn't know.

That made Donal hate himself more for what he considered his cowardice.

In two days, however, he found himself, with Felicity and his mother and father, on a packet bound for England, his questions still unanswered, his imagination worn and frayed.

Chapter 28

Once the trunks were unloaded, his parents settled in the second bedroom, while Donal made apologies for having only one guest room.

"When I was a bachelor, I didn't expect I'd be having many houseguests."

"Quite all right." Quinton's answer was hearty. He lifted Màiri's hand, kissing her fingers. "I imagine you won't mind sharin' a bed for two weeks, will you, me dear?"

Even after twenty-five years of marriage and four children, he could still make his wife blush. She pulled her hand from his and looked away. "Go on with you, Quinton, McCoy. Is that somethin' you say in front of your son?"

"I just did." He glanced at Felicity, who had returned from discussing the supper menu with the cook, and immediately looked concerned. "Lass, with only two bedrooms…are we evictin' you from yours? I ne'er thought o' that."

"Oh no, Father Quinton…"

That made Donal smile involuntarily. Not being able to call his father simply by his Christian name, she'd begun calling him *Father Quinton.* Apparently, his father liked that epithet if the way he reacted every time she said it was any indication.

"I…we…" She looked at Donal, then studied the

carpet, not willing to bring herself to admit she and Donal shared his bedchamber. "You're causing no problem at all."

"Glad o' that." Quinton hadn't missed the glance passing between his son and daughter-in-law. He paused, looked around, and said in a decisive tone, "Now that we're settled in, I think I'll go now an' get that business out o' th' way."

As Màiri and Felicity made protests that they'd only just arrived, he continued, "Best t' take care o' it so we can enjoy our visit. Donal, would you have your man get me hat an' call th' carriage round?"

After Donal did that, he caught his father's arm. "I'll walk you out, sir."

He ushered Quinton to the door, pulling it shut behind them as they waited on the stoop for Charles to appear with the carriage.

"Father, please tell me…"

"I need th' wench's name, son, and the address." Quinton put on his hat and smoothed the fingers of his gloves.

"Her name's Eleanor Nordin," Donal replied. They were both speaking in near-whispers, as if fearing either Felicity or Màiri were lurking with ears to the door. "Nell. Number 17 Riverview Mews…Father, what are you going to do?"

"We can go over that later," Quinton's reply told him nothing.

At that moment, Charles and the carriage arrived.

****

Three hours later, Quinton was back. He waved aside Donal's anxious greeting, asked when supper would be served, and inquired if he might have a before-dinner drink. During the meal, he ate with a hearty appetite, declared Donal's new cook a wonder, and then asked his son if he still had any of his grandfather's whiskey available.

Abandoning Felicity and Màiri to the parlor, as was the custom, Donal and his father settled themselves in the study where a low fire kept a sudden chill night wind at bay. Sewell, the newly-hired butler, poured and served the Bushmills while Donal was thankful he'd taken only a few bottles to Nell's.

Quinton waited until he'd enjoyed a long, slow swallow of whiskey, then set down his glass. "I know you're anxious to be told, son."

He proceeded to relate to Donal what had transpired during his visit to Riverview Mews.

****

Charles pulled the team to a halt before the little house, saying, as Quinton opened the carriage door and climbed out, "Shall I wait, Mr. McCoy?"

"Yes, this shouldna take long." Quinton wondered what the footman thought was going on…why the father was now visiting the son's mistress. That made him slam the carriage door a bit more violently than was needed.

He stalked up the walk.

There was a coach light hanging from a hook near the door, but it wasn't lit. In fact, it was so dark under the little porch eave he barely saw the bellpull. Peering down, he found it, gave it a vigorous jerk, then waited as he heard a distant clanging inside.

After several minutes, during which Quinton wondered if he would have to ring again, he heard hurried footsteps, and the locks being released.

The door swung open, revealing a mousy-haired

young girl wearing a drab with a pinafore apron over it.

Lord, surely she isn't... Quinton felt dismay as he realized the girl couldn't be over fifteen.

"Mr. Donal?" The girl spoke and that allayed Quinton's fears. "Why are you comin' to the front door? You gettin' formal of a sudden?"

Quinton stepped over the threshold and into the light. The girl recoiled slightly.

"Oh! Excuse me, sir." She bobbed a curtsey. "I thought you was...someone else."

"Quinton McCoy." Quinton introduced himself, adopting an officious air he hoped would quell the girl into not asking questions. "To see Miss Nordin."

He looked around, noting the well-appointed foyer and wonder how much of the cheques he sent for Donal's allowance went into furnishing it. *Damn, this place looks as good as McCoy Hall.*

"McCoy?" The girl gave him a sharp look tinged with suspicion. "You Mr. Donal's kin?" She looked past him to the carriage stopped at the curb. "Where is he?"

"Never you mind where Mr. Donal is." Quinton walked completely inside, taking off his hat and gloves and handing them to her. Automatically, she took them while he nodded approvingly that her surprise hadn't made her forget her place. "I wish to see Miss Nordin...Nell. Tell her I'm here."

"Yes, sir." Flossie set Quinton's hat on the credenza, bobbed another curtsey, and hurried to the stairs. "If you'll wait there, sir..." She ran up them.

Quinton continued studying the foyer and what he could see of the upstairs from where he stood. *Egad, the place is very nicely furnished.* He hadn't realized his son had such good taste, or...*surely the dolly didn't decorate it?* He didn't believe someone of a class other than the gentry or nobility could be so discriminating.

A door opened. He heard voices, two speakers. One raised in inquiring tones, the other was the girl's. The door shut again and the girl reappeared at the top of the stairs. She came down them, not speaking until she stood before him again.

"Miss Nell says you's to come up. She's feelin' poorly today an' don't want to attempt the stairs."

Uncharitably, Quinton thought it a pity she didn't try to navigate the stairs, fall, and break her neck. *That'd save us all some trouble.* In the next instant, he was ashamed of having such a thought. He was a fairly peaceful man, preferring talk to action and negotiation to argument, and to wish such harm to a woman he'd never met both distressed and startled him.

"Very well." He gestured to the stairs. "Show me the way?"

There was another curtsey and the girl started up the stairs again. She was on the fourth one before Quinton moved. She stopped, looking down at him.

"Well? Ain'tcha comin'?"

He didn't answer, simply stamped up beside her, then followed her to the top and down the hall to a door at the end of the corridor. Quinton waited while she opened the door, stuck her head in and said, "Here's Mr. McCoy, Miss Nell," then stepped back so he could walk past her. She pulled the door shut behind him, barely giving him time to get inside, its edge brushing the tails of his frockcoat.

Quinton looked around, taking in the elegance of the bedchamber and finding it comparable to the one at Elm Tree Mews he and Màiri had been given. *Damn, Donal, you've spent a pretty penny on this bit of fluff, havena you?*

The centerpiece of the room, however, was the four-poster bed. There was a movement from it and Quinton focused on the woman lying there. She was pretty, he admitted. Not as coarse as he expected, though definitely full-bosomed and round-hipped, as evidenced by the way the flimsy wrapper clung to her body. Briefly, he wondered how much was natural and how much changes brought about by the developing child. He also noted she was definitely older than his son.

"Mr. McCoy? Who are you?" She had a voice that, with a bit of training, would be a delight to hear. As it was, a lower-class accent came through sharp and abrasive, less than halfway grammatical, as well as hoarse, as if she'd been crying recently.

"I'm Donal's faithur."

"Thought you had to be, with that hair. He's spoke of you on occasion."

"Let's dispense with the social pleasantries, Miss Nordin," Quinton interrupted. He simply wanted to get this unpleasantness out of the way and escape. "I know who you are an' you know who I am, so I imagine you're also aware o' why I'm here."

"So, Donnie ran cryin' to Papa, did he?" Her voice curled with scorn. "Funny...I never thought him a Daddy's boy." She shrugged. "Goes to show how wrong someone can be. Are you goin' to give me the money for the doc?"

"No, I'm not."

"No?" The word came out in a near-wail. She was off the bed faster than he'd have expected someone in such a delicate condition to move, coming around it to stop a few feet from him. "Wot the 'ell am I supposed to do, then?"

"I'll tell you exactly what you're goin' t' do, Miss Nordin…an' I'm givin' you th' courtesy o' that title only because you're carryin' me grandchild." Quinton was studying her carefully as he spoke. *Well, Donal, you can pick the beauties.* He had to give his son credit for having an eye for women, even if this one was a conniving tart. "You're goin' t' have this child."

"No, I ain't." She looked up at him, jaw abruptly outthrust belligerently. Oddly, it made her even more attractive. "Who do you think you are? Comin' in 'ere and tellin' me wot I'm to do? I don't want no baby. I ain't the maternal type."

"I know exactly what you are," Quinton interrupted harshly. "You're a pretty piece of tail who attracted my son, gave him some years o' fun, an' then got caught."

"Through his carelessness," she flared.

"Whose fault it was isn't th' point," Quinton replied.

"Wot is, then?"

"Th' child."

"So…you wantin' me to 'ave it, then you're goin' to take it away, maybe?" She looked hopeful. "In that case, I'll need some compensation for my inconvenience."

"You'll get nothin' for yourself," Quinton snapped.

"Well now, that ain't fair."

"Shut up an' listen," he ordered. "Here's what's goin' t' happen, an' whether you consider it fair or not doesn't matter. 'Tis th' way 'tis goin' t' be."

"I'm listenin'," Nell replied reluctantly.

Reaching into his breast pocket, Quinton removed his cheque wallet, took something from it, and held it out to her.

After a moment's hesitation, Nell took it. Scowling, she looked at it. "Wot's this?"

"You can read, can't you?"

"Of course, I can read, but…"

"Then you see it's a cheque, made out t' you. You'll take it an' leave London an' go far enough away that word o' what happens t' you won't get back here. Once you've found such a place, you'll notify th' bank whose address is on that cheque, an' every month thereafter, you'll receive anaithur, which you'll use to pay for your lodging, meals, an' physician's care. Are you followin' me so far?"

Neal didn't answer. Her nod was given grudgingly.

"When your lying-in occurs, you'll notify th' bank. If th' child lives, o' that also, but naithin' else. I do not want t' know its gender nor whate'er name you choose t' call it. Thereafter, a cheque will arrive for its upkeep an' education, t' be terminated upon its twenty-first birthday." He paused, drawing in a deep breath. "Now then, is there any part o' what I've said that you *don't* understand?"

"Let me see if I got this right." Nell's voice trembled with sudden sarcasm. "You're payin' me to 'ave your son's baby, take care of it, and you don't want to know noffin' about it?"

"That's correct."

"I'm to go somewheres I ain't known, to live…alone?"

"You'll need a servant. You may take that girl…" Quinton nodded toward the door. "…with you. Th' money you receive should be enough t' pay her salary also."

"Nah, I don't mean Flossie. I might get lonely. Wot

if I meet some gentleman who'd want to marry me?"

"I doubt that's going t' happen, but if by some miracle, it does, go ahead." Since she looked to be agreeable, Quinton was generous. "The money will still come for me grandchild. But…" He held up a finger. "There'll be no whorin'. You'll live a clean an' decent life t' set a good example."

"The *only* example," she corrected. "I'm takin' it Donnie won't be comin' round to see the little tyke?"

"You'll never see me son again. If you attempt it, if you try t' embarrass him in any way, I'll have you arrested for extortion. I think that might earn you a transportation somewhere a li'l more unpleasant than England."

"You wouldn't!" She looked shocked. "I ain't no demander."

"I would, an' I think we've established what you are. You're a Judy who's going t' come out o' this pretty lucky, unless you attempt t' get greedy. An' t' ensure you don't try that li'l game, I've had my solicitor draw up a legal contract." Quinton pulled two sheets of folded paper from another pocket. He thrust them at her.

"What's that?" Nell drew back as if he held a gun.

"It's a declaration that you're acceptin' me money t' care for you before th' child's birth an' that I'll continue t' send you remuneration for its upkeep an' education until th' age stated." He'd had the paper written up during Donal's visit home. "Also, that if you ever make any move t' get further money from me or me son or attempt t' communicate with Donal in any way, you'll be prosecuted for extortion."

"You're a 'ard old bastard, ain't you?" She said it with something sounding near to admiration.

"Say what you will…do you agree?"

"Wot'll you do if I don't? If I don't sign that paper?"

Quinton had already thought of that. "I understand th' rents on this place come due in two days. If you don't sign, me son won't pay an' th' lease will lapse. You'll be out of here on your well-cushioned little arse an' back on the streets." He wasn't about to tell her he'd never allow her to go back to whoring. Let her assume he would. "How long will you be able t' play th' dolly-mop with a big belly, do you think? It'll be th' workhouse for you in about three months, I imagine."

Nell didn't answer. For an instant, she seemed to actually tremble, a deep red rising from her throat, flooding her face. She held her breath, then released it so loudly it seemed a gasp. Flinging herself into the chair, she pulled a quill from the pen holder and flipped open the inkwell. Dipping the quill into it, she scribbled her name at the bottom of the first paper with a splash of ink.

"Wouldn't you like t' read it first?" Quinton made his tone politely ironic.

She shook her head. "I think you explained it clear enough."

"In that case, sign th' second one, also." As she did, he continued, "That's your copy. I don't want you t' have any leeway t' say you weren't aware o' th' terms."

Nell signed the second sheet. Quinton retrieved the first, checked the signature, then affixed his own. He waved the page to make certain the ink was dry before he returned it to his pocket. Then, he signed the second page, also.

"What 'appens now?" she asked.

Quinton was certain he felt impotent fury smoldering under that mild question.

"Now, Miss Nordin?" He bowed slightly. "I bid you good evenin'." With that, he turned and walked to the door, pausing to look back. "As I said, the lease will expire in two days. I suggest you begin packing now."

Nell didn't answer.

As Quinton walked down the hall, he heard a crash behind him. He imagined the wall next to the door was now covered with ink from the inkwell shattered against it. He went down the stairs to where Flossie stood in the foyer. Picking up his hat from the credenza, she held it out to him.

"What's to h'appen to us, sir?" It was obvious she'd been listening outside the door.

"Nothin' bad." Abruptly, he wanted to soothe her, seeing her as the child she was, sorry she had to get caught up in this. He made his voice kindly. "In fact, it may be even better than your life up t' now."

Accepting his hat, he waited for her to open the door, then walked out, saying over his shoulder, "Best see t' your mistress. She's going t' need some assistance in packin'."

At the carriage, he climbed in, telling Charles to take him back to Elm Tree Mews.

****

"She's not t' get in touch with you again," he concluded.

"I'll never know whether I have a son or a daughter?" There was wistfulness in Donal's question.

"'Tis better that way, son." Quinton wondered what Donal thought would happen. Surely the lad didn't believe he could make repeated trips to some far village to see his child and keep it from his wife?

"In that case, why do I feel so guilty? The child will

live. Thanks to you, it'll have a good life." Donal dropped into a chair, resting his head in his hands. "Why do I feel as if a crime has been committed?"

"The feelin' will pass." Quinton knew that sounded cold. He pushed his own dismay aside. "Just keep tellin' yourself this is the best way…for th' child, for you, an' for Felicity."

"You're right, of course." Donal got to his feet, drawing in a deep breath. He let it out slowly. "Thank you, Father. That sounds so inadequate, but…"

Abruptly overcome with emotion, he knelt and threw his arms around Quinton, surprising his father by hugging him tightly.

"Here now, what's this?"

"Thank you for not…thank you," was muffled against his vest.

"You haven't done that since you were a wee one," Quinton muttered.

As if reprimanded, Donal released him and got to his feet. "Excuse me, sir. I forget myself."

Before Quinton could reply, there was a knock at the door. To Donal's call, Sewell opened the door and looked in. "Mrs. McCoy asked me to let you know supper is prepared and will be served whenever you and Mr. Quinton are ready, sir."

"Thank you, Sewell. We're ready now, aren't we, Father?" Donal glanced at Quinton, so formal it was shocking.

"As can be." Quinton forced a hearty note into his voice, a little dismayed by his son's expression.

Instead of the gratitude and relief he expected, Donal's face was devoid of emotion. He wondered if that was the only way his son could keep from showing exactly how he felt about what had transpired that evening.

****

At supper, though Donal ate steadily, he didn't enjoy the meal, seeming preoccupied. He made little conversation, letting Quinton and Felicity do most of the talking. Felicity noted the change, remarking how quiet he was, asking if he were unwell.

"I'm fine," Donal assured her. "I was simply thinking over that business transaction Father finalized today." His expression saddened as he said that.

"Did it go well, Father Quinton?" She looked at Quinton.

"I believe I can say it went better than expected," Quinton replied. He refused to look at his son.

Donal didn't comment. Instead, he held out his glass so the wine steward could refill it. *I am such a coward.* He would drink a great deal of wine that night.

Chapter 29

Spring, 1860

Donal Callum Seamus McCoy
#3 Elm Tree Mews, Sedley House
Chesterfield, Mayfair
London, England
The United Kingdom of Great Britain
My Dear Son,

I hope this letter finds you and Felicity well. You know it's not in my general nature to write letters but I've a special purpose in this one.

Lord Alisdaire has returned to Tipperary and has decided to be in residence for the spring and summer. Since this coincides with the beginning of the Season in Tipperary, he will be attending the first event of the year, to debut his daughter Fiona. I shall also be there. Along with Colin, I'd like you and Felicity in attendance so I may present you to His Lordship. He has never met any of my family, other than that one time when you were children. Indeed, I've not told him much about myself at all, although he's evinced curiosity on occasion. Mainly, I've maintained a business relationship. Since he will be here for at least the next six months or more, and I will be in his company fairly continuously, I believe it is time to adjust our association a bit.

I shall expect you sometime during the week of May

fourteenth, which is when the ball will be held. I sincerely hope there will be nothing to prevent your attending. Your business shouldn't suffer if you're absent for a few days. Indeed, nothing short of the fact of your wife being in a delicate way and unable to travel must prevent it.

Your mother is looking forward to seeing you. It has been nearly two years now since your last visit.

Your Father,
Quinton Aloysius Francis Xavier McCoy
McCoy Hall
Tipperary, Ireland
The United Kingdom of Great Britain
****

Frowning, Donal dropped the letter to the desk and sat staring at it. Previously, he'd enjoyed receiving a missive from his father, especially since his work now prevented him from going home as much as he liked. This one, however…

After buying into Roger Melton's business, he found himself being slowly drawn into learning about the workings of the importing industry. He was startled to discover that trade fascinating and was soon working alongside his uncle-in-law to make the company even more prosperous. Donal immersed himself in absorbing all the knowledge he could, to the point where Melton offered him a partnership. Thinking his association would by no means detract from his still being called a gentleman, because no one thought of Roger Melton as anything else, Donal accepted. In the current society, with the *nouveau riche* so prominent, character was becoming more important than bloodlines. It was entirely acceptable for a man to be in business and still be called a gentleman, as long as there was no dirt under his nails when he appeared in public. Indeed, the "captains of industry" were becoming very important to the country.

These days, the sign over their offices read, *Melton, Melton, & McCoy, Importers*.

If anyone had asked, Donal would've said his life was now complete. The business was going so well he was a wealthy man, with a home in Mayfair as well as a country estate which, though small, was sumptuous enough and had a fine stable of hunters. He had weekend house parties. He was still welcomed at Almack's, was looked up to in some circles, and had a small coterie of friends which, surprisingly, still included Joss.

His old friend has startled his former companion in debauchery by abruptly courting a smart young lady, marrying her, and settling down. *If you can do it, so can I.* That was his way of telling Donal of the happy event. *I'm following your lead, old chum, all the way.* So far, he seemed to be succeeding.

Donal and Felicity had been married almost a decade now, and Donal was as in love with her as ever. He considered himself a happy man, except…

Except for the fact that in every letter from Quinton and every visit they paid home, he was always asked the same question in some form or other: *When are you going to give me a grandchild?*

When he thought about it, Donal was always startled to realize he and Felicity had been married ten years. It certainly didn't seem as if it had been that long since the day he sat at his desk making that odious list and hearing Joss laugh because he added Felicity's name to it.

His wife was as beautiful as ever. She hadn't let

marriage or the years add weight to her small frame, and her ashen hair was still like gilt. Neither had her lovemaking suffered with the years.

Perhaps they hadn't been blessed with a child yet, but…so what? Donal admitted he wanted children. He'd like to see both himself and Felicity duplicated.

Occasionally, he thought perhaps he and Felicity should talk about why it hadn't yet happened. Then he'd remember how a couple of his friends had gone years before announcing a happy event and he'd think perhaps he and Felicity were also to be late bloomers. He set the thought aside to become lost in the activities of work and day-to-day living. In fact, the only time it now came to mind that he and his wife were still childless was when he received a very unsubtle reminder from his father.

As now.

Picking up the letter, Donal carefully re-folded it into its envelope shape and placed it in the drawer of his desk where it joined all the others written him by Quinton over the years. He had no idea why he was saving them. Some memento of his father for that time when Quinton would no longer be there to needle him with those blunt queries? Was he unconsciously hoarding them in hopes of having some keepsake of its grandfather to show that as yet nonexistent child he still wished to have?

He gave a heavy sigh. It appeared that last hope was never going to achieve fruition. *I'm almost thirty-five.* Felicity was twenty-eight. *Perhaps I'd best bring up the subject before it's too late.*

No time like the present, he supposed.

Leaving his study, he went up the corridor and through the foyer, passing the credenza with its lavish gold-framed mirror. He paused, studying his image in the glass. Donal saw nothing to complain about in that reflection…a fairly tall man, perhaps a few pounds overweight because he employed a very good cook…but well-dressed, definitely a gentleman in his prime. He glanced at his hair. As plentiful as ever.

Donal admitted he was vain when he inspected his hairline to make certain it wasn't receding, though he told himself he needn't worry. His father was now in his mid-fifties and still had a full head of hair. *Like father, like son…* Donal's own hair was as fiery and undisciplined as always, though he did now sport a very refined and modest but well-kept handlebar moustache.

Sewell was standing nearby, sorting the rest of the post after delivering Quinton's letter to the master.

"Where's Mrs. McCoy just now?" Donal asked, making his tone casual and then asking himself why he thought he had to do that. *Is it unusual for a man to ask his wife's whereabouts?* The house wasn't so big they could be in it and not be unaware of each other's presences.

"I believe she's in her study, sir. She said she was going over the list for her birthday celebration."

Birthday? Drat, he'd forgotten. Felicity's birthday was ten days away and she was planning a party. Quinton's request—and for that, he supposed he should read *order*—would definitely interfere with that. They could decline to go, of course, and incur the McCoy patriarch's wrath.

Thirty-five years old and still expected to jump-to when Father beckons, Donald inwardly fumed. Nevertheless…since it had, in a way, to do with Quinton's position as Alisdaire's steward, it was probably necessary they be present.

"Thank you, Sewell. If I'm needed, that's where I shall be, also." Donal spun on his heel and aimed himself in the direction of the little room, just past the library, that Felicity had designated her study.

The door was closed. He stopped, knocked, and to her call, opened it and went in.

****

Felicity was sitting at her secretary, a dainty little rolltop davenport. Fashioned of highly polished burr oak, it had been painted a delicate cream, its thick cabriole front legs scrolled with carved vines and rosebuds. Donal had commissioned a local cabinetmaker to build the piece as a surprise for her twenty-third birthday. All the furniture in the room was very fragile-looking and feminine, finished in bleached wood or painted cream color. Wanting to make certain the finish matched the other pieces in her study, he'd secretly sneaked into the room while she was out shopping and carefully scraped a bit of paint from the backside of one of the legs of a lamp table so the cabinetmaker could match it.

Donal rarely came into the room. Not because it was his wife's *sanctum sanctorum* and forbidden to him but because he felt out of place in such distinctly female surroundings. The room gave him the sense he was too large to perch on the delicate chairs with their bentwood backs of interwoven cane, his feet too clumsy to tread the flower-embroidered throw rugs.

Today, however, he overcame his feelings of ungainliness and stepped inside boldly.

"Did you need something, dear?" Pen poised, Felicity looked up from the list, absently offering her cheek to be kissed. Donal did it dutifully, but not without some enjoyment, even after all this time.

"Have you completed your guest list?" He nodded at the paper.

"I believe I have. I wanted to compare it to yours, however, to make certain we didn't duplicate and also that no one is omitted."

"I'm afraid I haven't started mine yet," he admitted. "You see…"

"Oh, Donal? Why not?" She looked a little exasperated, as if he were a child being deliberately disobedient. Almost immediately, however, her expression changed to a gentler one.

Felicity would be a good mother if the way she treated him when he didn't live up to her expectations was any evidence, he thought. That reminded him rather bluntly of his reason for being there.

"I've just received a letter from Father."

"I hope no one's ill." She turned back to the list, dipping the nib into the inkwell and studying the names a moment before writing one more.

"Everyone's fine," he replied. "Lord Alisdaire is in residence and is planning on presenting his daughter at the first ball of the Season."

"Oh?" She didn't look up.

"We've been invited," he continued. "Father wants His Lordship to meet his family. Finally. I think he's planning on currying a bit of favor, for some reason."

"That's wonderful. I'll have a chance to wear my new satin gown." She continued writing.

Donal didn't reply to that. At his silence, she looked up.

"What's the matter?"

"The ball is in two weeks…"

"…and so is my party…" She finished for him. "Oh." She glanced at him and then away.

"You see the problem." When she didn't answer but simply stared at the list, he continued, "I know how much you've been looking forward to this. I'll write Father, give my regrets, tell him we've plans which can't be changed…"

"No." With a sigh, she stopped him, laying a hand on his arm. "If Father Quinton wishes to introduce us to Lord Alisdaire, then we mustn't disappoint him. Will Colin be there?"

"Of course."

After graduation, Colin had come home to live with his parents. Quinton kept a watchful eye on his youngest, having decided he wasn't to be allowed to run wild among English females and become another Padraig. He kept track of the boy's activities in Tipperary, also.

"Then we must surely be there. We mustn't let your father down, especially if it's in regard to his employer."

That's exactly what Lord Alisdaire was, though very few people ever referred to the relationship between him and Quinton in such a way. Most merely characterized it as "Master McCoy's stewardship position."

"But the party…"

"We can postpone the party." She brushed her plans aside. "We'll simply have it when we come back. Four weeks from now will do just as well, perhaps even better since some of the flowers I wished to order won't be in full bloom until then."

"If you're certain?"

Donal didn't care one way or the other whether they went or stayed. He'd settled into being a stay-at-home, perhaps having a few people, such as Joss and his wife, over for a quiet supper on occasion. He wasn't really wild for their own parties, either. Those, both in Mayfair and at their country estate, were merely for Felicity's amusement. He simply stood around and looked elegant, and once or twice led his wife onto the dance floor, then returned to pontificate a bit before hosting his male guests into the study where they shared brandy and cigars.

"I'm certain." Thinking the matter settled, Felicity returned the pen to its holder and lifted the desktop, placing the list inside. When Donal didn't move but continued standing there, she asked, "Was there something else, dearest?"

"As a matter of fact…" Donal pulled one of the flimsy little chairs over and dropped onto it, wincing when it groaned slightly under his weight. He waited a moment, as if expecting it to collapse, and when it didn't, said, "There was more in Father's letter."

"Oh?" Felicity sounded only half-interested. She began searching through the desk, pushing aside items while holding up the lid with one hand. "Has he heard from that distant relative again?"

Our distant relative. That was how Quinton referred to Padraig now.

She shook her head. "Honestly, I don't know why he can't simply say *Padraig* and get it over with."

"Last we heard, Padraig was on his way to some place called the Nebraska Territory, and there's been no word since. Felicity," Donal caught her hand, stopping her search. "Father's again asked why we haven't had a child."

"Oh." She looked away, gently letting the davenport top close.

"Quite frankly, I'm tired of telling him to be patient. I'd really like to say it's none of his business. That's a very intimate thing and he's no right to keep hounding us about it, but…" He made a sound of defeat. "…I think we should talk about that."

"What do you mean, talk about it?"

"I mean…well…we love each other…and we make love with frightening frequency. I daresay if anyone knew how much, we'd be a scandal…but…" He stopped, taking a deep breath. "We've been married ten years now. Why don't we have a child?"

Felicity didn't answer. Donal was startled to see her face flush bright pink, then drain slowly white. She pulled her hands from his, only to have him leap to his feet and catch them again, holding them tightly.

"Are you all right? You look faint." He looked around, releasing her and waving one hand toward the bellpull. "I'll call…"

"I'm all right." She pushed him back into the chair. Again, it groaned under his weight. "I'm sorry. I didn't mean to frighten you. It's…well…it's simply that in all this time, in spite of how freely we've loved each other, that seems such a very private subject, and I suppose it startled me that you'd wish to speak of it." She gave a short laugh. "I'd imagined it would simply happen one day and we'd perpetuate the baby-under-the-cabbage-plant myth and wink and nod as everyone else does."

Donal didn't answer. He remembered how Joss had puffed out his chest like a pouter pigeon when he announced the expectation of his first son. There had been plenty of winks and nudges then…for the next two children, also. Lately, however…

Now that he thought about it, whenever Joss came

around, even when he and his wife visited, the children were always left at home, and they rarely spoke of them. Was his old friend attempting to be delicate about the lack of children in his own life?

"Do you think perhaps we should…?" Felicity was still speaking, making him give his attention back to her. "…should we consult a physician?"

"God, Felicity, could you…" *What would that involve?* He envisioned the doctor aiming a barrage of very personal and embarrassing questions at his wife. "Could you tolerate such a thing?"

"I believe I could manage." Felicity extricated her hands from his and placed them on his shoulders. She kissed him. "You know I want a family, Donal."

"I'm not acquainted with many physicians." Donal was rarely ill, even with a bout of the sniffles. On those few occasions, he'd consulted Barnell, the Melton family doctor, recommended by Uncle Roger.

"I'll arrange a call to Dr. Barnell." Felicity became very businesslike. "I'll tell him the problem and he'll take it from there."

She gave him a smile he thought a little too bright.

"Do you wish me to go with you?" Donal was unselfish enough to realize if something was amiss, it might reside with him rather than his wife.

"To hold my hand, you mean?" Felicity gave him an indulgent smile. "I assure you I don't fear physicians. Besides, I've known Dr. Barnell all my life."

"I meant…I suppose he might wish to ask me questions also."

"I hadn't thought of that." Her expression said she truly hadn't. She patted his hand. "Why don't we wait until I've seen Dr. Barnell and find out what he has to say?"

"Very well." He agreed, reluctantly.

"I suppose I should send a note to his office right now, requesting an appointment time." She reached to the back of the desk where a row of little pigeonhole drawers formed the hutch of the davenport. Pulling a box from one of the compartments, she opened it and took out a small sheet of stationary with the McCoy crest engraved in the upper left corner.

That had been an affectation of Quinton's after he became Alisdaire's steward, the blandishment of the family coat of arms, as if to remind His Lordship the McCoys had also been nobility, no matter their present demotion to gentility.

"Would you have Sewell call Charles to run this round and bring back an answer?"

"Of course." Donal turned to the door. "I'll send Father a reply, letting him know we'll be there. I suppose we should plan to arrive a few days before and stay a couple of weeks?"

Not looking up from the letter, she nodded.

"That means we'll have to start packing soon," he said. "We'll plan to have our own party when we return."

That made her look at him. Briefly, she simply sat there, before smiling gently. "Don't worry. Everything will be all right."

Donal turned away, calling to Sewell. As the butler came toward him, he wondered whether Felicity was talking about their party or about seeing the doctor.

Charles was dispatched with the letter and returned in several hours with an answer. Dr. Barnell could see her the following day around noon.

****

The next morning, Felicity rose, dressed, and shortly before the appointed time, left in the carriage, driven by Charles. Though he tried not to show it, Donal waited anxiously for her return. He refused to go to Melton, Melton, & McCoy that day, wanting to be present when she arrived home.

Little more than an hour later, Felicity was back.

Donal met her at the door, pulling her into the study as soon as she had given her pelisse to Sewell and pulled the pin from her hat.

"Well?" Immediately, he mentally flinched as he realized how worried he sounded, as well as how abrupt.

"I explained to Dr. Barnell my concerns," she replied. "He decided I should consult a specialist."

"Specialist?" Donal repeated the word as if he didn't know its meaning.

"A doctor who is trained specifically to treat female complaints and such," she explained. Pink stained her cheeks. "I take back what I said earlier. I really don't know how I managed not to blush terribly as I spoke to Dr. Barnell. Donal, how will I ever survive seeing someone who…"

"I'll go with you," he said in a rush.

"Yes, that was what I was going to say next," she replied. "Dr. Barnell said you should be there."

"Oh. I see." He felt a little taken aback by that, though he'd just volunteered.

"I'm to see him in three days."

"So soon?"

"Uncle Roger is Dr. Barnell's good friend, as well as his patient. I suppose he felt because of that he should rush things along."

"Yes, I suppose so." Donal's answer was off-handed. He rallied, lifting Felicity's hands and kissing them. "Well, I suppose we're off to see the...what's he called, anyway?"

"A gynecologist," she supplied.

"Right." He took a deep breath. "We're off to see the gynecologist on Thursday, then." He put his arm around Felicity's waist and guided her to the door. "I daresay he'll ask a few questions and set everything to rights immediately. Why don't we go into the parlor and have tea?"

In spite of his optimistic-sounding words, Donal felt a deep worry attempting to surface.

Chapter 30

Promptly at two o'clock, Donal and Felicity arrived at Dr. Blount's offices on Harley Street.

Harley Street had been part of the ninety-two acres of the Howard de Waldron estate, inherited from the Marylebone estates of the Dukes of Newcastle. Originating when Edward Harley, second Earl of Oxford and Earl Mortimer, began developing Cavendish Square and surrounds in 1715, there were now twenty physicians in residence, as well as various hospitals and clinics.

Because of its closeness to the railway stations, many well-known personages—artists, including J.M.W. Turner and Allan Ramsay, and politicians—lived there. It was also near Queen's College, a school for young women, which had been founded a few years previous.

Blount's surgery was rather quiet and understated in its location on the Street, as well as in its décor. Donal was surprised to see no carriages waiting about, other than their own. They went up the steps and into the building, walking into a small and well-lit but empty reception room.

"Are you certain we've come on the right day?" he asked, placing his hat on a nearby rack as he looked around at the comfortably arranged chairs and couches, and a door beyond, shut so there was no indication where it led.

"I'm sure," Felicity replied. She hung up her pelisse, also. "Thursday, at two in the afternoon. That's what Dr. Barnell said."

"Could he have meant next Thursday?" Donal questioned.

Before she could answer, the other door opened and a short, well-dressed man looked in.

"Mr. and Mrs. McCoy?" As Donal nodded, he continued, "I'm Dr. John Blount. Hope you haven't been waiting long."

"Only a few moments," Donal answered. He decided Blount, pink-cheeked and stout, looked more like his idea of Saint Nicholas, minus the white beard, than a physician.

"Please, come into my office." Blount stepped back, gesturing for them to precede him through the door.

They entered a short corridor as well-lit as the waiting room had been, the walls holding paintings as well as sconces converted to gaslight. He led them across the hall and into a small room with a desk, more comfortable chairs, and several bookcases.

The place was very neat. On the desk, there was an inkwell set and a large desk protector and blotter. Several folders lay to one side, neatly stacked. Incongruously, next to the folders, there was a small brass bell sitting on a little marble base. Donal was glad to see there was no articulated human skeleton hanging from a stand or anything else indicating this was a physician's office, not even a copy of Rembrandt's painting *The Anatomy Lesson.*

"We thought at first perhaps we'd come on the wrong day or were in the wrong place," he said. "The waiting room was so empty."

"My surgery is closed on Thursdays," Blount explained. When they looked surprised, he continued, "In cases of an infertility consultation, since it's such a sensitive subject, I generally have the couple come in on Thursdays. That way it's more discreet."

"That's very thoughtful," Felicity murmured, a faint flush touching her cheeks.

"The last thing I wish to do is cause anyone more discomfort," Blount answered. "There's usually enough of that already." He gestured to the two chairs before the desk, going around it. "Please be seated."

As Donal waited for Felicity to settle herself, then dropped into the other chair, the doctor picked up two of the folders, and opened them. Laying them side by side, he studied the first one.

"I've a copy of Dr. Barnell's medical notes on both of you. He was good enough to send them over."

"Yes," Felicity spoke up. "He asked my permission to do so while I was with him."

Blount nodded. "It says here you're twenty-eight, Mrs. McCoy?"

She nodded.

"You, Mr. McCoy, are thirty-five."

Donal nodded also, then, since the doctor was still looking down, said, "That's right."

"You've been married ten years and this is the first marriage for both of you."

"Yes. As a matter of fact…" Felicity caught Donal's hand. "Our tenth anniversary is coming up soon."

"Congratulations." The doctor looked up and smiled. "I've read through both case histories and I see nothing that stands out as a problem. Both of you seem to have managed to avoid having most of the childhood illnesses."

"We were fortunate," Donal said.

"Quite so, though if you were to contract them now, it might go bad with you," Blount pointed out. "Not to frighten you, but childhood diseases in adults can sometimes have a dire effect."

"Then I hope we manage to stay lucky," Donal murmured.

"Exactly." Blount looked up. "You've had few mishaps, also. In fact, the only thing I'd characterize as any kind of trauma at all was when you were thrown from your horse, Mrs. McCoy, when you were thirteen."

"You never mentioned that." Donal looked at Felicity, telling himself he shouldn't be worried now, since that incident had happened fifteen years before. Nevertheless, it was a bit of a shock, hearing of it now.

"It wasn't so bad," Felicity replied. "I was learning to jump. The hurdle was too high and my horse balked. I was also learning to ride sidesaddle and had a very unsteady seat. I sailed over his head and landed on the top cross-pole. It struck me in the…" She stopped, gesturing vaguely at her pelvic area. "…here. I wasn't really hurt, just badly bruised." She laughed. "For several weeks, I could barely move without crying."

"I'm glad that was all," Donal said, relaxing. "I suppose it's a good thing I didn't know before. Otherwise, I'd forbid you horseback riding at all."

"I suppose we should get started." Blount picked up the bell from his desk and shook it. It made a high-pitched but loud tinkling.

Almost immediately, the door to the right opened and a young woman came in. She wore what appeared to be a maid's uniform except that it was light blue and the pinafore apron over it was plain and had two large patch pockets.

"Yes, Father?" She stopped, hands clasped together in front of her.

"This is my daughter, Annabel," Blount said.

She nodded.

"She's my nursing assistant, as well as my secretary and clerk. I daresay my practice would suffer greatly without her."

"Please, Father, that's embarrassing." Nevertheless, Annabel looked pleased.

"Would you show Mrs. McCoy into the examination room?"

"Examination?" Felicity started slightly. "You mean you'll…"

"Don't worry, my dear. Since this part of the office visit is rather extensive and personal, I employ a midwife. I assure you, she's very experienced and I trust her diagnoses completely."

Felicity relaxed.

Holding out her hand, Annabel said, "Would you come this way, please, Mrs. McCoy?"

As Felicity stood, so did Donal.

"Oh, not you, Mr. McCoy," Blount said.

Donal looked at him questioningly.

"I'm afraid neither you nor I will be privy to this portion of the visit."

Donal sat down again, watching Felicity walk with Annabel into the other room. The door shut.

"Now then…" Blount took a sheet of foolscap out of a drawer, placing it in the second folder. "If you'll come with me, sir?"

"Am I to be examined also?" Donal told himself he shouldn't be surprised. Nevertheless, he was.

"Certainly," Blount answered, getting up from his desk and gesturing to a door on the left side of the room. He opened it and allowed Donal to walk through ahead of him. "I'm not one of those physicians who immediately assume childlessness is the wife's fault."

He followed Donal inside and shut the door.

"I hope that doesn't insult you." He laid the folder on a nearby table.

Near the door was a coat tree on which a white coat hung. Taking off his own frockcoat, Blount dropped it over a hook, took down the other, and put it on. That made him look less like St. Nick and more like a physician. He also took a pair of white cotton gloves from a pocket and pulled them on.

Picking up something lying folded on the table, he held it out.

"You'll need to change into this. You may do so behind there."

Donal took the item, shaking it open. It looked like a nightshirt, except it was completely open from neck to hem. There was a single button at the neck and one at the waist. He looked over his shoulder. In a corner of the room stood a tall dressing screen, a rather plain and utilitarian one, with two connected metal frames draped in white muslin. He walked behind it. The other side of the screen held a small stool and another coat tree.

"I didn't realize I'd have to undress," he said as he bent to slide off his boots.

"I do a very thorough exam," Blount replied. "Can't do that with trousers, a vest, and coat in the way."

"I suppose not." Donal carefully hung coat, vest, and

shirt on various hooks, then folded his trousers and placed them and his small clothes on the stool.

He held up the item Blount had given him, wondering if Felicity was even then dressed in a similar garment. He slid it on, buttoning the neck.

"Excuse me if I appear awkward," he said as he emerged, struggling to close the button at the waist. It was clumsy. "As you commented, I haven't been ill all that much, and I'm a bit ignorant of what a physical examination involves."

"Just sit there, please." Blount gestured at a chair. "Don't worry. Most men who've gone through this find it a bit daunting."

That wasn't the least encouraging. Donal didn't answer. He dropped into the chair. The shirt-front gaped and he awkwardly held it closed.

Blount sat in another chair, opening a drawer in the table, taking out something. The item was about a foot long, slightly resembling a very thin trumpet with a narrow flaring rim on one end.

"I say, is that thing made of ivory?"

"Why, yes, it is." Blount held up the item as if surprised Donal might recognize the material. "This is a cardiac auscultator, or a cardiac ear trumpet, if you will. It will enable me to listen to your heart and lungs and determine if they are working properly."

"My father's physician in Tipperary uses one of those, but his has a flexible tube. He called it a snake ear trumpet." Donal laughed ruefully. "As a child, I was always frightened of the thing. I kept expecting it to rear up and bite me."

Blount joined in with a quick laugh. "I assure you this one doesn't bite." He pushed the trumpet through the opening at the neck of the shirt, pressing the flared rib against Donal's chest. "Just breathe normally and don't speak.'"

Placing the other end of the trumpet against his ear, he leaned forward, listening intently. Abruptly, he straightened, nodded, and sat back.

"Normal heart rhythm. Very steady. Lungs sound good, too. Do you indulge in tobacco?"

"A cigar now and then. Nothing else." Donal murmured and wondered why he added that.

He and Joss had tried opium once but the lethargic disinterest and apathy resulting was something neither liked. Donal never wanted to feel he wasn't in control. He realized that, at this moment, he was definitely not in control. It wasn't a good sensation.

In short order, Blount checked his pulse, used a clinical thermometer to determine his temperature, palpated his throat and chest, and peered into his eyes.

Retrieving the folder, he rested it on a knee.

"Now then…" He'd found a pencil somewhere and scribbled on the sheet of paper in the folder, then sat with writing instrument poised. "I've a few questions."

"Certainly." Donal settled himself a little more into the chair. He started to cross his legs, then realized that wasn't too feasible while wearing that nightshirt thing.

"You were twenty-four when you married?"

"Twenty-five, actually. I managed a birthday during my courting." He'd barely noticed that and certainly hadn't celebrated it.

"Hm." Blount wrote. "College man?"

"That's right. Cambridge." Donal wondered what his education had to do with anything.

"This is going to be a very personal question, Mr.

McCoy."

The way the doctor said that made Donal unconsciously tense. He waited, not speaking.

"How sexually active have you been outside your marriage? Beginning with your first encounter and up to the present?"

"That is definitely a personal question." Donal allowed himself to become slightly insulted. "One I might question why you're asking."

"I suppose you have that right." Blount didn't appear worried by his anger. "I know how wild university lads can be, as well as young adult men...curious as well as experimental. I was once one myself. The question isn't mere curiosity but medically pertinent. I'm simply trying to ascertain if you placed yourself in danger of contracting some of the more malignant diseases of Venus."

"Dis..." Donal couldn't get the rest of the word out. He sat there, staring at the doctor.

"Some of those can cause sterility, as you may or may not be aware," Blount went on, mildly.

"Doctor, I assure you I've never put myself in harm's way where that factor is concerned." Donal realized he sounded completely prudish as he spoke.

"Surely you weren't a virgin when you wed?"

"At the age of twenty-five?" He nearly laughed at that absurdity. "No, but..." Why not simply admit it. He sighed. "While I was at Cambridge, I was no worse than any other youngster away from home and free for the first time. I'll admit I was a bit of a rake later, however. For three years before my marriage, I had a mistress but didn't limit myself to her. From the moment of my marriage to Felicity, however, I ceased all...uh...outside activity. I've been faithful to my wife since I placed that ring on her finger."

"In that case, you're to be commended." Blount looked unapologetic for eliciting this confession from him. He made more notes. "Did you practice birth and disease prevention?"

Donal didn't answer. He merely nodded. This was something he hadn't spoken of to anyone since that last argument with Nell. His thoughts shied like a frightened horse as an image of his long-ago mistress forced itself into his mind.

"What type?" the doctor persisted. "*Coitus interruptus*, the *préventif français*…"

"Yes, the latter." He couldn't bring himself to say it.

Blount wrote. He set down pencil and folder and looked up. "Now, Mr. McCoy, I must examine your genitalia."

"My…what?" Donal's voice went up. He swallowed, forcing his next words into a lower register. "I mean, is that really necessary? I assure you I'm fully capable of…" He gestured awkwardly. "…my…uh…marital duties."

"I'm afraid so." Blount made his answer sound so reasonable. "As much as I wish to believe you, I must determine you're telling me the truth as far as any exposure to a pox is concerned. Personal examination is the only way." He smiled slightly. "Please, don't take umbrage."

Donal surprised himself by smiling in return. "I understand, sir. However, I wish to say I'm unaccustomed to having my Percy fondled by anyone of the male gender, so excuse me if I flinch." He gestured as if surrendering. "What do I do?"

"Understood." Blount nodded. "You simply move your legs apart slightly."

As Donal obeyed, the doctor leaned forward, lifted the tail of the shirt, and folded it back over his thighs.

The examination was thorough but quick, and Donal thanked God for that. Blount's gloved fingers palpated his testicles, felt the length of his shaft, slid back his foreskin, and inspected the glans. His touch, though impersonal, was nevertheless disturbing. The doctor didn't laugh as Donal flinched slightly and reddened when his rod reacted by stiffening.

"I-I'm sorry…I assure you…" Donal tried to give a rationalization. All that came out was a mumble.

"Don't worry," Blount answered. "Unfortunately, the privates can't differentiate between a physician's examination and a lover's touch, though the brain can."

He unfolded the shirt, dropping it over Donal's knees, and sat back.

"It appears you're perfectly normal, and free from any disease. I know…" He held up a hand as Donal started to speak. "…you said so, but… Now, one last thing…"

He turned, took two small glass beakers from the table, holding them out.

Donal studied them, cautiously took both, and asked, "What am I supposed to do with these?"

"I wish a urine sample in that one." Blount pointed to the beaker in his left hand. "And a sample of your regenerative fluid in this." He tapped the one in Donal's right hand.

Donal took a deep breath. "Dr. Blount, I daresay you may think this necessary, and I'll gladly give you this one." He held up the left beaker. "But the other? Sir, I

278

don't…"

"I swear to you, this isn't mere prurience on my part, but a necessary part of the examination if I am to give you a thorough and honest diagnosis."

"In that case…" Donal got to his feet. "May I ask you to allow me the privacy of performing this…action…out of sight?"

Blount nodded, as if expecting this request.

Donal walked behind the screen. Setting the two vials on the floor, he carefully removed his clothing and hat from the stool, and sat upon it.

"I'd truly prefer to be alone for this." He raised his voice slightly.

"I can understand how you might consider this an invasion of privacy, Mr. McCoy."

He heard Blount get to his feet and open the door.

"I'll wait in my office. Simply call me when you've finished."

The door shut.

Oh God. Filling the urine cup was easy enough. The wish to get it over with made the flow quick, but the other? Nothing.

Considering himself so unusually sensitive that the mere brush of a hand roused him, Donal now didn't respond at all.

What am I going to do?

He forced a vision of Felicity lying on their bed in beautifully naked slumber. He thought of the things they did in the privacy of their bedchamber, of the stirring blood when he loved and worshipped her body as she in turn did his. Feeling he profaned the pleasure they shared, he managed to accomplish what the doctor requested.

He thanked God Blount had left the room and wasn't present to hear his groan of relief as he finished.

Afterward, he sat on the stool waiting for his shaking limbs to regain strength and his rapid breathing to lessen as he stared at the two beakers, at the pale amber liquid in one and the milky substance in the other. At last, he stood, picked up the glasses, and walked around the screen and to the door. Setting the beakers on the table, he opened the door.

"Doctor?"

Blount, in mid-stride, stopped pacing before the door. Without speaking, he came back in, immediately taking the beakers and carrying them over to another table at the back of the room, a table Donal hadn't noticed before. On the table was an odd instrument consisting of a downward-slanting rod with a rounded cup on the top. It was attached to a stand and a mirror with a candle behind it.

Taking a small pipette with a suction blub on the end, he drew out a small amount of urine, dropped it onto a glass square, and set the piece under the end of the rod. Then he leaned over it, placing his eye against the rounded cup. He moved the candle and magnifying glass back and forth.

"No problems there," he announced.

The same procedure was accomplished for the other material, after which Blount straightened and gestured to the rod. "Would you care to look? Since this came from your body, you have the right to see what it contains."

Cautiously, Donal placed one eye against the cup as the doctor had. At first, he didn't see anything except a dark spot. Then Blount moved the candle slightly and a mass of squirming, wiggly things, looking like nothing more than minute tadpoles, sprang toward his eye. He jerked backward, realized he was seeing what was on the glass square and looked again.

It was fascinating…and shocking.

He straightened. "That was in my… What are they?"

"Sperm, my dear Mr. McCoy. The partial essence of life."

"Each of those…things…contains the body of a complete human being?" He couldn't believe it, bent to take another look.

"If you're thinking of *preformation*," the doctor said. "I'm not certain of that theory. Some people believe there's more to creating a child than the material you yourself supply. I'm one of those. I believe the wife also offers something. A child comes from two people, not simply one while the other carries it."

Realizing Donal was staring at him, he laughed slightly.

"Sorry. I'm getting on one of my soapboxes again."

"As you get off your soapbox, Doctor, tell me what *that* means." Donal gestured at the microscope.

"It means that it appears there's an abundance of those little swimmers. You're an extremely fertile man, Mr. McCoy. Congratulations. You could people a small village all by yourself."

Before he could stop himself, Donal sighed. Blount smiled.

"Now then, I'll leave you to get dressed. The midwife should be finished with her exam by now. I'll review her report and I should have an answer for you."

He went out.

Donal hurried behind the screen, dressing as quickly as possible. He paused before a little mirror on the wall to make certain he was presentable, then went through the door back into Blount's office.

Chapter 31

When Donal emerged from the exam room, he found Felicity sitting in the same chair as before. She was calm, not a hair out of place, her clothing smooth and unwrinkled, no evidence she'd been through any such near-humiliation as he had. He wondered again what exactly the midwife did in the way of an examination, then decided he didn't want to know. Felicity didn't appear ruffled or embarrassed in any way, so perhaps it wasn't as shameful as what he'd gone through.

"Come in, Mr. McCoy. Sit, please." Blount looked up from reading a paper covered with short sentences.

As Donal took his seat beside Felicity, she gave him a quick, anxious smile.

Blount continued to read, frowning slightly. Abruptly, the frown deepened, changing to a scowl. He read a few more lines, sighed, and looked up, closing the folder. His gaze traveled from Donal to Felicity but he didn't speak.

"Well, Doctor?" Donal couldn't stand it any longer.

"Mr. McCoy…Mrs. McCoy…" For the first time, the doctor looked hesitant.

"What is it?" Felicity asked, abruptly alarmed.

"I'm afraid I have bad news."

"Bad news? How can that be?" Donal shook his head. "You said I…"

"I'm afraid it isn't you, Mr. McCoy." He looked at Felicity.

Donal's heart sank. *No. Oh God, no.*

"That riding accident you had as a child…"

"It was nothing." Felicity shook her head, denying something, but looking as if she wasn't certain what. "Dr. Barnell said I was all right."

"I'm afraid Dr. Barnell was wrong." Blount's tone became gentle, as if he were speaking to a small, frightened child. "According to Mrs. Patrick's report, you have something called ovarian adhesions."

"Wh-what's that?" Felicity's voice trembled.

"Apparently when your body struck the cross-pole, you had massive internal bruising. There was barely an outward sign of trauma, but inside…" He paused, closed his eyes briefly, then opened them to give her an apologetic look. "Your reproductive organs were so damaged, they quite literally became bonded together and atrophied. You've never had regular courses, have you?" He asked that very quietly.

She shook her head. "I have…uh…cramps…for a few days. I lie down and they go away." She looked stricken. "I thought that was the way it was supposed to be."

"Unfortunately, that isn't the case." Blount sighed and said the fatal words. "I'm afraid you can never have a child. Mrs. McCoy."

He stopped as Felicity put a hand to her mouth and bowed her head. Donal slid forward in his chair, putting his arms around her. He pulled her body against his.

"Is there no way to…"

"I'm afraid not. There's nothing to be done. In fact, there may be future danger of a cancer of some kind developing, and if that happens, removal of the affected organs will be necessary."

"Oh no…" Felicity's moan of despair stabbed into Donal's heart.

"Come, sweetheart." He stood, pulling Felicity with him. "Please forgive me, Doctor. I fear I should take my wife home. This has been quite a shock."

Blount rose and came around the desk.

"I understand." His hand on Donal's shoulder was gentle. He looked as if he were suffering as much as Felicity.

"Please send me your statement. I'll see it's paid." With a nod, Donal hurried Felicity out.

She stumbled alongside him, not making a sound. In the reception room, they paused only long enough for Donal to retrieve his hat and her pelisse.

Charles gave them both a startled look as he saw them leave the office. Like a good servant, he didn't comment as he opened the door so they could climb into the carriage.

Felicity stayed silent until they reached home. Once there, Donal helped her from the carriage. She pulled away from him and hurried inside.

By the time he finished giving instructions to Charles and was in the foyer, he saw Sewell putting her pelisse and bonnet into the closet and Felicity disappearing up the stairs. Thrusting his hat at the butler, he followed.

She'd gone into their bedroom. As Donal entered, he saw she was emptying the drawers of the dresser he'd moved into the room for her things. Pantalets, chemises, and stockings lay on the bed in a mad jumble as if flung wildly.

"What are you doing?"

She went to the wardrobe, pausing in pulling a dress off a hanger. "I'm moving my things to the other bedroom."

"In God's name, why?"

"Because having marital relations is primarily for the creation of a child. Because I can't give you a child. Because you'll no longer want me since I'm…flawed."

"Don't say that."

"I swear I didn't know, Donal." She looked away, continuing to fumble with the dress in her hands. "Perhaps it will be best if we…separate. I'll leave."

"What?" He couldn't believe what she'd said. "Where would you go?"

"Home. I'm certain Mother and Uncle Roger will take me back, and then…I… If you wish to divorce me and find someone more…suitable…"

"For God's sake, Felicity." He caught her, pulling her away from the wardrobe, jerking the dress from her hands and tossing it back inside. "I love you. I don't give a damn what the primary reason for marital relations is. If it's some kind of sin to want to love my wife whether it produces issue or not, then I'm a sinner of the first order. Because I love you and I'll continue loving you no matter what."

He caught her chin in his hand, turning her head. She looked at him with those pale eyes swimming in tears.

"If it's to be only you and me, then that's the way it'll be. I don't care. It would be good to have a child, but it's not necessary. If Father demands a grandchild, he can get it from Colin or Padraig or Bridie. I have you and that's all I want." He shook her gently. "Do you understand?"

She leaned against him, sobbing. Donal put his arms around her. He held her until the tears stopped and she stood silent in his embrace.

"Come on." He guided her to the bed, pushed her to sit upon it, and knelt to unbutton her shoes and lay them aside. Turning her, he opened the back of her dress, maneuvered aside the corset cover, and loosened her laces. Hands on her shoulders, he pushed her onto the pillows. "Lie down. Rest. This has been a trying experience."

Felicity didn't answer, didn't make a sound except to exhale a watery sigh. He brushed back her hair, kissed her on the forehead, and said, "I'll have Mrs. Harris make tea. You rest. After you've calmed a bit, we'll sit in the parlor…and talk."

She managed a nod, then rolled over, hugging the pillow.

Donal tiptoed out. He went down the stairs to his study. Sewell saw him and followed.

"Is everything all right, sir? Mrs. McCoy looked a bit discommoded."

"I'll explain later, Sewell." Donal didn't feel like talking just then. He threw himself into a chair.

Sewell was aware where they had gone, but not the reason. *Am I supposed to let the staff know? How the hell do I say something like that?*

"For now, pour me a brandy, have some tea brewed for Mrs. McCoy, and then don't bother me for a while."

"Yes, sir." Sewell obeyed. Setting a small snifter by Donal's elbow, he went out, closing the door behind him.

Donal didn't drink the brandy right away. He sat staring into the fireplace, seeing again Felicity's tear-stained face, feeling once more that icy stab of lost hope as he heard the doctor's words. *I'm afraid you can never have a child, Mrs. McCoy.*

There must be something we can do…but what? For the moment he couldn't think, brain drowning in despair, not for himself but for his beloved wife.

Chapter 32

There must be some way.

For quite some time Donal simply sat there, that stricken look on Felicity's face rushing again and again through his mind. At last, he seized the glass and gulped down the brandy, not savoring it at all, barely feeling its burn. Picking up the decanter Sewell had placed on the table, he poured another glassful and drank it also.

There must be a way. It wasn't fair that Felicity be denied a child, or the right to be a mother, when other women, women who didn't want children, who wouldn't be loving mothers, could…

…Nell's face flashed into his mind.

Nell didn't want my child…

He hadn't thought about her in years and now, twice in one day. He wondered if he should've admitted to Blount he'd already fathered a child. That would've immediately put the blame on Felicity, without all the examinations and such.

Perhaps he had to be slightly drunk to see the answer.

Getting to his feet, Donal set down the glass so sharply he swore he heard the crystal crack. He was out the door and up the stairs, taking them two at a time, not giving himself a chance to think and perhaps talk himself out of what he knew was a harebrained scheme even as he thought it…because he hoped it might work, if it didn't mean the end to his marriage.

He didn't knock at the door but slammed against it, throwing it open and dashing inside.

"Felicity."

Lying on the bed, she jerked slightly at his call and pushed herself upright.

"Donal? What is it?" Her voice was full but drowsy.

She raised the little handkerchief she held to her face. He imagined she'd cried herself to sleep.

"Felicity…" He fell to his knees by the bed, taking her hands and holding them tightly. "I've an answer, if you're willing. If you don't decide to leave me."

"What in the world are you talking about? Why should *I* wish to leave *you*?" Her laugh was sad as well as sardonic. "I should think it's the other way around."

"Didn't I say don't talk like that?" He brushed any thought of their separating aside. "I want no one but you, but when I tell you, you may decide you don't want *me*."

"Donal, you're not making sense."

"Just hear me out, and then…"

"I'm listening." She was staring at him as if she thought he'd gone a little mad.

Perhaps he had.

"First, I've a confession to make. That's the preface to everything."

"Donal, what could you possibly…" She was confused.

She'd every right to be, he admitted.

"Listen."

"Very well but get off your knees. Sit by me."

Still clasping her hands, he dropped onto the bed. "Felicity…" How to say it? No gentle way, just blurt it out. He took a deep breath. "Before we married, I kept a woman."

She didn't speak, eyes widening.

"During our courtship, every time I left you, I went to her." He hurried on, trying to get it all said before she denounced him.

"Donal, why?"

"Because I was a fool, I suppose. That's the only reason I can find. I was afraid to admit I was falling in love with you and I used her to deny it." He saw disbelief and what he supposed was the shock of anger on her face. He went on desperately, "After we were married, I realized I wanted no one but you and when we returned to London, I decided to tell her so."

"That business you had shortly after we returned?" she guessed.

"I went to see her with the specific purpose of breaking off with her. She told me she was with child. She wanted money to get rid of it."

"Oh, Donal!" The horror of such an act twisted her expression.

"I didn't know what to do. I couldn't…" He shook his head. "I know it was cowardly, but I decided I had to tell Father."

"That's why we made that sudden trip to Tipperary, and why he and your mother came back with us." Felicity said that as if she now understood a great deal.

He nodded. "Father paid her to go away and never get in touch with me."

"Why are you telling me this now? I didn't know. You kept it hidden well. Why confess at this late date?"

It was almost the same thing Quinton had asked him that day in his study.

"Because I've always been filled with remorse about

the child," he admitted. "I know she didn't want it and she's probably only tolerating it because of Father's cheques. Because… Felicity, if I could find that child and bring it here, could you find it in your heart to love it?"

"That's asking quite a lot, Donal."

To his ears, her voice sounded cold.

"If you say you won't, then I beg you not to leave me, but to forgive me." *I'll grovel, if I have to. I mustn't lose you.*

To his surprise, she smiled, hand going to his cheek. "I love you, Donal. If you bring your child here…It might be difficult to love another woman's baby, but I know I can love that part of you that is in it. How could I not?"

"Then you'd want it? If it can be found?"

"You say *It*. Was it a boy or a girl?"

"I never knew," he admitted. "She was forbidden notifying me."

"Do it, Donal." Felicity's eyes were lit with a brilliant flaring of what he could only call *hope*. "Find your child and let's raise it as it should be…as a gentleman's offspring."

"When did I get so lucky?" He caught her hand, kissing it.

"If you don't know where she went and haven't heard from her in all this time, how will you find them?" Felicity became abruptly practical.

"I've heard there are people in London who can be hired to do that sort of thing," Donal's answer was vague. He'd already realized the bank probably wouldn't tell him anything. "I'll ask around. Someone will know. Joss." He brightened. "I'll ask Joss. He knows all sorts of things."

****

"You want to do what?" Joss's look was comical with astonishment.

"I need to find someone," Donal repeated patiently.

"Who?" Joss finished his wine. "Has your footman run off with the good silver?"

"I'd rather not say."

"Secret, eh?" Joss pretended hurt. "Well now, Don. I think you know you can trust me. After all we've done together? At this point in our lives, I'm the keeper of more keys to secrets than I wish."

He held up his empty glass.

"Nevertheless, I feel the fewer people knowing about this, the better. Are you aware of anyone who can be hired to do this sort of…uh…enquiry work?" Donal carefully refilled Joss's glass.

"As a matter of fact, I do. One of my father's clerks absconded with a small amount. Chap found the cove in two days. He's now working off paying back the money out of his wages. Papa wouldn't have him arrested, didn't want the scandal known." Joss set down his glass and steepled his fingers, peering over them at Donal. "Shall I get in touch with him?"

"If you would." Donal was startled by the gratitude in his voice.

|Joss frowned but pretended not to hear that.

"Gent's name is Doyle. He was a Peeler, stationed at Whitehall Place, what they're now calling Scotland Yard. Inspector, I think. Retired but got bored so he opened an enquiry agency. *Private Consulting and Investigations*." Joss raised his glass in a salute, then drank it down. "I'll send word round to him tonight."

Chapter 33

"Mr. McCoy, there a gentleman to see you." Sewell presented the tray on which a small cream-colored card lay.

Donal took the card, studying it intently. Good stock paper, delicate cream color, ink black in a simple but elegant font. It wasn't a business card but had only a name engraved upon it. *Sean Michael Doyle, Esquire.*

It had been four days since he'd spoken to Joss, and he despaired of hearing from the enquiry agent, thinking his friend had decided not to get mixed up in what might become a sordid affair. Though Joss seemed to accept that Donal refused to tell him because he wanted to keep everything as quiet as possible, his residual guilt built a wild and distorted scenario wherein Joss found out, told everyone, and he and Felicity were driven from London, the aftermath of which was that Felicity divorced him and he returned to Tipperary in disgrace to be disowned by his father. It was a close approximation to the way he'd felt as he traveled home after Nell's announcement.

Common sense told Donal Joss would never do such a thing, but his own conscience insisted he might.

Doyle, ushered in by Sewell, was nothing like he expected. He was a rather short man, with fairly regular but nondescript features, his name and coloring indicating him to be dark Irish. He was dressed in somber but somewhat stylish clothing and wearing a low-crowned hat. That surprised Donal, who'd thought to see someone in a derby and clothed in a garish houndstooth-check and ill-cut suit accompanied by hobnailed boots. Doyle's boots were highly polished Wellingtons.

"Sean Doyle, sir." He held out a hand which Donal accepted, noting the firmness of his grasp.

His delivery was nothing as expected, either, for he spoke with the received pronunciation of an English-educated Irishman, similar to Donal's own speech.

"Oxford?" Donal wondered aloud.

"Cambridge." Doyle smiled. "Matriculated there, as did you, if I'm correct."

Donal didn't ask how he knew. He decided Joss had told him, that they were old school chums, though Doyle might've investigated him before coming round, or perhaps he was trained to detect education from accents. He had no idea what a man from the Yard was trained to do.

"Please, sit." He gestured at a nearby chair.

"Thank you." Doyle eased himself into the chair, continuing, "Rather disappointed my parents when I decided to become a Bobbie and then got myself promoted to Scotland Yard's upper forces, but they accepted it and were rather proud finally of my achievements, I believe." He smiled, as if realizing he was straying from the purpose of his visit. "But I digress. Mr. Joselyn said you've someone you wish found?"

He reached into a breast pocket and brought out a small notebook. Opening it and taking out a little stub of a pencil, he held it poised over the blank page.

"That's correct." Donal explained the hows and whyfores, glossing over as much as possible, thankful Doyle didn't press him. Except for asking a question to clarify some remark, he didn't speak, though he wrote swiftly in what appeared to be some type of shortened script of his own devising.

When Donal finished, he said, "Neither you nor your father have heard from her in all this time?"

"She was instructed to notify only the bank of the child's birth and that it lived," Donal answered. "She was never to contact either of us."

"Hm." The sound was rather neutral, telling Donal nothing. "Which bank was that?"

"Barclay's," Donal told him. "My father has both business and personal accounts there, as do I. He never told me how he handled it, but I think he set up some kind of Trust from which the bank could issue funds on the strength of his signed permission."

"That's good to know," Doyle said. He placed the pencil inside the notebook, closed it, and returned it to his pocket. "Well, I'll see what I can do. When I find out anything, shall I come in person or will you wish a written report?"

Donald considered. "I suppose progress reports can be done by letter." He didn't want the servants getting curious and wondering why a stranger kept coming round. "The final one…when…*if* you find her, should be done in person."

"Don't worry, Mr. McCoy." Doyle stood, offering his hand again.

Once more, Donal considered that firm handshake and hoped it indicated a steadfast type who wouldn't stop until he was successful at the task given him.

"I'll find her. As we used to say at the Yard, *Doyle's on the case*." He winked. "I had a ninety-nine percent success rate."

Here's hoping this isn't the one percent you couldn't solve, Donal thought as he rang for Sewell to show Doyle out.

He told himself he should feel optimistic. He'd hired a man who was confident he could find Nell, but… *He's trying to find a woman who disappeared ten years ago. The bank's the only one knowing where she went. He won't be able to simply walk in and ask where those cheques are being sent. That's confidential information and they aren't going to tell. What can he find out?*

Donal felt he had truly sent Sean Doyle on a wild goose chase.

Chapter 34

Time for their departure for Tipperary neared with
no word from Doyle. Donal tried to stifle his
disappointment. He'd hoped to have the matter settled
before seeing his father, wanting to announce his plan to
Quinton even if he had to lie to the rest of the family. He
doubted the falsehood of adoption of an orphan would be
believed. His mother and Colin would see through his
fabrications as soon as they set eyes on the child, but
what did that matter if everyone else believed it?

He'd already formed a picture of the child in his
mind. Regardless of its gender, it would be his image,
with only a lingering likeness to Nell. Perhaps, if a
daughter, it might have her small stature, but otherwise,
it would have his hair color and his green eyes.

However it looked, he was going to love it and that,
with Felicity's assurance she would also, made him
impatient to learn whether he had a son or daughter, so
he could begin planning its future…whether he would
send it to Eton and Cambridge or to a school for young
ladies before arranging a fortuitous marriage.

Felicity had gone about her packing and then settled
herself in her study to begin making plans for accepting
the young stranger into their lives. Donal himself was
realistic enough to have a few misgivings.

The child would be nearly ten years old and have
lived in a fatherless home all those years. He refused to

believe there would be a stepfather in the picture, but if there was, he'd have no legal claim.

What if he doesn't want to leave his mother? From what he remembered of Nell, he couldn't conceive her being sacrificing and loving enough to make anyone not a cynical adult want to stay with her. *What if he hates me, holds my abandonment against me and refuses to accept me?* That might happen. *Wouldn't that be ironic? We accept the child but the child won't accept us...no, not us,* for he couldn't believe anyone wouldn't like Felicity. *Won't accept* me?

Studying Felicity's happiness, Donal adopted her optimism. *He'll love me, I'm his father. He'll forgive me and understand. He'll fit in and we'll be the happy family we should be.*

That's why the silence from Doyle was so nerve-wracking, though he pretended otherwise. In spite of his earlier doubts, he'd now convinced himself the enquiry agent would have no trouble picking up Nell's trail and finding his quarry. Hadn't he said he had a ninety-nine percent success rate in the cases he'd solved for the Yard?

Nevertheless, the day they were to leave for the ship bound for Ireland came closer and closer, and still there was no word.

****

"Mr. McCoy?" Sewell stood in the study doorway. "That gentleman who was here a few weeks ago. Mr. Doyle? He's back, requesting to see you."

"Certainly, Sewell." Donal struggled to keep the eagerness out of his voice. "Send him in. By all means."

It was the day before they were to leave. Donal had finished his packing and was in his study, enjoying a glass of wine while waiting for supper to be announced. He stood, setting the glass he held on the mantel shelf. *Thank God. At last.* He turned to face the door as Sewell returned to the entrance.

It took only a few moments for the butler to usher Doyle into the study. Without being told, he pulled shut the door as he had on the agent's first visit, leaving them in privacy.

"Doyle, come in." Donal came forward, offering his hand, which the agent grasped, then released. "I haven't received any progress reports." He laughed slightly. "I thought perhaps you'd given up and were hesitant to admit it."

"Oh, I've made progress," Doyle replied. His tone sounded slightly rueful, however.

"Please, be seated." Donal gestured to a chair.

The agent hesitated as if uncertain. His manner seemed tentative and slightly abstracted, making a vague uneasiness stir in Donal's mind.

"This was a fairly simple case, so I thought rather than sending you a progress report, I'd simply come round and give my findings in person." Doyle sat. He fell silent.

"Well?" Donal tried to keep the eagerness out of his tone and knew he failed.

"Well…" Briefly, the agent looked anywhere except at Donal, before meeting his gaze directly. "I've completed my search."

Again, he stopped.

"And?" Donal was confused by this odd hesitancy, as well as a little perturbed. *What is it? Why can't he simply say what he has to say?* "Did you find her? Frankly, I thought you'd have a bit of difficulty."

300

"As I said, it was fairly simple, if one knew who to go to," Doyle answered. He still held his hat, hadn't given it to Sewell, and now studied it, rolling it around and around in his hands, instead of looking at Donal. "I have a contact at the bank. I asked him to do a bit of unauthorized checking on your father's accounts, and it was easy enough to get the address of where the cheques were being sent."

"So much for confidentiality, then." Donal laughed. "I daresay the bank wouldn't be happy if they knew they had an employee who was also working for you."

"I assure you the man immediately forgot whatever he found," Doyle said, very seriously.

"Of course." Impatient to learn more, Donal brushed that aside.

"In fact, what I learned at the bank made any further inquiry unnecessary, but I decided to follow through to make absolutely certain. Thoroughness, you know."

That was an odd statement but Donal chose not to question it. He waited.

Doyle removed that little notebook from his pocket. Opening it, he read from a page.

"A week after Miss Nordin left London, the bank was notified she would be living in Littleton-on-Thames, a small town some fifty miles from here. It's not really on the Thames but situated on a riverlet branching off from the main river..." Briefly, his voice trailed away and he sat a moment as if pondering that statement before continuing. "No matter. I went to Littleton, discovering she had rented a small cottage there, declaring herself the widow of a soldier and living on his pension. She took the girl Flossie Winters with her as a maid and housekeeper."

Donal realized he hadn't thought of what might've happened to young Flossie in all this. A new guilt sprang up. He quickly quashed it as he asked, "So you found her? What did she say? Is she going to let the child go? Will there be any problem?"

Doyle didn't answer. Again, he averted his gaze.

"What is it?" Exasperated, Donal stood. "Damn it, Doyle. Why are you acting so strangely?"

"I…" The agent shook his head. "I'm sorry. I suppose there's no way but to say it."

He looked up, eyes meeting Donal's. In them, Donal thought he saw sadness and apology.

"Miss Nordin is dead, sir."

"Dead?" That wasn't what Donal expected him to say. That Nell would fight, perhaps wanted more money to let his child come to him…yes, but that she had died? "How?"

"There was a fever, about eight years ago." Doyle spoke as if he hadn't heard Donal's question. "A good many of the townspeople died. Miss Nordin was one of the first casualties."

"Who's been caring for my child all this time, if his mother's dead?"

"The child died, too. I'm sorry to be so blunt." Doyle hurried on, as if to get it said and out of the way. "They were both ill about a week, then succumbed."

Donal blinked, shaking his head as if he didn't understand. *Surely, I misunderstood. He didn't say…* He struggled to find some reason, some validity in what he'd been told. "The money…where has the money been going all this time?"

"Someone notified the bank. They stopped issuing the cheques, but since your father had said he wanted to know nothing concerning it, it's simply been sitting in the account, collecting interest all this time—Sir!"

Doyle was on his feet as Donal took a step, wavered, and his knees buckled. He felt strong hands catch his arms, pushing him into his chair. As he leaned back, head lolling, eyes closed, he heard the tinkling of crystal and liquid being poured. A glass was thrust into his hand.

"Drink that."

Automatically, he raised the glass. Without opening his eyes, he tasted the rich flavor of brandy, drank one swallow, then thrust it aside. It was pulled from his hands and set on the mantel.

"All this time? They've both been dead?" He repeated the words, shaking his head, as if he couldn't translate their meaning. *It can't be.*

Donald opened his eyes. The first thing he saw was Doyle's own brown ones, worried and sympathetic. The agent was hovering. He glanced at the bellpull by the hearth.

"Shall I call your butler?"

Donal shook his head. "Y-you're certain?" *Please, say no, say you made a mistake.*

"Positive, sir. I spoke to the doctor who treated them. Got a copy of the death certifications. He's been holding them in case any relatives showed up, asking. I even went to the cemetery and saw the graves." Doyle fumbled in another pocket, bringing out several folded papers. "I made rubbings of the headstones."

He held out the papers.

Donal took them, two large sheets of cheap foolscap, the coarse kind employed by artists for making sketches. They were folded into quarters. Inside were two official-looking documents on stiffer, better-grade bond. Very carefully, he set those on the table. *I won't look at those. I can't.*

He didn't open the larger sheets, but instead, asked, in a very quiet voice, forcing himself not to let it tremble, "Tell me, Doyle…did I have a son, or a daughter?"

"A son." Doyle's forefinger tapped the sheet he held.

Donal opened it to its full length, staring at the black charcoal smears across the cream-colored page. When the sheet was placed over the stone and charcoal rubbed back and forth, the edges of letters were thrown into relief:

Quinton Donal Nordin
May 1, 1851 – November 12, 1853.

She named him after Father and me. Donal didn't look at the other paper. Nor would he look at the death certificates. Not now. Later, perhaps, when his shock had lessened. He wished he'd tried to find Nell. *Why didn't I? Why did I have to be such a coward and let Father handle this?*

Too late now. He could berate himself all he wished. *It didn't matter. My son is dead. My child I never knew.*

"If it matters…the doctor said he was a smart little lad. Had your red hair."

"Thank you, Mr. Doyle." He was startled by how calm his voice sounded when inside he was screaming with grief. "I appreciate your thoroughness. If you'll send me a statement, I'll see your services are remunerated."

The same thing he'd said to Dr. Blount. *Yes, thank you for dashing my hopes and rending my heart to shreds. Let me pay you for destroying my only expectation of immortality.* He knew he had no one to blame but himself.

Doyle didn't answer.

As if in a daze, Donal got to his feet, tugging gently on the bellpull. When Sewell appeared, he said, "Mr. Doyle is leaving, Sewell. Please see him out."

So very polite, so British. *Mustn't forget our manners, even in the face of total bereavement.* In that moment, he wanted to fling himself to the floor and scream. Beat his fists against the cold marble of the hearth until his fists turned black and the skin burst and blood poured forth over the stones. *What good would it do?* His son would still be dead, his part of the family name would still disappear.

With a murmured, "I'm sorry, sir," Doyle followed Sewell out.

Once they were gone, Donal dropped the papers into the chair. He wanted to throw them into the fire but knew they had to be saved. He retrieved the brandy glass and drank every drop, set it back on the mantel, and took a deep breath.

I have to tell Felicity. That was going to be even worse than learning of it himself.

Sewell met him at the door. "Is anything wrong, Mr. Donal? You appear…saddened."

"Some…business information didn't go as I wished, that's all." He smiled quietly. "Thank you for being concerned, Sewell." *Saddened? Sewell, I want to rend my garments, rub ashes into my hair.* "I must speak to Mrs. McCoy. Please see we're not disturbed."

"Yes, sir."

Donal swept past the butler and went down the hallway to Felicity's study. *How am I going to say this? How can I break her heart again? She's been so happy since I told her.*

The study door was open. He could see Felicity sitting at that delicate little davenport. He knew what she was doing, making another of her interminable lists, this one holding items she intended to buy for the nursery. He'd laughed when she began it, reminding her the child would be a ten-year-old, too big for infantile toys. She changed the list to one for redecorating the guest bedroom for a youngster, and now…

"Felicity…"

"Oh, Donal." She looked up and smiled, pen poised. "Tell me…"

He saw then she held small squares of color, paint swatches, shades of blue and pink and a couple in a pale yellow almost cream.

"Which color should we choose? I'm leaning toward this blue." She indicated one of the squares in a robin's-egg pastel. "I suppose it would be best to wait and discover if we have a son or not, but…"

"Felicity," he tried again.

"I know I'm impatient," she continued, ignoring his interruption. "I can't help it. Oh, Donal, I'm so excited."

"Felicity!"

That stopped her. For the first time, she saw how upset he appeared.

"Donal? What is it? You're… What's happened?" Setting down her pen, she got to her feet.

He shut the door, coming to her and taking her hands. "I've some bad news." He pushed her back into her chair.

"Bad news?" Her gaze swept over his face. "Sewell said you had a visitor. Was it that Mr. Doyle?" At his faint nod, she guessed, "He couldn't find them."

"No. He found them. He…" Donal pulled her into his arms, bowing his head. "Oh God, Felicity…"

"Donal, what is it?" She was frightened now, pulling away to stare at him, confused by seeing her husband whom she'd thought so controlled when in public obviously on the verge of tears.

"Paint the room white. There won't be any reason to redecorate." His voice broke. "He's dead…"

The explanation came pouring out. Through tears, Donal spoke the cruel words telling his wife the child they'd believed would come to them was dead, had been dead for years. Felicity cried then, too and in her sobs, Donal realized she wasn't crying for herself or her own loss but for him, as well as for that unknown little boy who'd never known his father and now never would.

When at last she was silent, Donal whispered, "I'm being punished, Felicity. This is God's way of punishing me for being so selfish and such a coward."

"Don't be foolish." Her words were so sharp Donal stared at her. "God wouldn't kill an innocent child and make me childless to punish you. He'd…he'd smite you dead or something."

"Then I wish he would, because I'd gladly die to give my child back its life and make you whole." He meant that, closing his eyes and actually waiting for a lightning bolt to slash through the ceiling and strike him.

It didn't happen, of course, and he simply stood there, disappointed that he would continue to live.

"What do we do now?" she asked, blinking and stifling another sob.

"Go on, I suppose. Back to the way things were before I received Father's letter and we went to see Dr. Blount. To our old life. We've a trip to make to

Tipperary." He wondered how he was going to bear being in his father's company, hearing his question again, seeing his sister's children without envy.

"I suppose you're right." Her sigh was so deep it shook her body. She pulled out of his arms and returned to the desk.

Picking up the list, she replaced the pen in its holder. Then she carefully folded the paper and tore it into several pieces, dropping them into the little wastepaper basket by the desk. She looked up at him.

"I do have a few more things to pack, so I should get to them since we'll be leaving in the morning." She walked past him into the hall, adding as if in afterthought, "I suppose it's a good thing I didn't order those toys and clothing."

"Felicity." He caught her hands as she passed, spinning her around. "I love you."

"I know that, Donal." She sounded surprised, as if he didn't have to tell her, as if he shouldn't doubt she knew.

"I only hope my love will be enough." He humbled himself to say that.

"I suppose it will have to be, won't it?" She kissed his cheek. "Don't worry. It'll be all right."

The same thing she'd said before they saw Dr. Blount. *We've both repeated ourselves today,* he thought, and that didn't console him one bit.

Chapter 35

In Donal's opinion, the first ball of the Tipperary season wasn't much to speak of.

Harrington's might consider itself the Almack's of Tipperary, but as far as he was concerned, the place couldn't hold a candle to that more austere club. It was built on the same grand scale, in some parts an exact replica, as if the architect visited the former and copied it. There were dining rooms and a large ballroom, as well as smaller rooms for card games and such, but no heavy gambling or serious games of chance were permitted. Refreshments were the same dry cake and buttered toast, with white soup added, while ratafia, orgeat, and tea reigned supreme in the refreshment department. The only exception was that among the punchbowls there was one designated a wine punch, Irishmen being of a disposition such that they weren't all expected to sip those other mild beverages.

Once inside, Donal told himself to stop making comparisons and enjoy himself, and he found eventually he was able to do that with ease. He knew most of the guests, having grown up with their sons and daughters. Other than being re-introduced to them, a formality for those he hadn't seen during his visits home, there were no new people to meet. He was startled to see several of the girls he'd known were now ushering their own daughters into the ballroom. That sent a pang he knew

Felicity was probably also experiencing, that some of the women he'd played with as a child had children old enough to now have their own debuts.

She smiled at him, as if acknowledging they had the same thought, then turned to speak to someone calling to her. Donal looked back at an old university friend who was expounding on some subject. *That's the way it must be now. It was fairly easy.* Soon, even that small stab of regret would also disappear.

He hoped.

Lord Alisdaire was fashionably late in arriving. Donal was surprised by his appearance. He might be wearing an evening suit of the latest cut, but Donal found him to be a near-caricature of the absentminded, bumbling English lord, though he was certain most of the man's demeanor was an act. It had to be. Surely the Crown wouldn't appoint someone so seemingly dimwitted as landlord for so much Irish real estate. Before Quinton could speak, His Lordship made introductions himself. He seemed unable to remember Colin's name, however, and kept confusing him with Padraig, much to Quinton's irritation.

Donal marveled that his father was able to hide his exasperation as Alisdaire persisted in speaking of the exile.

Lady Alisdaire wasn't much better, apparently as airheaded as her spouse, chattering on incessantly, though Felicity and his mother seemed to find her conversation fascinating. Indeed, the three women were soon speaking together as if they were old friends.

The old lady, Alisdaire's mother, was a pip. Donal warmed to her immediately, even if she also made Padraig the subject.

"From all I've heard, that boy was full of dash-fire, but deserving of the infernal cut by our entire society as well as his family."

"Good God, Mother, where do you get those phrases?" Alisdaire asked. "You sound as if you've been hobnobbing with the footmen again."

"You should try it, Robert," the old lady rejoined. "That's the best way to get the gossip while it's still fresh."

If Donal had met her in his university days, before the fire in his blood had been contained by Felicity's passion, he thought he and the old duchess might at that moment be hovering around a punchbowl, perhaps spiking it with a shot of two of Bushmills and laughing at the other guests' reactions.

The fourth person in His Lordship's party was his daughter, Fiona, his son Samuel being away at school and not expected home until after the ball. She was a pretty little thing, demure-looking, but once or twice he caught her sending Colin a surprisingly bold glance. Colin appeared interested in her as well. She stood for quite some time, silent, listening to her grandmother and father natter on about Padraig and that wild part of the United States where he'd supposedly gone. At last, however, it appeared she'd had enough and, unlike any of them, wasn't afraid to say so.

"Father, could we please change the subject?" Her voice was soft and melodious. "You promised us no gossiping tonight."

Yes, definitely a saucy bit under that quietly fashionable white debutante's gown.

"Now you're doing exactly that, and leaving us standing here unintroduced." She glanced around, caught Colin's eye and dimpled.

Her eyes were blue, like the sky at noon, contrasting with her deep brown, almost sable hair, twisted into thick curls at the back of her head with little tendrils escaping to drape in front of her ears and at the nape of her neck. "Do I have to present myself to this gentleman?"

She looked directly at Colin as she said it, tossing a curl over her shoulder.

Follow-me-lad curls. That said a great deal, too. Donal wondered if Colin was catching all the not-so-subtle signals the girl was sending him.

If his attention meant anything, Colin was. He took the initiative, introducing himself instead of waiting, and immediately swept her away for a dance.

Then the young idiot had the stupidity to drag her off the dance floor and into the darkness of one of the terraces. Who knows what would've happened if Quinton and Lord Robert hadn't missed them?

Donal was certain no one believed that cock-and-bull story both Colin and the girl told of her becoming faint and his taking her onto the terrace for some fresh air. They all pretended to accept it, but...

On the ride home, Colin appeared thoughtful. Of course, Felicity and Màiri were talking so, he wouldn't have been able to get a word in anyway. Donal doubted if anyone noticed his younger brother's silence. *God, I think he's actually interested in the girl. Seriously interested.* That surprised Donal, but his next thought was, *Well, why not? He's nearly twenty-eight now. Why shouldn't he begin seeking a wife?* Where better to begin than a debutante ball?

It was almost as difficult to realize Colin was that old as it had been to accept him as an adult when he'd graduated from Eton. Donal still didn't understand why Quinton insisted Colin return home after leaving Cambridge, nor why he hadn't tried to rush the boy into marriage as he'd done Donal, as he himself had been. Perhaps that was their mother's doing. Hanging onto the baby as long as possible.

Once home, Quinton dismissed the servants who'd waited up, telling Cormac to lock up. With an invitation to Colin to join them, he and Donal retired to his study while Màiri and Felicity pleaded exhaustion and went to their rooms.

Colin politely excused himself.

"I'm a bit tired, Da," he stated. "All that dancin', I suppose. Th' exercise an' excitement fair wore me out." He cocked his head to one side as if thinking. "Do you suppose th' lasses feel that way, too?"

Without waiting for an answer, he started up the stairs. Quinton didn't shut the door but set about serving himself and Donal. Giving his son a brandy glass, he sat to one side of the hearth, though it was still too warm for a fire to be lit. Donal took a chair on the other side.

"Where will you be sleepin' tonight?" It was a casual-sounding question and at the same time an intrusive one, especially for a father to ask a married son.

"Isn't that rather personal?" Donal managed to temper the sharpness of his reply with, "In my bed. Where else would I sleep, sir?"

"In your wife's, perhaps?"

"Father, you aren't going to start that again, are you?" Donal surprised himself with an unmistakable whine in his voice, that of a child who feels he's being unfairly reprimanded.

"You've been married quite some time now, Donal,

an' I've yet t' be given th' happy news that Felicity's with child." Quinton paused to take a sip of his brandy. "Why haven't I?"

"Must you ask that?" After all that had happened, though his father had yet to know, Donal was completely affronted.

He lowered his voice slightly, as through the door Colin's footsteps sounded on the stairs.

"I'm afraid I must." Quinton was unsympathetic to any embarrassment he was causing his son. "I arranged t' pay off that dolly-mop you dabbed, so I know there's no reason you can't sire a legitimate child." There was a slight pause. "She didn't lie, did she?"

"Sometimes these things take time," he hedged, without answering Quinton's question directly. He thought he heard Colin's steps stop. *Is the little twit eavesdropping?*

"Not usually." Quinton wasn't going to take that excuse. "You were born a year after your maithur an' I were wed…an' Padraig a year after that, an' Bridget eighteen months later, an' Colin…"

"I don't need to be reminded of the birthdates of my siblings." This time, Donal didn't hide his irritation. "I'm quite aware how old we all are."

"No matter how many times you visit, son, when you're in this house, you never once visit your wife o' an evenin'." Quinton returned to the original subject.

"Have you been listening outside my door?" Donal's tone went icy.

"Not exactly," Quinton answered. "But there is a board in the floor in front o' th' door t' Felicity's room that creaks when stepped upon. 'Tis been silent so far."

"So, you *have* been listening. God, my own

father…spying on me." Donal rolled his eyes heavenward.

"'Tisn't spyin'," Quinton denied. "I simply have trouble sleepin' on occasion an'…"

Donal sighed. "Very well, Father, if you must know… The truth is, I didn't think it proper for Felicity and myself to…" He found he couldn't find any term to describe the marriage act that wouldn't make him flush, even after all this time. "…not in my parents' home."

"Not proper? Codswallop! Your presence here doesn't stop your maithur an' me from… Ne'er mind that." Quinton sighed and turned serious. "Donal, you're me heir an' therefore you must give me a grandchild. Must I find your bastard an' legitimize it so th' McCoy name can continue?"

"Father…" Gulping down the rest of his brandy, Donal gave a sharp cough and got to his feet. He placed the goblet upon a table and went to the study door.

Immediately, he heard the sound of someone going up the stairs at a run. *Colin* was *listening. Oh, Lord.* He shut the door.

"I'm afraid I've some unhappy news." He turned, leaning against the closed door as if attempting to draw strength from its solidness against his back.

"What?" Quinton stiffened. He raised his brandy glass.

"Wait." Donal came toward him, placing a hand on his arm to prevent him from drinking. "Let me tell you first."

"Is it that bad?" Quinton rested the glass against the chair arm. "What has happened, son?"

"I…we…"

Donal had deliberately not thought of how he would

tell Quinton, not wishing to have that uppermost in his mind and interfering with his enjoyment of their visit and the ball. Now, he wished he had. Being cowardly again. *It has to be done. Now's as good a time as ever.*

He shook his head, sighed, and said, "Felicity and I won't be having children, sir."

"What do you mean you won't be havin' children?" Quinton stared at him as if he'd begun spouting German or some other foreign language.

"Let me rephrase that." Donal fell back on his somber, stolid British affectation. "We *can't* have children."

"Nonsense," Quinton snorted. "You're a McCoy." As if his lineage made him productive. "O' course you can."

"No, we can't." Donal made his tone dogmatic.

Quinton was quiet a moment, seeming to think that over. "Have you been t' a physician? This isn't something you've simply decided on your own?"

"We went to a specialist. On Harley Street." Donal didn't know why he added that. Perhaps because that address seemed to give anything more authenticity? He braced himself, dreading Quinton's next question, knowing exactly what his father was going to say, and was determined he wasn't going to have Quinton lay the blame on Felicity.

He fell into his chair, looking away from his father, and let the entire story come pouring out, of the visit to Dr. Blount, of hiring Doyle, and the outcome of the agent's investigations.

"I...see," was all Quinton said as he seized his goblet and drank the remaining brandy without pausing. Then he sat there, staring at the empty glass, not moving.

"But…I've been paying all these years…the bank…"

He stopped.

"The money hasn't been touched. Someone notified the bank." Donal ventured when he didn't speak. "No one's touched that money for nearly eight years."

"Damn th' money." Quinton grated the words as if they were difficult to get out. "I can have anaithur grandchild. There's Colin, an' maybe Padraig, but you… Donal, you'll ne'er…" He drew in a deep breath, his expression one of shock and sincere sadness. "An' that poor li'l lad…"

"Please, Father. Could we let the subject drop?"

"O' course, son." Quinton's answer was so meek, Donal gave him a sharp stare.

"It would please me if you don't mention this to anyone."

"As if I would." Quinton took exception to that statement, relenting to add, "I will have t' tell your maithur. Some time."

"Of course, but lay the blame on me…and *never* say anything to Felicity."

"I'd ne'er do that," Quinton swore.

They were both silent a moment. Quinton got up and went to the mantel, selecting a smaller glass, pouring whiskey into it.

"Don't like t' mix me drinkin', but tonight…" He looked at Donal. "Will you have one, son?"

Donal shook his head. "I think I need some sleep." He stood also. "If you'll excuse me, Father?"

He was dismissed with an absent nod. As Donal left the study, Quinton spoke again.

"Donal, me child, I'm so sorry."

That made Donal turn to look at Quinton. He was

shocked to see a tear roll down Quinton's cheek. He didn't answer but went out, closing the door behind him.

Quinton took the whiskey decanter and placed it on the table before seating himself again. Passing a hand over his eyes, he wiped away his tears.

****

Once out of his father's sight, Donal returned to his own room. He was startled to feel a sudden lightening inside. It was as if now he'd shed himself of some heavy, dark secret. *I had no idea Father's wishes were weighing on me so.*

In spite of what he'd told Quinton, however, he wasn't sleepy. Far from it. He was wide awake and wanting to see Felicity, to tell her what he'd done, to see if she would experience the same liberation as he. He also felt a sudden and surprising desire to make love to her, something he'd never before experienced while in his father's house.

He waited until he heard Quinton's footsteps come up the stairs and disappear down the hall to his own rooms. They didn't stop at his mother's door, so he wasn't going to tell Màiri of their conversation tonight, at least. Once he heard Quinton's door shut, he undressed and put on the nightshirt he hypocritically wore when visiting his parents. Rollo always laughed when he took it out of his case. He was glad he'd told the valet not to wait up tonight.

Pulling on his dressing gown and buttoning it, he opened his door and peered into the hallway. The corridor was darkened except for two gas sconces lighting each end, enough illumination for him to see his way to Felicity's room. Not that he needed anything showing him its location. He stepped into the hall, pulling the door shut behind him.

As he neared the door, he heard that telltale squeak. Odd how he'd never noticed it before, but now that it had been brought to his attention… He wondered if Quinton would hear, also. Would he be listening tonight, after all he'd been told?

Gently, he rubbed his knuckles against the door, whispering, "Felicity?"

There was movement inside. The door opened.

"Donal? What…"

Finger to his lips, he brushed past her into the room. "What are you doing here? You never…"

"That charade is over." He spun to look at her.

She was wearing a simple muslin nightshift, made elaborate with smocking on its yoke and embroidery at the neck. Wide bands of eyelet ran the length of the front and sleeves, giving brief but enticing glimpses of bare flesh. It was a nightgown Donal recently had bought her on a whim, something for her to wear briefly before he took it off her.

God, you're lovely. He could feel his love growing simply by being near her.

"What do you mean?"

"I told Father everything tonight," he said. "I hadn't planned it, but he started in and…" He shrugged.

"So he knows it all?" For a moment, she looked distressed. "About my accident, and…"

Shaking his head, he broke off whatever else he'd been about to say. "I love you, Felicity. I refuse to have you shamed in any way. No matter what, I will always feel I caused this, and I'll take the blame…"

"Donal," she interrupted, "earlier, I felt the oddest sensation…" She smiled. "As if something had been lifted from my heart. Some deep burden I hadn't really realized I was carrying…or that it was so heavy."

"When…when was that?"

"Not long before you knocked on my door." She looked surprised. "Was that when you told Father Quinton? Are we so attuned?"

He bowed his head.

"What happens now?"

"Father knows, and that's all that matters. He'll keep our secret. From now on, it'll be as we planned. When we leave here, we'll continue our lives and be happy. If someone mentions we don't have a child, we'll simply say, 'That's the way it is.' We won't be sad and we won't dwell on it." Donal spoke with determination, as much for himself as for her. "We've each other and we're all we need. You do understand that?"

She nodded.

"And you accept it as I have?"

Again, she nodded, not speaking.

"In that case, get yourself into bed, my lady." Taking her hand, he led her to the bed, turned back the covers she'd pushed aside when she came to the door, and waited while she sat on its edge. "Now then…"

"What are you planning?" she asked, a slight smile tilting her lips.

"I, madam, am going to get into this bed and make love to you, to prove what I say." Unbuttoning his dressing gown, Donal tossed it onto a nearby chair. That cumbersome nightshirt followed. Sliding in beside his wife, he took her in his arms.

As he kissed her, he remembered that long-ago day, when reading his father's letter, how rebellious he'd felt, and how he considered marriage a chore he had to get out of the way. Now, he wondered why he'd ever had such a ridiculous thought.

"I love you, Felicity. You're my present and my future, and you're all I'll ever need."

A word about the author…

Toni V. Sweeney has lived thirty years in the South, a score in the Middle West, and a decade on the Pacific Coast and now she's trying for her second thirty on the Great Plains.

Since the publication of her first novel in 1989, Toni has written 92 novels, with 89 of them being published. This includes several series.

https://www.facebook.com/profile.php?id=100048 587829251